Ambitionz As A Ridah

Written by:
Frank Rice

Cadmus Publishing
www.cadmuspublishing.com

Copyright © 2021 Frank Rice

Published by Cadmus Publishing
www.cadmuspublishing.com

ISBN: 978-1-63751-038-4

All rights reserved. Copyright under Berne Copyright Convention, Universal Copyright Convention, and Pan-American Copyright Convention. No part of this book may be reproduced, stored in a retrieval system, or transmitted in any form, or by any means, electronic, mechanical, photocopying, recording or otherwise, without prior permission of the author.

This is a work of fiction; therefore, names, characters, places, and incidents are the products of the author's imagination or are used fictitiously. Any resemblance to actual events, locales, or persons, living or dead, is entirely coincidental.

Contents

Prologue..1

Chapter 1 2

Chapter 2 6

Chapter 3 11

Chapter 4 20

Chapter 5 45

Chapter 6 57

Chapter 7 65

Chapter 8 73

Chapter 9 79

Chapter 10...87

Chapter 11...110

Chapter 12...132

Chapter 13...152

Chapter 14...173

Chapter 15...193

PROLOGUE

 The ghetto is like a battle field, but if you haven't ever been there then you know nothing about it. It's time to open the eyes of the ones who haven't ever been there to let them know that a solider isn't just a person who goes to war for their country, but they are also teens going to war just to survive in the streets. But when is enough, enough? Cause violence is getting out of hand and just like on the battle field too many are dying too young. It's easier to get a gun than an education in my city and now that crime has moved into our schools, the youth don't have childhoods anymore because their parents worry that if they go outside to play that they'll get shot or start hanging with the wrong crowd. And we can't blame the parents because some of them do their best to raise their children right. So, who do you blame? It's hard to say because crime has been around for a. long time and without evil there could be no good and vice versa without good there could be no evil.

 But if you take the time to look around, you could see where it's coming from and though it's just my opinion I blame the nation. And until America wakes up, it will continue to have these kinds of nightmares. And Oh, my bad for not introducing myself at first. My name is Darrell Drakeford, but everybody calls me Drama. It's funny how certain situations can change your whole perspective on life, and a week ago if you would've asked me to speak on something like what I just said you probably would've just gotten a cold glare. Then again, I wish I could've thought of or understood a concept like this a week ago, cause if I did, we wouldn't even be having this conversation right now.

Chapter 1

East End

Standing in line in the small chow hall of the Richmond Juvenile Detention Center waiting to get their dinner trays, two teens, one dark skin, medium height, with a low cut and the other a light skin dude who's a few inches taller also with a low cut and wearing a state issued green jump suit and orange shirt like his friend, stand in line mean mugging the other juveniles whose pod is on the other side of the chow hall sitting down eating.

"I'm saying Big Bro you go home tomorrow so I'll pop that nigga's top if you want me to." The light skin kid says to the dark skin one.

"Naw Joe, Rock gave me the order so I gotta eat this nigga myself homie." Big Bro says to Joe as they keep up with the line while, they both stare hard at a fat light skin kid who's dressed like them, eating a cheeseburger and french-fries not paying them any mind as the two different older male staff members stand at the top of the brick divider that separates the two pods in the chow hall.

When both Big Bro and Joe get their trays and small cartons of milk, they are told by their short cock eyed, fat pod officer to sit at a table that's right next to the medium height divider because of the detention centers organized seating arrangement.

"It must be meant to happen." Big Bro says to Joe as they look over the clean white brick divider where the fat kid is right beside them on the other side of the divider oblivious to the danger he is in while they go to sit down and eat their meal as well.

"Sit down and shut up!" the officer snaps at Big Bro who sucks his teeth while sitting down as him and Joe eat and drink as fast as they can, so they won't be hungry on lockdown.

"Damn, yall must was hungry as a motherfucker." One of the other teens sitting at the four-person table with them says while they ignore him as the other pod is told to dump their trays and get in line.

"Here it go." Big Bro says with a mouth full of food as he washes it down with chocolate milk.

"Shit I'm going too." Joe says as they both stand up.

"Sit down! You raise your hand before you move, this is your last warning Drakeford! Yours too Young!" Their fat pod officer is saying before they jump over the divider and rush the fat kid instantly knocking him to the floor from wild punches before they start stomping him and the two scared pod officers blow their whistles but don't intervene as they scream "STOP FIGHTING!" before getting on their walkie talkies and calling for assistance. Stomping the fat kids head in the ground, blood from his head and mouth get all over their jumper pants legs but they don't stop even though pod officers can be seen through the glass around the chow hall running to and in as they all rush Joe and Big Bro who start fighting them before their slammed on the table and put on the floor in handcuffs.

"Take Drakeford to a cell in intake and take Young back to the pod and lock him in his cell." One of the LT.'s says as the nurse stands by to help the fat kid they beat up; as pod officers surround him to see how bad he's beaten while they drag Big Bro and Joe out of the chow hall and in separate directions.

"East Side my nigga!" Big Bro yells to Joe who replies, "All the time, Blatttt!"

When they get Big Bro in intake one of the big black pod officers says, "Are any of these rooms open?"

"We just got two new intakes, but we can send one of them to population and yall can put him in there." Replies the lady at the receiving desk as they take Big Bro to the last corner cell with a big three at the top of the door and push him in.

Taking the handcuffs off him they signal for the woman to shut the door and they stand in front of it until it shuts, and they check it to make sure it's locked as Big Bro stands at the door cursing and kicking the door.

"Keep that shit up we gone come in there and hog tie your ass." the officer says playing with the handcuffs before he stops, and they walk off. Looking out the door into a room with nothing but chairs and a lady sitting at the desk in the middle of the room, Big Bro sees his eleven-year-old short, Dark skin brother being escorted out of a back room where they dress new intakes.

Sitting him down in one of the chairs the officer says something to the lady at the desk who replies, "He's going in two."

"A Darrell, what the fuck you doing in here?" asks Big Bro.

"Who is that?" Asks his Brother sitting in the chair wearing the state issued dark green jumper and a green shirt holding his sheets, blankets and hygiene in a clear plastic bag.

"It's yo big brother nigga." replies Big Bro as the officer hears him and says "Uh oh, we got Ralph and Darell Drakeford here again. Make sure tomorrow when he's released into population that it's logged that they be kept separate from each other as well as Joseph Young, Jeremy White, George Tall, Michael Vince, Todd Allston, Kwame Toliver, and especially Novel Sharp."

"Is he in a gang?" Asks the woman writing down the names.

"I don't know but his brother over there is and he just responded to a hit sent out by Todd Allston on Charles Meech who is a known wanna be Blood who is testifying against Todd." Replies the officer as Big Bro yells "Maine you don't know what the fuck you talking about ain't nobody send me to do shit, that's yall motherfucking problem yall think yall know everything."

"Shut up, you don't suppose to have that jumper on in that cell any way so gone take that off and have it ready for me when I get there." The officer replies.

"I ain't giving you shit, come take it!" Big Bro Screams while bouncing with his fist balled up.

"Open room three." The officer says getting mad as the lady at the desk does what he asks.

As he approaches the room, little Darrell springs up, runs and punches him in the back of the head screaming "You ain't gone do shit to my brother!"

Running out swinging Big Bro as well pummels the big bad officer who balls up while they both swing wildly on him. Panicking the lady at the desk gets on the phone screaming "Their attacking a staff member! We need help in intake! Brown is being assaulted! Brown is being assaulted!" Knocking him over a chair arm and to the ground they only get to stomp him for a few seconds before they are bum rushed by a room full of staff members who now assault them before throwing them in room two and three and closing the door.

"Yall pussy motherfuckers! Why yall do that to my little brother! I'm gone come up here and kill one of yall ass when I go home tomorrow! Watch I'm gone have every Blood in this bitch setting it on yall ass! I swear to GOD! That's word on the five! " Big Bro is yelling from behind the door now wearing nothing but his orange state shirt, drawers and socks as the sweaty staff members leave out of intake with one placing their shoes and jumpers by their doors as Darrell screams" Fuck the police!" As he kicks the door.

"You gone want your sheets and shit. Keep that dumb shit up and I bet you won't get it. " The officer says to him.

"I don't give a fuck! Suck my dick you bitch ass nigga! As soon as I get in population I'm gone set it on one of yall ass anyway! " Screams Darrell as Big Bro kicks his door as well.

"We'll see, "the officer says leaving out of intake.

"Hold up nigga, you better give me my shit!" Darrell screams kicking the door even harder as the woman at the desk tries her best to ignore the noise.

"A yo, bitch! Give my brother his shit I know you hear me you dumb ass bitch! Don't even worry about it, I'm gone show you my dick all night long anyway."

"Yeah bitch! Me too!"

"A Darrell, what the hell you get locked up for?"

"Me and J.R got chased and he flipped the jeep. He had to go to the hospital and shit, but yo, what pod Yummy and them in?"

"Yummy in C-pod, Travis and Vel in G, Pooh and Tyron in D and me and Joe was in F pod with Nobel and George, but they moved them to F pod to separate us and that's where all the homies at. Me and Joe just set it on Mousey snitch ass. They got him in C so if you go to that pod yall get that pussy bitch! Replies Big Bro as they stay up talking all night.

CHAPTER 2

Fairmount Ave, East End
The Next Day April 17, 1996

"Blaatttt!!! Yeah, yeah, yeah, yeah!" A teenager in his early twenties says as him and a group of other male and females all wearing red somewhere on them stand on the corner of the ice-stained snow filled ground as Big Bro walks toward them wearing a red Skully, and a wheat snow suit with the matching Timberland boots, smiling, happy to see them. Getting up to them they dap each other up with a hand shake that forms a B before making a five-point star with their hands.

"Damn, nigga I ain't seen you in a minute you done got bigger and everything." One of the teens say with a smirk.

"Gone with that bullshit, I ain't been gone for nothing but seven months and we set it before I left." replies Big Bro.

"So, was the dawgs holding it down in there?" asks dude.

"Come on now Bloodshed you know we held it down, and now that I'm out Joe and Nobel's in charge plus my lil brother just got locked up yesterday and we banked that pig Brown, so you already know what it is." replies Big Bro.

"OK, that's what's up." A few of them say.

"I don't know if you know or heard yet, but Prime got killed. Nigga's caught him in his whip by his self slippin, we got the nigga's though, it was bitch ass Black Mont and them. But anyway, I run the set now and I was waiting for you to come home before I told you I'm putting you up under me cause I like how you move and think before you pop off plus I like the loyalty and family values you show." Bloodshed say's to him.

"That's what's up" he replies calmly and nods in agreement as his breath can be seen in front of him because of the cold weather.

"Yall trying to go over Missy crib and lay back? Cause it's cold as a bitch out here." Asks one of the females as they agree and start walking across the street up the block in a close pack with Big Bro and Bloodshed up front talking and laughing.

When they all get to Missy's house they all stand on her large porch as one of the females ring the door bell and they wait until they see someone look out of the down stairs front window before opening the door a few seconds later and looking up at them. "What?" Asks the little girl wearing thick lensed glasses while staring up at them look down on her. "Where yo sister at and why yo lil bad ass ain't at school?" Asks the girl.

"Cause I ain't got to go to school if I don't want to. Why you ain't in school?" Replies the little girl as they all laugh, and Missy appears behind her and tells her "Move Pumpkin. "Get out they way so they can come in the house."

"I'm gone tell mama you let all them people in the house." Pumpkin says stepping out of their way as they all make their way in the house.

"And I'm gone tell her what I caught you and that boy across the street doing." Replies Missy as they all make their way up the steps toward her room.

"We won't be doing nothing!" Pumpkin screams.

"Un huh, I saw yall you little whore and don't try to come in my room either. "Missy says as Pumpkin follows them to the stairs before saying "I got my own room I don't need to come in your room anyway, with your ugly friends." As she storms off toward her own room and slams the door.

"Your lil sister crazy." One of the females say to Missy as she shuts the door to her room and they all have a seat on the couch and around her Queen size bed.

"Passion, you and I both know you and Ladybug's little sisters are way worse than Pumpkin; and hey baby! I didn't even notice that was you." Missy is saying to Passion before noticing Big Bro take his skull cap off and she walks toward him with a big smile giving him a hug and a kiss before saying to the rest of them. "Yall know I'm gone have to put yall out my room right quick so yall gone have to go down stairs or something."

"Damn, your draws just fell off didn't it Tammy." Ladybug say's calling her by her real name.

"Whatever, Brenda. Get out. "Missy say's with a smile before Kissing Big Bro again as they all get up and pile out of the room, closing the door behind them.

As they both quickly get undressed looking at each other smiling nothing needs to be said as they both plan on letting their bodies do the talking as they climb into her bed and she gets on top of him and say's "don't hurt me." As she looks down into his eyes and clinches her teeth as she puts him inside of her and moans as her body slowly adjusts to the size of his erection as she rock's back and forth moaning and gripping at his chest as he massages her back and ass.

"Ralph, Ralph." She start's saying erotically and moaning out his name as she speeds up until her body lock's up and she start's shaking as she cums hard while he suck's her titties and she moans in his ear.

"Where my sister at?" Asks pumpkin giving the group sitting in her living and dining room the third degree as they talk and smoke cigarette's while looking at music videos on the floor model T.V.

"I don't know little girl, why don't you go look at Barney or something? "say's one of the dudes before she walks to Passion and Ladybug and asks the same question.

"Where yo mama at?" Asks one of the dudes before she turns to him and asks "Where yo mama at?" And everybody bursts out laughing even her before asking both Passion and Ladybug again.

"Where my sister?"

"She went to the store right quick, she be back." Replies Passion playing with the little girl's hair as she sits her between her legs on the floor.

"Why yall got all these boy's with yall and how come all yall got on the same color?" Asks Pumpkin playing with a doll baby she pick's off the floor. "It means were friends." Replies Passion.

"I'm gone tell my mama I want some red clothes too." Pumpkin say's as Passion smiles and giggles.

(Twenty Fourth St. East End) Later that evening

"I be glad when I turn eighteen in seven months and get my accident money, so I can take Darell and get out here! "Big Bro say's storming away from his grandfather who's sitting in a lazy boy in front of the television screaming, "Take his bad ass, both of yall can get the hell out of my house right now. And don't think you taking, all that money after all we done did for yall." As Big Bro walk's out the back door slamming it behind him.

"What's up dawg?" asks Bloodshed • standing in his back yard smoking a blunt.

"As soon as I come in the house his old ass start trippin, I hate that motherfucker. All he wanna do is talk shit about me and my brother and ask about our accident money." Replies Big Bro as they walk out of the back yard and up the alley.

"So, what they gone do about yo brother? " asks Bloodshed, passing him the blunt.

"Probably put him on house arrest, he be out next week." Replies Big Bro inhaling and then exhaling the weed smoke.

"You got all yo lit and shit on cap?" asks Bloodshed. "Yeah, you trying to hear me spit flame?" Asks Big Bro.

"Naw, I just wanted to know if you had everything." Replies Bloodshed getting the blunt back as they turn left through somebody's yard and come out on the main street as they walk to the side walk.

"That weed kicking in with that liquor yet?" Asks Bloodshed passing the blunt back.

"It is. I think that's why that old motherfucker started cussing me out." Big Bro says with a slight giggle as the city bus rides past them and some occupants on the bus look at the two of them without them even noticing.

"Maine, we can lay up at some bitch's house tonight. You ain't gotta go back in there if you don't want to. Matter fact shit, the homie just hit us with a pack, so we can just sit on the block and grind all night even though you don't need it. Yeah, Passion told me bout all them clothes Tammy brought for you for when you got out." Bloodshed says with a smile.

"Shit, I'm wearing one of the outfit's right now Skully and everything."

Replies Big Bro giving him five and throwing up the B as Bloodshed, say's "blaaat that's what's up." As they laugh while walking down the street.

"Yo word to Blood, that bitch love you yo. She ain't even been looking at niggas let alone talking to them, if I was you, on some real shit I'd marry that bitch cause you. OH SHIT!" Bloodshed is saying before the four dudes who rode past them on the bus come around the corner and pull out guns and start shooting at them pop pop pop pop pop pop pop and then take off running as both Big Bro and Bloodshed lay face first in the snow.

Hearing the shooting stop Big Bro slowly lifts his head up and looks around the now deserted snow filled street.

"A yo Bloodshed get up them nigga's gone." Big Bro says sitting up and nudging Bloodshed who doesn't move.

"Come on man, stop playing. Get up before them niggas come back." Big Bro says before glancing back down at Bloodshed and seeing a hole in the back of his red Skully as well as his blood starting to stain the white snow.

"OH SHIT!" Big Bro screams turning him over and seeing another hole in his fore head as his eyes and mouth hang completely open as Big Bro holds him and rocks as he looks around and screams "A yo somebody help us!" But sees nobody before looking down at Bloodshed and shaking his head as his tears fall upon his face before he takes his hand and closes his eyes as he sits in the snow rocking and holding him.

CHAPTER 3

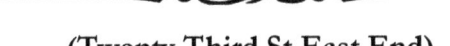

(Twenty Third St East End)
Three Years Later (September 24, 1999)

As the street lights come on and the day turns to night while the cool summer air continues to blow slightly, lights from cars can be seen driving up and down Twenty third street in Churchill as different types of rap music can be heard blaring from the speakers of cars as they drive by the people standing and walking the street.

Sitting on the trunk of a dark red baby caddie a taller much older Big Bro talks on his phone while a crew of three other men stand around the car by the side walk selling drugs.

"I'm saying Blood, is it a go or what?" Asks a taller and much bigger Joe. Holding the phone away from his face Big Bro replies "Hold up, I'm trying to catch up with the nigga now on three way" Before he continues to talk on his phone as a black Pathfinder slowly pulls up and parks a car behind his caddie and everyone in the group puts their hands on their guns except Big Bro who pays the jeep banging Foxy Brown "Foxy Bells" No attention as it stops and hands come out of the window as to say.

"Don't shoot, we're not armed."

"Damn Nobel, Joe and Quarter. What's wrong with yall niggas tonight?" They hear a female ask from the passenger side.

"Who da fuck is that?" Asks the dude standing next to Joe with a blue bandanna hanging out the left side of his back pocket showing that he is the only Crip in that Blood group.

"Quarter don't play with me you know my voice." The light skin female says as she gets out of the jeep.

"Oh, damn. My bad. What's up Tammy or is it Missy today?" Asks Quarter.

"I'm feeling good, so I guess I'm Missy for right now. Hey Joe." She says to Quarter and speaks to Joe as she walks over to them and looks at Big Bro who has had his back to them the whole time as he talks on his phone. Looking back at them not wanting to bother Big Bro while he is on the phone having what sounds like a business conversation she says "Damn Nobel, you look like you ready to kill somebody out here. Why you got your face all balled up for?" Looking at the brown skin dude standing closest to Big Bro.

"What? And who else you got in that fucking jeep?" barks Nobel in an unfriendly tone with his hand put in clear view holding his berretta as he stands beside Big Bro as if he is protecting him from the world while Big Bro doesn't even bother to turn around while he talks on his phone like he doesn't have a care in the world from knowing that as long as he has his niggas around him he is safe from any harm.

Looking at Nobel and thinking "What the fuck is wrong with you, I'm his girl, and maybe you need one or need to go jerk off." Tammy says "Don't trip, them just my girls Wendy, Pam, Tameka and Kim. We on our way to the club and when I saw yall I asked Wendy to pull over, so I can speak to yall and come talk to my man."

"Well hi and bye we busy right now." Nobel says smartly as Quarter and Joe serve drugs to the passing crack heads that stagger over to them.

"And! You ain't the only person over here, A Joe you heard from Passion?" Tammy asks getting irritated at Nobel and Big Bro for acting like he doesn't hear her standing there.

"I thought Passion got killed?" Asks Joe looking at Quarter who gives him a I don't know hunch of the shoulders.

"Man, she knows Passion got killed, she just want some conversation. I guess you wanna know if Ladybug still the police? Stop asking shit you already know, you see the man on the phone so carry yo ass." Nobel says making her feel mad and frustrated before Big Bro taps Nobel on the shoulder and hands him some money and points at Tammy.

Sucking his teeth, he hands the money to her while Big Bro stays on the phone. Smiling from ear to ear she says "Thanks baby. I mean Big Bro." Before she turns and walks back to the Pathfinder and gets in smiling at Nobel as the driver pulls off and beeps the horn when they drive past Big Bro who waves back.

"Why you keep giving them hoes money?" Nobel asks out loud.

"Why do I keep giving you money?" Replies Big Bro before he continues talking on the phone while Nobel gets quiet. SCREECH! A car bends around the corner causing everyone to instantly whip out their guns as Big Bro hops off the trunk just as the car that bent the corner blasting Biggie's "Respect" slams on brakes beside the caddie.

"What you jump off the car for wit yo scared ass?" the young dark skin kid in the driver seat asks.

Looking at his fourteen-year-old brother Big Bro screams "What the fuck is wrong with you! Don't you know niggas almost smoked yo dumb ass wit that stupid shit! And you lucky you my little brother cause if it was anybody else I'd been pulling they ass out the window of the car and beating the shit out of them!" Big Bro says in an angry tone as Drama laughs at the fact that he just scared his hard core big brother.

"Dat shit ain't funny shawty and I know that ain't no junkie car either cause you don't sell coke, so don't be bringing them stolen cars round here making shit hot wit all that dumb ass joy riding! " Big Bro is saying as a

police car comes down the street and Drama peels off just as they put their lights on to chase him.

"Dis little nigga crazy." Big Bro says watching the police try to chase Drama in the car. Walking to the side walk where Quarter, Nobel, and Joe are, Big Bro tries to erase the anger from his face.

"Man, yo lil brother bad as a motherfucker." Quarter says with a light chuckle.

"Who you telling? who you think named that lil bastard? All this little motherfucker wants to do is steal cars all day long. He done been kicked out of every school in Richmond and he think I ain't gone make his ass get a job." Big Bro replies as he tones down his upset demeanor.

"So, what this nigga gone do?" Asks Nobel inquiring about the phone call Big Bro was just having. "He said we gone have to wait until next Thursday cause the feds is down on them niggas hard as a motherfucker."

"Thursday? What the fuck this nigga expects us to do until then?!" Asks Nobel in an upset tone.

"Shawty come on with that ungrateful bullshit. The man said the feds watching him, so you should be happy the nigga taking the risks he taking to make sure we get this shit!" Big Bro screams on Nobel who doesn't reply as he looks at the ground in silence trying his best to mask his anger.

"Alright. So, on a brighter note, is yall niggas trying to go to the club tonight or what?" Quarter asks trying to ease the tension in the air.

"I don't care, it ain't like we got shit else to do." Replies Big Bro in a calmer tone before his phone rings and he answer it.

While he talks on the phone a white caddie with a burgundy rag top pulls over to the curb playing "ATF" by DMX and Joe, Quarter and Nobel seeing the tinted-up car all stand around Big Bro as the driver cuts the car off before two dark skin males emerge from the front passenger and driver side of the car. Noticing who it is Joe says "What's poppin Varsity, what's poppin Lil One." as they walk over to where they are standing around Big Bro.

"What's up nigga?" they both seem to smile and say at the same time as they all greet each other with daps and hugs while Big Bro hangs his phone up and greets them as well. "Ain't shit where the weed at round this motherfucker?" Varsity asks with a smile.

"Traymond got some weed but outside of that I don't know cause we just sold him our last Q.P." Replies Big Bro.

"Shit! I don't fuck with that nigga, he got too much larceny with him. He'll fuck around and sell a nigga some parsley." Lil One says after hearing who has the weed.

"That nigga be on some bullshit like that?" asks Quarter lighting a cigarette.

"Hell yeah. That's why niggas keep sticking his pussy ass up." Replies Varsity.

"Damn, I wish I would've knew that shit. I wouldn't have sold his pussy ass a motherfucking thing." Big Bro says before his phone rings again and he answers it.

"Yall seen J.V and them today?" Asks Varsity.

"Naw, I don't be knowing them dudes like that. And I can see you being around J.V and Lil one, but for you to be twenty yall sure do be hanging around them young ass niggas a lot." Replies Quarter.

"I fuck with them niggas and somebody gotta try to keep their young asses out of trouble." Varsity say as he glances up and down the block.

"How the fuck you start hanging with them niggas anyway?" Asks Nobel.

"I met them through J.V and J.V use to steal cars so I guess that's how they met." replies Varsity.

Before Nobel chuckles to his self and says" Nigga, yall three niggas is too old to be hanging with them young ass niggas." Looking at Nobel and not seeing the humor in his statement.

Varsity replies, "A real nigga is a real nigga despite their age, so they gone be my niggas regardless."

"I mean, it ain't nothing wrong with that. Do you, you know." Nobel says with a straight face before Big Bro hangs up and whispers something in Nobel's ear to which he takes out his phone and starts dialing some numbers.

"A yo V, we bout to take care of something right quick, and I ain't trying to have you caught up in the middle of it so I'm gone get at yall later on. And if I come across some trees I'm gone call you." Big Bro says giving Varsity five and then Lil One.

"Alright then, I'll holla at you my nigga." Varsity replies to Big Bro before him and Lil one give Quarter five and then walk back to the car, getting in, and pulling off.

George Mason Square

"So, what's up J.V is you getting in the car or what?" Drama asks a short dark skin male with a low cut.

"Nigga I just seen you getting chased in that shit. I'm not getting in that hot ass car." replies J.V while standing on the curb beside the car.

"Nigga I got chased in an Oldsmobile, this a Lincoln. And I just got this shit. So, come on and ride with a nigga yo." Drama says while playing with the brakes making the car rock back and forth.

"Naw I'm good, I'm not fucking with you tonight. I'm bout to go lay it down anyway." J.V says as he stands in front of the apartment he shares with his girlfriend.

Sucking his teeth Drama says, "Alright then yo." with a look and tone that says he's a little upset before he pulls off with the music blasting Biggie's "The What".

While driving down the street he sees one of his younger friends standing in front of an alley, making a U-turn in the street he turns the car around and drives back to where he saw him standing.

Pulling up to the curb beside the tall dark skin male, Drama says with a smile "What's up Trigger? What the fuck you standing right here for?"

Returning his smile, Trigger replies "What's up nigga?" as a tall light skin male in his teens with a low cut comes out of the alley walking toward them fixing his pants at the same time with a young female prostitute behind him that keeps walking down the street without paying them any attention.

Stopping beside Trigger the light skin teen looks at Drama who looks at Trigger confused and asks, "Who is that?" As he gets out of the car with the music still blasting.

"Oh, dat's my nigga Hova. He just moved next door to me a couple of days ago. He from Newport News." Replies Trigger.

Twisting up his face Hova corrects him saying "Bad News, not Newport News."

"What's up shawty? My name Drama." Replies Drama introducing his self as he gives him five.

"Damn you look young as a motherfucker, I know that ain't your whip." Hova says while looking at the whip that Drama hopped out of.

"Naw I'm fourteen. That ain't my whip. I stole that shit from out Henrico this morning."

"Man, yall young niggas out here is out of control." "Young? How old is you?"

"I'm seventeen bouts to turn eighteen in a few weeks."

"That ain't old. You called me young like you was Varsity or J.V age or something." Drama says sitting on the hood of the car.

"When you get out?" Trigger interrupts them asking Drama.

"Day before yesterday." Replies Drama who looks up and down the street to make sure that no police are around.

"Where everybody else at?" He asks looking back at Trigger.

"Well Lil One being Lil One so my guess is he somewhere making a freak movie, and you know if you ain't over eighteen he ain't even gone open the door for a nigga when he doing that shit. I don't know where G-Way or

J.V at and Varsity been missing all day, but you know how he is. Yummy,

Pooh, and Tyrone got some whips, they round here somewhere and Vel in da alley getting his dick sucked by crackhead Sharon but as long as they been in the alley they probably fucking." Replies Trigger giving him the rundown of the where bouts of their small crew before Vel finally makes his way out of the alley. Walking towards them, he smiles when he notices Drama who says.

"Look at yo black ass nigga, you keep fucking with them plucks yo dick gone fall off." As they give each other five and a hug.

"When the fuck you get out?" He asks.

"Day before yesterday. Yall niggas ain't got no rides out here." Replies Drama ready to bounce before the police see the car sitting in park.

"Fuck naw! This nigga flipped the got damn Blazer on the highway yesterday and we won't even be getting chased." Vel says pointing at Trigger.

"Nigga, the tire popped, and that bitch flipped itself. I told yall I ain't wanna play that stupid ass cops and robbers shit anyway. This nigga Yummy keep bumping the fucking jeep, so I speed up and the motherfucking tire pop, then the next thing I know we rolling sideways down the motherfucking highway. We had cars flying past us and everything. I ain't doing that shit no more." Replies Vel.

"That's cause you can't fucking drive. And when he bumped you, you was supposed to let him get in front of you, so you could chase him. That's why he kept bumping you." Trigger says as Drama asks, "So yall ain't got no whips?"

"Naw we on foot. Pooh and Yummy had a Blazer earlier and Tyrone just den pulled a Lex, but I ain't seen him since." Replies Vel speaking on the other half of their crew.

"That nigga Tyrone need to come up off my den puller too. He done had my shit for a minute now, and he stealing all types of exotic shit with my shit." Drama says as everyone lets out a slight chuckle.

"You steal cars?" Drama asks Hova

"I done rode in them before, but nah, I don't know how to steal them." "Well yall niggas come on and ride wit me and let me teach you a little

something." Replies Drama with a smile looking at Hova before he walks to the driver side of the stolen Lincoln and gets in as they all pile in before Drama uses a screw driver to start the car up, puts it in drive and pulls off.

"Where we going to do this at cause I'm hungry as a bitch." Asks Trigger.

"I was going out Henrico by Regency unless yall wanna go somewhere else?"

"I don't give a fuck where we go just as long as you stop and let me get something to eat." Trigger says rubbing his stomach.

"Alright I'll stop at Wendy's or somewhere on the way." Replies Drama turning the car deck up.

(Twenty Third St East End)

"I'll be back," Big Bro says to his homies as he gets in the passenger seat of an old model caddie driven by an older dark skin man. Getting in the back seat, Nobel shuts the door and the man pulls off.

"So, what did you wanna talk to me about?" The man asks Big Bro in a nervous tone as he continuingly glances at Nobel through the rear-view mirror.

"Fuck you keep looking at me for!" Nobel screams at him as he watches him watch him while Big Bro sits in silence listening to the oldies, but goodies play on the radio.

"I was only checking my rear view." Dude replies nervously.

"So, you just gone lie in my face like that!" Asks Nobel forcefully as the man timidly looks towards Big Bro for some help but he ignores them both and enjoys the music.

"And you gone ignore me?!" Nobel continues with a hint of being pissed off in his voice.

"Come on youngsta, I don't want no problems with you." the man replies trying to defuse a potential situation.

"Well stop fucking lying and looking in my face like I'm trying to steal something out of this raggedy ass car!" Nobel says in a harsh tone as not once has Big Bro's humble facial expression changed which seems to scare the man more than the screaming Nobel is doing.

"So is there a certain place we. " dude is asking as Big Bro holds up one finger then points at the radio as "A Change Gone Come" by Sam Cook plays on radio. Taking a deep breath, the man puts his eyes back on the road and continues to drive while Big Bro listens to the song.

As the song goes off Big Bro says, "Pull up in this next alley and park." "The alley?" Asks the man as Big Bro confirms it with a silent nod which sends fear surging through the man's body but he does what he's told and pulls into the alley and parks.

"Cut the car off." Big Bro says in a calm tone as the man does what he's told and asks, "You still ain't tell me what this was about."

"I think you know what this is about." Replies Big Bro in his same calm tone. Thinking to his self for a brief moment the man's eyes widen, and he quickly says," I gave them that money for Neka Boo and Troy's bail, I don't know why Rell and them keep saying that."

Looking at him with a simple look on his face, Big Bro says "Whatever, hold up, I gotta piss." Before getting out of the car as dudes heart thumps in his chest and he nervously looks in his rear view to see why Nobel is so quiet and sees he has a gun pointed at the back of his head before Nobel pulls the trigger and blows his brains all over the wind shield.

Getting out of the car Nobel walks the opposite way of Big Bro who gets in a van that was following them and they pick Nobel up at the other end of the alley. As the two girls in the front seat talk, Big Bro and Nobel change their clothes with some clothes that were laid out across the back seat in the van.

"A yo Tah Tah take us to the Cinemax out Henrico. What movie yall trying to go see?" Asks Big Bro.

"It don't matter. I ain't been to the movies in a while anyway." Replies Tah Tah driving while "Trying 2 Do Something" by Master P plays from the speaker as they try to decide what movie they want to go see.

Chapter 4

**(Venable St East End)
Da Next Day (September 25,1999)**

"Get yo lil bad ass up!" Big Bro says playfully while snatching Drama up who is in the bed of his room knocked out snoring. Jumping up out of his dreams from shock, Drama stares at his brother like a scared child for a brief second.

"What you jumping for wit yo scared ass?" Big Bro mocks him from yesterday while laughing at the look on his face.

"What you in my room playing for? You see a nigga was sleep." Drama says a bit angry.

"Nigga I don't care if you get mad. What the fuck I tell you bout stealing them damn cars?" Big Bro says punching him in the chest as Drama covers up.

"Maine stop hitting me. I'm not trying to hear dat shit. I don't be telling you what to do."

"That's cause you Fourteen and I'm Twenty Darrell." Big Bro says with a laugh that shows he loves his little brother.

"You trying to be funny.Ralph.what kind of name is Ralph anyway? That shit sounds like a noise that would come out of a fat bitch ass." Replies Drama as they both laugh.

"If you stop bringing them fat shitty ass bitches over here you'll stop hearing it so much." Big Bro cuts in as he lights a blunt and sits on the edge of the bed where Drama is still laying.

"Let me hit that shit, it better be that haze too." Drama says reaching for the blunt.

"Hold up, I just lit it. I'm gone pass it to you." Big Bro says hitting the blunt a few more times before passing it to him.

"Damn yo, I can still remember when ma use to catch us smoking and go the fuck off." Drama says hitting the blunt as a look of sadness grows on his brothers face from the remark.

"Yeah, GOD bless her soul. She tried her best to raise us. died trying." Big Bro replies shaking his head as he gets the blunt back and takes a long pull while he thinks back on the car accident that killed their mother.

"Boy yall always into something! And I always gotta take off work to take one of yall back to school." Their mother scolds a young Big Bro and Drama who she calls Ralph and Darrell while they both sit in the back seat of their mother's old light tan Chevrolet Caviler.

"But ma, they were picking on him and one of them pushed him." Ralph says trying to defend why his little brother got suspended on the second day of his first year in middle school. Sitting next to his brother Darrell doesn't say a word.

"How the hell do you know? You're in high school, so what the hell are you even doing at a middle school anyway? And I talked to the principle, so stop lying to me cause she told me she watched the whole thing and ain't nobody pushed nobody!

You worse than your damn father with all that damn lying and trying to be tough. And you see where that got him KILLED!

Shot to death in the streets for trying to be a gangster and I'm not gone keep putting up with the " She never got to finish her words. While arguing with them in the back seat she ran a stop sign and was blindsided by a drunk driver driving a black pickup truck.

"Big Bro!" Drama yells punching him in the back and snapping him back to reality.

"Give me the blunt Maine, you just holding the shit letting it burn." He says as Big Bro gives him the blunt and unwraps his red flag off his hand and ties it on his head before he stands up still a little shook of the memory he just remembered.

"You must be high as a bitch cause you trippin'." Drama says hitting the blunt while staring at his brother who just ignores the comment and asks, "You need some money?"

"Yeah." Replies Drama as Big Bro goes in his pocket and pulls out a knot and throws it to Drama before leaving out the room.

"Good look yo." Drama says not even paying attention to the money as he lays back in his own thoughts smoking the rest of the blunt. Grabbing his keys off the night stand Big Bro leaves out of the apartment, gets in his caddie and pulls off dialing some numbers on his car phone he lets it ring until somebody picks up.

"Hello?" The voice asks.

"A yo, Nobel, meet me at the Palace in bout ten minutes." Big Bro says to Nobel who's on the toilet taking a shit.

"Alright." Nobel says as he jumps off the toilet and flushes it without wiping his ass.

Hanging up Big Bro continues to drive until he gets to a rundown grey house. Pulling over, he cuts the car off gets out and walks to the back of the house. Hitting the window when he gets to the back, a tall brown skin guy in fatigues and a black shirt opens the boarded door with an Uzi hanging on a strap across his chest.

"What's poppin Big Bro?" Dude says as Big Bro walks in and past him into a room full of crackheads as he walks through the kitchen, looking around, both rooms of what they call the Palace are full.

Smiling, Big Bro walks to a room door that has two other men standing in front of it like the two men at the back door. Pulling out his key he walks to the door as the men step to the side while he unlocks the door, walks in and locks it behind him.

Seeing Quarter and some other dude looking at T.V. sitting beside Joe on a couch as he comes in he looks at Quarter and says, "let me holla at you right quick."

Walking to the corner of the room Big Bro asks him "Who is dat yo?"
"How you figure I know him?"

"Stop playing wit me. We all Bloods and you the only Crip and dude got on a blue flag." Replies Big Bro with a look of seriousness as Nobel comes in the room and Joe who already knows what their talking about minds his business as he counts money.

"Dat's Vega yo, he's one of my most trusted and he just happened to be with me when I stopped by to check on the Palace." Replies Quarter.

"Nigga you should know the rules better than I do. We open at 5 a.m. and close at 9 p.m. You don't ride wit drugs and money when making a drop, obey the laws and the back rooms to the Palace is off limits!" Big Bro says getting loud. "I know the rules, why you raising your voice?" Asks Quarter in a defensive tone.

"Cause you keep breaking da motherfuckers like they don't apply to you!" Replies Big Bro as Noble comes over but Big Bro waves him off.

"My bad then damn. Neva happen again." Quarter says trying to end the argument as Vega looks a bit uncomfortable.

"Listen shawty, I love you, but I can't afford to fuck dis up so last time Maine tighten up." Big Bro says with a look of death in his eyes.

"You right, dis yo shit and I gotta respect that, so like I said, never happen again." Quarter says as they both stare each other down for a few seconds before Quarter walks off, says something to Vega and they both leave.

"What's up? I'll go pop both they ass right now. Just give me the word." Nobel says seriously.

"Be easy homie, everybody makes mistakes." Big Bro says in a calm tone to Nobel as he sits down beside Joe with Nobel sitting down beside him.

"What's poppin' Blood?" Joe asks giving him five and throwing up a B. "How long them niggas been over here?" Asks Nobel to Joe.

"Can't answer that Blood. You know Quarter work the first shift. I just came in for my shift and made sure the money was straight. I don't question Big Bro so I just thought he was hired help." Replies Joe as Big Bro looks at the floor with his hands over his face still thinking about what Drama brought up and how he got from there to here After Ralphs and Darrell's mother died they sued the driver of the truck. But after paying lawyer's fees, all they walked away with was thirty thousand dollars to be split between the two of them.

While living with their grandparents all they kept talking about was the money that they had won, and greed was in their eyes. So, Ralph, being the older brother felt like it was his responsibility to take care of his little brother Darrell so he moved out and took his little brother with him to an apartment duplex he paid for with some of his half of the thirty thousand dollars and he also brought furniture and appliances as well as drugs to supply a steady income and not rely so much on the lawsuit money which was almost all gone from the purchase of his car.

He still remembers the greedy look in his grandparent's eyes and the remarks they made when he and his brother were awarded the money. He felt like he couldn't trust his family and it was that same feeling that led him to join the Bloods at the age of fifteen with some of his close friends.

All the while though he watched over his little brother Darrell as if he were his father and that's how he got the nick name Big Bro which was given to him by a highly respected 0.G of the Mad Stone Gangsta Bloods before he was killed in a drive by shooting years later. He said he gave it to him because he handles responsibilities like a big brother should.

And as Big Bro put in work for his new set and home the more he came up in the organization, his name and reputation grew dangerously large in the streets along with his rank while little Darrell looked up to him as his idol.

"You alright?" Asks Nobel with general concern as he passes him one of the bottles of Henny he just got out of the liquor cabinet.

"I'm straight." Replies Big Bro in a sullen tone taking the bottle and twisting the top off before taking a huge gulp as if he were drinking water.

"One more day out the way." Nobel says taking a sip of his own Henny while Joe looks at cartoons on TV in silence as always while drinking a bottle of Tanqueray.

Thirty First-St. East End

Walking down the street, Trigger Pooh, Yummy and Tyrone laugh and joke with each other while Yummy dribbles a basketball. "Come on nigga, Tell us where the Lexus at. I'm trying to push that shit." Yummy says to Tyrone.

"No sir, that shit banging. Bitches on my dick and everything cause of that car. So, I know I ain't gone let you make that no hotter than it already is."

"That's fucked up, it ain't like you can't get another one." Yummy says trying to convince him to tell him where he parked his stolen Lexus.

"This shit got spree wells and TV's. I took the PlayStation out, and when I'm finished with the car I'm gone strip that shit." Tyrone says as they cross the street walking toward a crowd of dudes on the corner hustling and Trigger notices some of them staring at them as if it were a problem between them.

"A yall niggas be on point." He tells his homies while never taking his eyes off the crowd as they get within their distance.

"Why, what's up?" Asks Pooh looking around. "Them niggas right there staring at us." Trigger replies in a low tone as they get to where the crowd is standing, and they break up and stand directly in front of them.

"Which one of yall niggas named Tyrone?!" Asks the shortest one in the group with an aggressive tone.

"Why, what's up?" Asks Trigger.

"I ain't talking to you Trigger. Which one of yall little niggas named Tyrone?" He repeats his question staring down Pooh, Yummy and Tyrone.

"My name Tyrone, what's up?" He asks curiously as dude simultaneously snatches him up by the collar of his shirt and puts a chrome nine with an extended clip in his face and barks "Where the fuck my Lex at?!"

"What Lex? I ain't got no Lex, I'm walking." Replies Tyrone fearing for his life.

"My shit got stolen and everybody done already told me they seen yo little punk ass driving it!" Dude screams pushing the barrel of the gun against Tyrone's temple. Getting tired of seeing dude take advantage of his young friend, Trigger grabs Tyrone and yanks him away from dude while saying "Hold up Rah Rah, you don't even know if this the same person " before one of Rah Rah's home boys say, "Fuck all that shit Rah, clap that bitch ass nigga!"

Trembling with tears in his eyes and fear shooting through his chest Tyrone thinks Rah Rah is about to shoot him so with an act of desperation he swings a haymaker at Rah Rah and to his surprise knocks him to the ground with Rah Rah looking as shocked as he did as he watches Tyrone, Yummy and Pooh running away through someone yard with his niggas chasing them.

Getting up, he immediately joins the chase with a wounded ego which makes him shoot wildly the second he sees Yummy and Pooh jumping a gate into someone's yard. Getting on the sidewalk in front of the house, they see Trigger running down the middle of the street as more gun shots can be heard exploding behind them and hitting everything.

Looking back, Tyrone, who is running on the sidewalk sees Pooh, and Yummy trailing behind them so he yells "Come on niggas," before hearing someone scream and sees Yummy fall to the ground.

Stopping, Pooh tries to help him up as Tyrone stops and calls Trigger who stops and looks back only to see Rah Rah and his boys getting closer to Pooh and Yummy, so he yells "Come on! Fuck that!" before taking back off running while Tyrone hesitates but does the same.

"Don't just leave the nigga!" Pooh yells at them watching them both vanish around the corner before hearing a voice behind him say "You should've just left his ass."

Turning around and looking up with fear in his eyes, the last thing he sees is the flash from the barrel of a gun.

"You might as well kill this one too. You know he done seen too much." Rah Rah tells dude who just shot Pooh in the face. Ignoring his pleas, dude finishes Yummy off and the two of them run their separate ways while the others continues to chase Trigger and Tyrone. Still running, Trigger and Tyrone reach Twenty fifth street before their too out of breath to continue running. Stopping on the side of some ones house, they both breath heavy as sweat pours down their faces while they both silently look in front of and behind them.

After at least ten minutes pass they decide that it should be safe to come from out of their hiding spot. Slowly making their way out into the front yard they don't notice any visible threats so they make their way out of the gate and towards Twenty fourth street while cautiously keeping an eye on their surroundings.

As soon as they get on the side street they calm down a bit and Trigger asks, "You don't think they killed them, do you?" But Tyrone, feeling bad about abandoning his friends doesn't reply he just shakes his head and hunches his shoulders as to say I don't know.

Hearing a car horn beeping behind them, they both freeze out of sheer terror as they slowly look back hearing 2 Pac's "Blasphemy" and seeing Varsity to which they both rush to and inside of his car.

"What the fuck wrong with yall?" He asks seeing they are both visibly shaken.

"I think niggas just killed Yummy and Pooh." Replies Trigger in a nervous tone.

"What?" Asks Varsity a bit shocked by the statement and stopping the car. "Why you say that?" He continues to inquire.

"Alright look. We was going over Kirk house to play basketball when Rah Rah, Rell, Tank, Little Ricky, Greg, and Desmond stopped us and Rah Rah put his gun in Tyrone face " Trigger is saying before someone behind

them beeps the horn and they all look back and see an older man behind them. Remembering he is stopped in the middle of the street, he pulls off while Trigger continues to tell him the rest of the story.

"Any way he was putting the gun all in Tyrone's face so I pulled Tyrone back toward me and then niggas started trying to boost Rah Rah head up to shoot us, so Tyrone swung and knocked him out " He is saying before

Varsity looks over at Trigger and then back at Tyrone asking "He knocked him out?"

"Yeah, but look, after he hit the nigga we took off running and Pooh fell jumping a gate, so after Yummy helped him up, we was already ahead of them and that's when the shooting started and when we got on Thirty third, Yummy got hit and Pooh stopped but them niggas was right behind them, so it won't nothing we could do and we kept running." Trigger says as the smell from their sweaty shirts forces Varsity to let down all the windows in the car.

"So, did you see them shoot either of them after that?" Asks Varsity driving now back toward Thirty third street.

"Naw we kept running, but we heard shooting." Replies Trigger before noticing they are driving back towards the way they just came so he quickly asks, "Where we going?"

"To make sure niggas ain't dead, and yall ain't got shit to worry about, cause if either of them did get shot the police should be out there by now and even if they ain't, we might can get the niggas to the hospital." Replies Varsity while Tyrone nervously gets low in the back seat.

"I don't know. Suppose the niggas see us before we get there?" Asks Trigger a bit apprehensive.

"Fuck 'em I'm strapped. So, they can act crazy if they want to, cause we gone be acting crazy together." Replies Varsity.

When they get to Thirty third street they can clearly see up ahead of them a crowd of people, police cars and an ambulance.

"They got the yellow tape up and the street blocked off so I ain't gone even attempt to drive all the way down there" Varsity says before pulling over and parking the car.

"What are you ready to do?" Tyrone asks finally speaking up as his heart pounds hard in his chest.

"I'm bout to go see what's going on." Replies Varsity cutting the car off. "Hell naw, we just got shot at round here, and this where they be at. I'm not gone get caught slippin' in this car looking stupid, you can drop me off somewhere." Tyrone says while Varsity ignores him and gets out of the car to see what's going on.

Not seeing no one he knows, he stands at the front of the yellow tape and asks the young dude standing beside him "What happened yo?"

Pausing before he answers, the young dude looks him up and down before saying "Two niggas just got killed, but ain't nobody saying shit though." the young dude lets it be known as Varsity looks him back up and down before walking off back towards his car.

When he gets back to his Dodge Intrepid he sees Trigger laying low in the front seat, but notices that Tyrone is gone.

"Where Tyrone go?"

"He found out Yummy and Pooh got killed so he got out and ran. I don't know where the fuck he went." Trigger says in a calm sad tone as Varsity starts his car up and pulls off.

Twenty-Six St East End

"You know I love you right?" Tammy asks Big Bro before she sits her naked body on top of his and starts riding him.

Moaning and calling his name, Big Bro just lays there with his mind elsewhere. Riding him faster trying to get his attention she fakes an orgasm. "OOH GOD!" She yells out as her moans get louder as they fill her bedroom.

"Tell me it's good to you." She repeats over and over to no reply as she rides him harder. Feeling a strong orgasm coming, Big Bro snaps out of his deep concentration and grabs both of her ass cheeks as he comes inside of the condom inside of her.

"Yesss!" She says erotically feeling him come in her before she bends down and kisses his chest up to his mouth as their tongues wrestle with each other.

"Are you alright?" She asks staring in his eyes.

"I don't know. I've been feeling kinda strange lately." replies Big Bro.

"You care to talk about it?" Asks Tammy.

"It's nothing to talk about, I've just been feeling weird like something bout to happen. I don't know. I can't explain dat shit." Replies Big Bro sitting up.

"You just probably tired and need some sleep." She says rubbing his chest.

"Can I ask you something serious?" "Sure, why not?"

"Do you ever feel like motherfuckers only hang around you for what you can do for them?"

"Are you directing that at me cause if so it's not like that." "That's not directed at you I just wanted your opinion."

"Well I don't know. Cause my girls are my girls. We've had our arguments, but I never looked at it like they hang around me for what I have, but if that's what's bothering you I" Tammy is saying before he cuts her off.

"Hold up, hold up, hold up. I'm not talking about me, I was speaking in general."

"I know, I'm just saying. I love you, and when you worry I worry and I don't want nothing to happen to you, cause I don't know what I'll do." Tammy says which makes Big Bro smile.

"I'm glad to hear you feel like that." He says to her giving her a kiss on the lips before he gets up and starts getting dressed.

"Where you going?"

"I got money to make and I know you don't want no broke ass nigga." He says to her putting his shirt on.

"I'd be with you if you did or didn't have money. And I don't know if you believe me or not but that's the truth." She says still laying in the bed with the covers over her as she stares at him.

"I'll call you later." He says to her as he leaves out of her room and house to his car where he gets in and pulls off with the music blasting.

George Mason Square

"Dat's fucked up yo." J.V says after Trigger tells him what happened as Hova, Trigger, Varsity, Vel and G Way sit on his porch.

"So, what's up, yall gone get some get back?" Asks Hova.

"Them niggas getting money, we ain't built like that." replies Vel. "So, what, yall just gone let it go?" Hova asks in disbelief.

"I mean, what we gone do? We ain't even got no guns and it's like a thousand of them niggas, that's suicide." replies Vel.

"This nigga named Trigger and yall ain't got no guns?" asks Hove confused.

"Hold up shawty, my name Trigger cause niggas ain't got to tell me to shoot they gotta tell me to stop shooting. We just ain't got no burnas, the shits kept getting tore off." Replies Trigger a bit irritated.

"I think Lil One got some burnas, but to go to war with them niggas, I don't know." Varsity says smoking a cigarette.

"Well call the nigga, and see if he'll let us use some of the joints." G Way says to J.V who goes in his apartment to get the phone. Coming back out with the cordless phone to his ear telling Lil One what happened they all sit and wait on his answer. When he hangs up J.V says, "He said he'll let us get three joints, but he wants the shit back."

"Bet, now we can get at des niggas." Trigger says hyper but deep down knowing they're going against the odds.

"So, what's up when yall trying to do this?" Asks Hova.

"A hold up right quick. I don't really know you, but I know you just moved round here, so I know you don't know these niggas yall bout to go get at and these niggas right here ain't neva killed nobody so I hope you bout yo business. And since yall riding that's on ya11. But yall already know what it's gone be." Varsity says to Hova and everyone else.

"I feel what you saying, and even though I don't know yall like that, I'm willing to ride for family, and right now yall my fam. They got at us, so we gotta get back at them." Hova says to Varsity.

"Well that's on yall cause like I said I know yall niggas, but if that's how yall trying to carry it, oh well, cause them was yall niggas." Varsity says getting up and walking off from being tired of watching them front for Hova before he gets to his car, gets in and pulls off.

"Like I said, fuck it, let's get at these niggas." Replies Trigger. "How you feel about it?" Hova asks Vel who's been quiet this whole time.

"I ain't got shit to say about it, I just move when my niggas move."
"Alright then that's what it is. Come on let's go get the guns." Hova says walking off the porch as Vel, Trigger, and G Way follow as they walk to a stolen caddie and Vel gets in the front seat.

"You coming?" G Way asks J.V from the passenger seat.

"Naw yo, me and Jasmine " J.V is saying before Vel pulls off not trying to hear his excuse. Sucking his teeth J.V goes back in the apartment while dialing some numbers on his cordless phone.

Waking up from hearing his phone ring, Drama looks for his phone before he finds it beside the bed on the floor.

"Who is this?" He asks picking it up still half asleep.

"A yo Drama dis J.V, yo look, this nigga Hova bout to send yo niggas on a suicide mission."

"What you talking bout?" Asks Drama.

"The niggas Rah Rah and them killed Pooh and Yummy behind a Lex Tyrone stole and now Hova done boost them niggas up to shoot out with them niggas,"

"What?!" Drama asks now fully awake. "When the fuck all this happened?"

"A few hours ago. I'm telling you shawty, Hova don't know what the fuck he bout to get them young niggas into."

"Dat's fucked up! I'm telling you Maine I'm getting tired of nigga's pushing shit at us like we ain't gone do shit. Why niggas ain't call me? You know they scared of my brother."

"Call you for what? It's like Varsity said, we ain't never killed nobody, we just steal cars."

"Well it's about time we start, cause I'm tired of this shit!" Drama says with anger in his voice and his adrenaline rushing. Inhaling and exhaling hard

J.V asks, "So what is you getting ready to do?" "Where you at."

"At my house."

"Stay right there, I'm on my way." Drama says hanging the phone up, throwing some clothes on and running out the house after grabbing one of his brothers guns. Running up the block, Drama turns the corner and goes into an alley where a green Grand Cherokee is sitting.

Getting in, he takes a screw driver out of his pocket, sticks it in the broken-up neck of the tilted steering column and starts the jeep up as Jay Z "Devils" blares through the speakers as he backs out of the alley into the street before putting it in drive and pulling off.

"What's up with Varsity and J.V?" Asks Hova.

"I don't know. They the oldest and J.V a sometime nigga, and if money ain't involved they don't really be with it." Replies G Way as Hova drives.

"So, what's up with Drama? Where this nigga at?" Asks Hova.

"I don't know, but I bet J.V done called him and let him know what we bout to go do." Replies G Way.

When they get to Lil Ones crib around South Side, he is standing on the side walk as they pull up behind his minivan. Getting out the car they all give Lil One five.

"So, what the fuck is yall young asses ready to kick off?" Asks Lil One.

"Fuck that shit. Them niggas killed Pooh and Yummy! "Trigger snaps. "Alright, but that's on yall cause I already know what it is with them niggas. The guns over there in the bushes."

Lil One says pointing to the bushes as Hova and Vel walk over to the bushes where they see three AK's. Looking around they pick them up and put them in the car before they walk back over to where G Way, Lil One, and Trigger are.

"I don't know when yall niggas started killing niggas on some Rambo shit, but yall niggas be safe and don't jump out the window on some dumb shit. Get who you gone get and be the fuck out cause yall know it's a lot of them niggas around there." Lil One says being the oldest and wisest while playing with the cross charm on his long gold chain.

"Don't worry about it we got this." Hova says giving him five as he stares in his eyes before, he walks back to the car while they talk and dap up Lil One before walking to the car as well and getting in as Hova pulls off.

Bill Robinson East End

"What's up Maine?" Ask Quarter to Big Bro as they stand on the side lines watching Nobel and Joe play basketball with some other people in the park.

"Why does everybody keep asking me that?" Big Bro asks his self out loud,

"I mean it just looks like somethings bothering you." replies Quarter drinking a beer.

"Ain't nothing wrong, I'm alright." Replies Big Bro taking a deep breath before he sits on the ground and Quarter kneels down beside him.

"Shit will be alright. I be having days like that too." Quarter says giving him the forty ounce. Taking a swig, he tells him "I'm bout tired of all this crazy shit I be doing, cause if something happens to me then who gone keep Drama in line?" Asks Big Bro as Quarter stares at him kinda funny before asking "What the fuck is you talking about?"

"I don't know homie I just had a lot of shit on my mind lately." "I mean what, we got beef with somebody or something?"

"Nah, it ain't nothing like that. I guess it's just my mind playing tricks on me." Replies Big Bro before his phone starts ringing. "Hello?"

"A yo Big this Varsity. Yo some niggas done got into it with some niggas we fuck with and the young ones is screaming war. I done told them to chill, but they mind was made up so I called Drama to check on him but he ain't in… " Varsity is saying before Big Bro stands up and cuts him off. "Who going to war, what the fuck is you talking bout and, where my little brother at?" asks Big Bro in an angry tone.

"I don't know where Drama at, that's why I called you. And they supposed to go shoot out with Rah Rah and them for killing Pooh and Yummy." Varsity says as Big Bro just hangs up. Heart pounding and his adrenaline rushing he yells "A yo we got some shit we need to take care of! Yall niggas need to come on!" Causing the whole basketball court to stop and look in his direction.

"What's up?" Nobel asks walking towards him as Big Bro Storms off the court on his phone while Joe and Quarter follow.

Thirty Third St

Sitting in his room with tears flowing uncontrollably from his eyes, Tyrone sits on his bed staring into space mumbling to himself as his left leg shakes while his phone rings, but he sits as if he doesn't hear it. Standing up he looks frantically around his room before he snaps and flips the mattress off his bed onto the floor. Picking the phone up, he throws it at the wall and screams "FUCK DIS SHIT!" before he storms out of his room and out of the house. Walking up his block to the stolen Lexus, he gets in it and pulls off fast with tears still falling from his eyes.

"I'm gone kill all those niggas! I swear to GOD! I'm gone kill them niggas!" He says out loud out of pure anger while blasting "Homies and Thugs" by Scarface as he accelerates the speed while driving towards only he knows where.

"Watch, I'm telling you, these niggas done fucked up! I'm telling you, cause they don't know who the fuck they fucking with." He says out loud to his self-flying through the streets.

When he gets to Lil Ones crib he slams on the brakes, puts the car in park by the curb before he jumps out and runs to Lil Ones door knocking as hard as he can but not getting any answer as he continues to knock "FUCK!!!" He screams before running back to the car, jumping in and pulling off just as fast as a little girl chasing her puppy runs out into the street.

Not being able to hit the brakes fast enough, he hits the girl and the dog sending her rolling over top of the car cracking the windshield as he hears a woman scream when the car comes to a stop.

Now in shock, he steps on the gas and side swipes a Dodge truck as he bends the corner and a police car that was sitting at the corner puts its lights on and gives chase. Looking in the rear view and seeing the police car behind him, for a split second, he thinks about stopping, but he doesn't as he steps on the gas and breaks while he bends corners trying to ditch the police car.

Thirty First St. East End

TAT TAT TAT TAT TAT TAT TAT TAT TAT TAT TAT TAT TAT TAT TAT TAT TAT TAT TAT TAT TAT TAT TAT TAT TAT TAT TAT TAT TAT TAT TAT TAT TAT TAT TAT TAT TAT TAT TAT TAT TAT

TAT TAT bullets erupt on the block after Hova parks the car in the middle of the block and they get out spraying at everything moving and hitting everything moving and standing as they catch the whole block off guard.

As everyone tries to run, the semi-automatic shots cut them down and don't even allow anyone else to attempt to return fire as "FUCK YALL NIGGAS" and "WHAT'S UP NOW NIGGA!!" Gets drowned out by the gun fire from the AK's. TAT TAT TAT TAT TAT TAT TAT TAT TAT

SCREECHHH they all jump back in the car and leave just as fast as they came while the shots still echo on the block. … … …

Making a hard right without tapping the breaks, Tyrone hits the edge of the curb sending the car flying in the air before it hits the ground and slides on its roof only slowing down and stopping after hitting a parked car.

Getting out with his gun drawn the cop radios for back up for the fifth time as he approaches the car slowly and sees Tyrone's lifeless body hanging half way out of the car and half way under the roof. Lowering his gun, he gets back on his radio trying to call for help.

Twenty First St East End

"What the fuck happened out here?" Quarter says as he gets out of one of the nine cars and trucks they pulled up in as everyone who gets out of the cars and trucks clearly show gang affiliation with red or blue flags on their arms or tied around their necks or fore heads.

Seeing bodies lying everywhere and what looks like the whole police station as well as every ambulance in the city pull up, they leave the guns in the cars and stay close by them as Big Bro walks toward the scene looking for any sign of Drama as the police block off the scene.

"Stop right there sir unless you wanna be arrested." A young officer says putting his hand out. Wanting to punch the young white boy in the face, Big Bro listens to what he says as he continues to look around for Drama.

"Your brother is looking for you." Joe says to Drama as him and J.V walk up looking just as surprised as them.

"DAMN!" Drama says with a smile as some Bloods call Big Bro. "Do you got a gun on you?" Joe asks Drama.

"Hell yeah, and from the look of this shit out here everybody else needs to have one too." Drama says jokingly.

"Give it to me. I will give it back, but you don't need to have a gun on you right now." Joe says as Drama sucks his teeth and gives him the gun off of his waist as Joe walks off and Big Bro walks up giving Drama a big hug from being happy that he's alive.

"What's all this for?" asks Drama.

"Just tell me you ain't had nothing to do with this."

"Hell naw, I just got here." Drama says looking on the other side of the street and seeing mean mugs come from Rell, Rah Rah and very few others.

"What the fuck yall looking at? Yall lucky yall ain't lying beside them motherfuckers!!!" Drama yells to them as Big Bro and everybody else with him turns around and some of the dudes with Big Bro throws up gang signs while others hold their hands up as if saying "What's up, what yall trying to do?" As a few officers and news people watch the whole thing before both groups turn and walk off.

Second Ave. North Side LATER THAT DAY

"Man can I leave yet?" Drama say's to Big Bro who has had him with him all day in various spots as they now sit in what looks like a shot house from all the people coming in and out buying various drinks.

"What you don't wanna hang with ya big brother no more?" Big Bro replies with a smile as he looks kinda drunk. "I mean I ain't got no problem hanging with you, but my niggas out there and you saw how them niggas was looking at me." Drama say drinking a Styrofoam cup full of Absolute.

"You don't even gotta worry about them niggas, we already on top of that and as far as yo niggas go if they were smart they be laying low because I be putting in work like a motherfucker but even I ain't even seen no shit like dat so you need to just be easy for a couple of days." Big Bro says in a concerned tone as Joe and a few other eyes are glued to the TV as they watch the news and they make what happened out as a gang war between the Bloods and Crips.

"Man, dat's some BULLSHIT!" One of them screams at the TV seeing their selves on TV throwing up gang signs at Rah Rah and them.

"Them people think they know every motherfucking thing and don't know shit. And how the fuck they gone say between Bloods and Crips when our whole crowd had on red and blue flags." Dude say's to the dude beside him.

"Joe told me he took a gun from you. What you doing with a gun, huh?

What, you done killed somebody before?" asks Big Bro.

"Naw, but I will when it comes to my niggas." Replies Drama. "Yeah, well I don't believe you. I bet you won't kill nobody cause dat shit ain't as easy as you think." Big Bro say's.

"Shittt, what you wanna bet? Cause it ain't nothing to pull the trigger dat shit don't take no rocket scientist to figure that out." Replies Drama.

"Oh yeah, well come with me right quick." Big Bro says as they both get up and walk to the back of the house.

"A yo Mitch let me holla at you right quick." Big Bro says to the guy who's been selling the liquor all night as he follows them out the house into the back yard.

"What's up Big Bro? "Asks Mitch.

"Remember what I was hollering at you about earlier? When am I gone get that?" Asks Big Bro.

"Hold on now Big Bro I told you business been kinda slow and I got you when it start to. ."he is saying before Big Bro slaps him hard across the face and then punches him knocking him to the ground before taking his gun out of the back of his waist handing it to Drama and saying" I'M your brother, ride for me, kill his ass."

"You want me to kill him for real?" Drama asks holding the chrome four five directly at dude.

"I'm serious, kill him! Ain't nobody gone say shit" replies Big Bro as Drama stares directly into dudes scared face with his adrenaline now rushing, but his finger just can't squeeze the trigger.

"Come on bad ass, hurry up, it's getting cold out here." Big Bro says pushing him before Drama hands him the gun back, gets mad and walks back in the back door.

"Like I said. So, stop snatching ass." Big Bro yell's at Drama before turning back to dude and saying" I don't care if you gotta sell ya ass. I want my money ASAP." before he walks back in the crib.

"SO, What happen gangsta?" asks Big Bro to Drama." "You right, I can be a man and admit that." Replies Drama.

"Well don't be running around with no gun if you ain't gone use it just as fast as you picked it up." Big Bro says putting his arms around his neck giving him a hug clearly showing he loves his little brother.

"So, you gone chill wit me tonight or what?" Asks Big Bro seeing it's getting late by the clock on the wall.

"Yeah, I'll hang around." Replies Drama drinking another cup of Absolute.

"Well let's go over some bitch's house then. What's up with some of them older hoes you be talking too?" Ask Big Bro.

"I just fuck bitches and leave 'em, cause when you stick around they start to want shit." Replies Drama.

"Preach pimp, but I know you got some hoes house we can go over." Big Bro says taking his phone out of his pocket. "Let me see that shit, I'll see what I can do." Replies Drama getting the phone, thinking and then dialing some numbers.

"Look, it's my shift tonight so I'm bout to bounce Blood so, I'll get at you." Joe says throwing up their set before leaving as a couple of other dudes follow and Big Bro walks out with them.

"Thank you, young man." Mitch says to Drama who just looks at him without replying as he continues to dial numbers in the phone and letting it ring.

"Hello?" A female asks answering the phone. "Can I speak to Jessica?"

"This is she who is this?" she asks before Drama lets her know and they start a conversation.

While on the porch Big Bro smokes a blunt talking to a black skinny older man.

"So, everything alright with ya'11?" Asks the man.

"I mean, I don't know what happened cause we had just got round there, and they were staring at us." Replies Big Bro about earlier.

"Well them young boys is scared to death Maine, and I thought they was gangsta's. You should see them jumping and ducking every time someone walks or drives by."

"Ain't none of them talk to the police, did it?"

"Yeah, everybody did, they had to. But I don't think anybody said anything." Replies the man as Nobel pulls up in a Lincoln, gets out and walks over to them.

"Let me holla at you right quick." He says to Big Bro who walks off with Nobel after giving the man five before walking in the shot house.

" Look we officially out of everything so I just called Joe and told him to shut down for today and I went to holla at them little niggas from earlier and a long story short they said they don't want no problems and they trying to squash the shit cause fiends scared to come through, cops everywhere and money getting fucked up." Nobel says to Big Bro.

"Well they need to talk to Trigger and them cause as long as they ain't fucking with Drama I ain't got shit to do with it.

"They chopped it up with Hova. I had him with me when we all went over there, and they talked for whatever that was worth and then they shook hands so I guess the shit dead, but I still told him they need to stay from round there for a couple of days until shit cool down." Nobel says.

"So, where the hell did you find him at?" Asks Big Bro.

"At some accident by Lil Ones crib. A little girl and her dog got hit by a drunk driver."

"Damn." Big Bro says smoking the last of the blunt and throwing it.

"Maine, we need to be getting on. Fuck all that shit, cause them niggas money ain't the only ones who's getting fucked up and I been looking for a better connect who can meet the supply and demand we need every time without all the hassle." Noble says as they lean on the trunk of the Lincoln as Drama comes out of the shot house.

"We good. And shit will be up and jumping tomorrow, so all that new connect shit is not poppin' cause you just can't trust everybody." Replies Big Bro as Drama gets to where they are.

"So, what's up with them little kids?" Big Bro says jokingly to Drama.

"Shut the fuck up. And shawty is eighteen. Just cause I'm young don't mean I ain't got older hoes. She lives with her mom's though, so we can't be making no whole lot of noise."

"Alright, well let's go round there then. A look Nobel, I'm gone get at you tomorrow and we gone grind out all day alright."

Big Bro says to Drama and then to Nobel as he gives both of them five and gets back in the Lincoln as Big Bro and Drama walk to his caddie, gets in and pulls off.

Forest Hill South Side

When they get to her crib she is staring out of her bed room window with the light on.

"Well at least I know she ain't ugly, and her friend bet not be either." Big Bro says jokingly as he parks and they get out of the car and walk to and on her porch and wait for her to open the door. When she opens the door, Big Bro sees that she is a short light skin older looking girl with straight hair going down the sides of her face and through her baggy black T shirt you can tell she has some very big titties.

"Yall be quiet when yall come in here cause I'm not trying to hear my mommas mouth." She says letting them in as they walk past her mother's room and lil sisters down the hall to her room when they get up the stairs.

"And she phat and I don't think she got no draws on." Big Bro says to Drama as they both smile before they get in her room and she closes and locks the bed room door.

"I'm still waiting for Mashonda." She says laying on her bed and flipping through the channels on her big screen TV as they sit on the pink couch in her room staring at her skin shine off the light in her room as she lays on her stomach with one leg in the air.

"What are yall so quiet for and why are yall staring at me like that." She says with a smile knowing they're looking at her legs and can smell the scented lotion she had just put on.

"Ain't nobody looking at you, we looking at the TV" replies Drama. "Whatever, so that's your brother? What's your name?" she asks. "Big Bro and what's yo name?"

"Jessica." She replies as she picks her phone up and dials some numbers.

"She's calling the police. She knows I'm too old to be over here." Big Bro whispers to Drama as they both bust out laughing from being drunk.

"Shh!" She says turning the TV up some as they quiet down but continue to laugh a little, "this bitch still in the house, she not coming." Jessica says hanging the phone up.

"well if you want me to leave I'll go. Just call me when you ready for me to come pick you up." Big Bro says. "You ain't gotta go nowhere it ain't like we doing nothing." Replies Jessica.

"So, what's up then, you smoke weed?" Asks Big Bro. "Occasionally." She replies.

"Well shit, you trying to blow now?" Asks Big Bro. "I don't care."

"Jessica?" They hear her mother call out.

"Oh shit, my mamma coming, get in the closet."

"Hell naw, you get in the closet." Drama says to her jokingly.

"I'm serious." She says in a whisper as they hide in the closet as her mama knocks on the door and she get up unlocks it and opens it.

"Huh?" She asks her mother. "Who are you in there talking to?"

"Mashonda and Tevin on speaker phone." She replies as her mother glances in the room.

"I was on my way to the bath room and heard laughing, and said to myself I know this child ain't got nobody in here this time of night."

"I don't know nobody who would be over here this time of night." Replies Jessica with a smile.

"Well. turn that TV down before you wake your little sister up, and I don't know what I had to eat but it is running through me." Her mother says as Jessica can hear Drama and Big Bro in the closet laughing so she laughs as well.

"That's not funny." Her mother says before farting and saying "OOH." Before she quickly walks off and Jessica shuts the door embarrassed as Drama and Big Bro both fall out of the closet laughing.

"I know she ain't just fart. Fuck that she just gotta catch me in here." "And that shit sounded wet." They say on the floor laughing.

"Yall be quiet." She says laughing as well while still standing at the door listening to hear if she is coming back.

When she hears her door shut, she sits back on her bed tripping off the tears Drama and Big Bro have in their eyes from laughing so hard.

"Is yall finished?" She asks.

"Come on now you know that shit was funny." Drama says as they sit back on the couch in her room.

Yall drunk too?" She asks.

"Yeah. But is you still trying to get high or what?" asks Big Bro. "Don't matter." She says getting up going to the dresser, pulling out some scented candles and lighting them as Drama and Big Bro both roll up while throwing the blunt stuffing in her little trash can. Giving her the blunt, she cuts the light off as they all blaze up and a movie plays on the TV. Coughing she asks "yall want me to smoke this whole thing by myself?"

"Yeah." Replies Drama looking at the TV "Let me blow you a gun." Big Bro tells her.

"Blow me a gun? What the hell is that?" She asks.

"Look, give me your blunt and close your mouth and one of your nostrils. And when I blow, inhale through your other. nostril." He says as she does it and damn near chokes.

"I don't wanna do that no more." She says still coughing and hitting her chest as he gives her blunt back.

"All that coughing, you gone be high as a motherfucker." Drama says staring between her legs as she sits on the bed not knowing her shirt is up and her draws are showing as she sits with her legs open showing her black silk panties. Looking at Drama she follows his eyes and notices what he's looking at before she fixes her shirt.

"Thank you anyway." Drama says as they both smile. "What yall talking about?" Asks Big Bro.

"Nothing." Replies Drama looking at Jessica and then looking back at the TV

"Yall wanna fuck me, don't you?" Jessica asks with a smile which catches them both off guard as they both now smile at her.

"Where that come from." Asks Drama.

"I see how yall keep looking at me, and don't no dudes come over no girl's house this late just to smoke weed. So that's why I asked that." She says still smoking the blunt.

"Shawty, we came to chill, and yo friend ain't show up. plus, you said my brother can come cause ain't nobody " Drama is saying before she says "Shhh Yall wanna see me strip?"

"HELL YEAH!" Big Bro says tired of Drama beating around the bush as she giggles, puts her blunt out in the ash tray with literally no ashes before she climbs on the bed and slowly dances as she smiles before lifting her shirt off slowly which shows a matching red bra and panties. Turning around she dips low and shakes her ass at them which looks like it's clapping.

"OK!" Big Bro says taking out some money and throwing it at her before she eases off the bed, sits on Drama's lap and acts like she's riding him as she takes her bra off exposing her titties before she gets up and bends over in front of Big Bro before sitting on his lap and riding him backwards as he feels her titties while she undoes his belt and pants before standing up and sliding her draws off as she goes back to Drama and pulls his sweatpants and boxers down before sitting slowly down on his dick as she tells Big Bro to stand in front of her.

Pulling out his dick, she sucks on it while riding Drama, moaning and slurping as she goes faster on both of them while they grunt, and she does what she does like a pro.

Switching, Big Bro hits it from the back and she sucks Drama off while throwing her ass back as Big Bro hits it from the back.

Pulling out, Big Bro busses on her ass while rubbing his dick on her butt cheeks as she is bent over still sucking Dramas balls before deep throating his dick and sucking it until he busses in her mouth while she swallows it all and continues until it's no more left.

Smiling, she asks "Now you see why I don't smoke weed?" "Shit! I would kill a nigga mamma to get you a blunt." replies Big Bro as they get dressed and she picks up her clothes and says "Yall be quiet." Before she leaves out of her room and goes in the bathroom.

"Look Drama, I'm gone asks you first. What's her phone number?" "Hell naw, that's my little freak nasty. And she a church girl so her mamma make her stay in the house."

"Come on Maine, don't let me find out your name is captain save a hoe." "You damn right. Look in the sky it's a bird, it's a plane, it's me, the older chick handcuffer captain save a hoe." Drama replies as they both laugh.

"Shit I'm ready to bounce now." Big Bro says now channel surfing.

Sparking his blunt back up Drama says, "Maybe you need to chill with me more often, huh?"

"No doubt." Replies Big Bro giving him five as they both look at the cartoon channel until she comes back in the room.

"Damn what you went in there and took a bath?" Asks Drama.

"I might be a little freak, but I'm not trifling. I went and brushed my teeth and washed up." She replies with a yawn.

"So what yall ready to do?" She asks.

"Damn, what you trying to kick us out?" Asks Big Bro.

I'm just tired from our little get together. And I know yall probably ready to bounce anyway." She states in a nonchalant tone.

"I love you." Big Bro says smiling "But for real it is kinda late, but you know I wouldn't mind chilling with you more often." continues Big Bro while getting up.

"Don't be a stranger then. And tell your brother he need to call me more often." She says to Big Bro looking over at Drama with a smile as she talks to him as if he isn't in the room.

"I'll make sure he does that." Big Bro says opening his arms as she gives him a hug and then does the same to Drama but a little longer.

"You better call me." She says as she lets him go and they make their way out of her room and down the hall where they all can hear her mother snoring.

"Damn, who in there with her?" Big Bro asks jokingly.

"Shit, maybe we need to go check and see if anybody in her closet, snoring like that." He continues as the three of them laugh while they walk down the stairs before giving her another hug before they leave out, get in the caddie and pull off blasting "The Message" By Nas.

Chapter 5

Twenty Sixth St. East End
Next Day (Thursday) September 26,1999

Waking up and rolling over onto an empty space on the bed, Big Bro realizes his girl has already left for work. Laying on his back in the empty bed, he yawns as he watches her ceiling fan slowly rotate above him before he stretches and starts making his way off of her Queen size water bed in his boxer's and into the bathroom. After getting his self together he comes out of the bathroom and make his way to the kitchen, opening the refrigerator he takes out a half empty gallon of milk and takes the box of Cinnamon Toast Crunch off of the top of the refrigerator before shutting the door of the refrigerator and placing the milk and cereal on the counter before he begins to get a bowl and spoon.

Pennsylvania St., West End

Watching a few of his homies stand in the street fighting jumping in a new recruit Joe glances from them to his watch before saying "alright, time." To which they all stop. Heavily winded they lock B's with the new recruit who is bleeding and pretty banged up but happy to have gotten it over with and now be officially considered Damu.

As they all walk over to Joe he locks B's with the skinny dark skin male and says "You rumbled like a true solider out their little nigga, so that's what I'm gone name you. And from here on out you gone be known as that Bloody Solja you feel me?"

Smiling with a busted lip, he accepts his new name with pride before one of the homies gives him his red flag and they all walk down to the corner talking while some stay and stand post in front of Joe while watching the block which seems to literally be filled with other Damus of all ages and genders doing everything from sitting on porches with music blasting from the house to selling drugs and shooting dice.

"I like that little nigga." Joe says out loud to no one in particular as one of the Damus in front of him silently nods in agreement.

"A yo Kreep, did Bags handle that business yesterday?" inquires Joe to the Damu who just agreed with him to which he shakes his head saying no without speaking, which he hardly ever does. Sucking his teeth Joe doesn't say anything as he looks down toward the corner and loudly says "SOOO WOOOP!" To which it seems like the whole block erupts with the response as he waves for the new homie and those who are with him to come to him.

Church Hill

Fully dressed now in all black, Big Bro drives his caddie to his crib. Upon getting to and in the duplex, he walks to Drama's room first and sees him asleep so he shuts his door and goes to his own room. Checking the caller, I.D, he doesn't see anyone important has called so he puts the phone back on the charger before getting up and leaving back out of the duplex.

Getting in his car he notices he's low on gas so he decides to get that out of the way before he starts his day.

Starting his car up and letting all of his windows down, he turns up "The Promise" by Foxy Brown and pulls off. When he pulls up in Parsleys gas station he gets out and makes his way toward the cashier's window to pay for his gas. Getting to the window he stands in a short line with some people of various ages that he doesn't recognize so he stands in silence until it is his turn at the window to which he pays for his gas and buys some candy before walking back to his car and pumping his gas watching cars ride past him up and down the street.

"Big Bro!" He hears someone call out to him in which he looks behind him and smiles at the familiar face as the light skin girl pushes a baby stroller with her son in it toward him.

"Hey Lauren where you on your way to?" He asks her as she gets to him and stops.

"Bout to take little Steve round Creighton over his daddy house." She replies smiling in his face as he looks down at little Steve and smiles before looking back up at her and saying.

"That little nigga look just like his daddy."

"Don't remind me." She replies in a joking manner.

"Well don't let me hold you up or nothing cause I was just speaking." She continues before they say their goodbyes and she continues on her way and he looks at her ass as she walks away and he continues to fill up his gas tank.

Second Ave. North Side

"I'm gone be up the block." One of the two Damus who was standing in front of Joe named Kapone says to Solja who gets out of the passenger seat of an Infinity jeep and shuts the door as Kapone pulls off and Solja makes his way toward his first mission without a trace of fear on his face ignoring the rest of the people standing around or walking the strip.

Getting up the steps to the porch of a grey house, he pulls a nine-millimeter from his waist line and rings the doorbell. After a few moments a female's voice asks, "Who is it?"

"Dap, is Bags here?" He asks using the name Bags knows him by. "Hold on." Replies the female as he stands at the door with his adrenaline rushing.

Minutes later he hears Bags loud voice talking to someone in the house before the door comes open and they lock eyes in a friendly way. Smiling, Bags who isn't paying attention to the fact that Solja has his hand behind his back asks, "What's up shawty?" Before Solja takes his hand from behind his back and with no words shoots him point blank in the face five times as he was told before he runs off of the porch with a trail of screams being heard from behind him in the house.

Williamsburg Rd.

"Did you hear that they are enforcing a six o'clock curfew tonight because of that shit that happened yesterday?" Hova asks Noble from the passenger seat of Nobel's Crown Victoria as Nobel drives down Williamsburg road banging "Hail Mary" by 2 Pac.

"Yeah, I saw it." Nobel simply replies as the music plays before looking over at him and saying "So you a little gangsta huh? I like that right there."

Smiling Hova replies "I mean sometimes a nigga gotta do what a nigga gotta do. Especially when a nigga force his hand."

"That's right." Nobel says in agreement as he nods to his statement. "See, I can fuck with a nigga like you. That's why I got you with me now. You got the heart. You just need a nigga to show you the game and when I'm finished with you a nigga ain't gone be able to tell you shit. Alright," Nobel continues as he smiles at Hova and gives him five.

17th Street, South Side Later That Afternoon

"Where the fuck is Hova at?" Trigger asks Lil One as him Drama, and J.V sit on the porch smoking weed.

"I don't know that dude like that." Replies Lil One exhaling smoke from his nose looking out toward the empty street.

"It's boring as a mother fucker." Drama says to no one in particular. "That's cause it's hot as a motherfucker round here with all these police constantly riding up and down the street." Lil One says to him before standing up and spitting off the porch before going in the house.

Looking at J.V Drama smiles and says, "You ugly as a bitch shawty." "I'm glad you think so, cause if you thought I looked good we'd be rolling around on the ground out here." replies J.V.

"What? Shawty we both know the only person that's gone be rolling around on the ground is you after I knock yo ass out." Drama says as they all start laughing and G Way pulls up in front of Lil Ones crib listening to NWA in a stolen black Dynasty.

"Look at this nigga Lil One gone cuss his ass out again for pulling up in front of his crib in that shit." Trigger says as they watch G Way make his way towards them.

"What's up my niggas?" he asks as they all speak and J.V hands him a blunt.

"Lil One gone say something about you having that car parked right there." Trigger tells him.

"Oh yeah, why?" Asks G Way.

"Cause its police everywhere out this motherfucker." replies Triggers "Oh, well yall trying to go somewhere then?" Asks G Way.

"We waiting for Vel to come back with something now." Replies Drama as Lil One comes out of the house eating ice cream. Looking at G Way and then looking at the Dynasty parked behind three of his cars, he blurts out "Oh hell no!!! You gone have to move that shit! RIGHT NOW!"

"I know I was about to do it anyway. Well look, I'm gone holla at yall later, I ain't trying to wait around for Vel." G Way says giving the blunt back to J.V.

"Where you bout to go?" Asks Drama not really wanting to wait around for Vel either.

"I don't know, somewhere." Replies G Way giving them all five.

"I'll roll with you." Drama says getting up and walking with G Way to the Dynasty and getting in the passenger seat. Getting in the driver seat G Way pulls a screw driver out of his pocket and places it in the broken-out space where the cars ignition used to be before he glow pieced it.

Turning the screw driver, he starts the car up and pulls off while Drama rewinds the "Fuck the Police" song that was playing in the tape deck.

"Shit was crazy as a mother fucker yesterday." G Way says as Drama constantly pushes the rewind and play buttons trying to catch the beginning of the song.

"Hell yeah. I was gone stay in the house today but I said fuck that shit." Replies Drama letting the song play as he leans back in the seat while G Way stops at a stop sign before making a right.

"Shit!" He says seeing a police car driving directly towards them.

Seeing what he's looking at Drama calmly replies, "Maine fuck them people, this South Side they ain't fucking with us." As like he said the police car rides right past them. Looking in the rear-view mirror G-way watches the cop car keep straight.

"Yeah, yall was rights It's hot round here. You trying to go out Petersburg and get something? Cause I done had this shit for a few days now." Asks G-way as Drama passes him a blunt and chokes.

Hitting his chest, he says "I don't give a fuck."

Broad Street

Sitting inside of a black Yukon Denali eating some pizza and cheese sticks from pizza Hut listening to Nas "Street Dreams" Big Bro, Joe and a few others talk about Solja as Kreep drives.

"That's what's up. But he needs to think things through more carefully next time cause if he doing his like that, that nigga gone end up in jail." Big Bro says before sipping his soda through a straw.

"Yeah, I had talked to him. The little homies gone get him right though." Replies Joe with his hand over his mouth as he chews his food.

"What's up with the other three new homies?" Asks Big Bro keeping up with what is taking place in his set.

"Prime Time and Rule straight. But ain't nobody viewed C.K in a while. Word is he caught a dope and gun case and done got an investigation started on us and I told Bags he needed to take care of that since he brought the nigga in the hood and vouched for him, but he took shit for a joke but this Mad Stone Gangsta Blood set don't play that shit so you already be knowing how that ended." Replies Joe as he locks B' and throws it up with Big Bro to emphasize his point and Kreep says "That's right." As he drives them back around the West End. When they get back around the strip everyone is basically doing what they we're doing before they left. Pulling up behind Big Bros caddie Kreep parks and cuts the truck off as everyone exits the truck but Joe and Big Bro who choose to remain in the truck and watch the block from behind it's tinted windows while they both continue to eat.

That's Solja right there standing between Point Blank and Black Out." Joe says as Big Bro leans toward Joes side of the window and sees Solja drinking a forty ounce and talking to Black Out.

"Yeah, I ain't never seen him before." Replies Big Bro.

"He a good nigga. I fuck with him." Joe says now eating the rest of his medium size pizza as Big Bro lights a blunt and takes a hard pull, inhaling and holding it in.

"A Joe." he says looking over at him and exhaling a cloud of smoke "On some G shit, I know we all grew up together, but as we grew up I feel like some of us grew apart, and lately I can't explain the feeling I've been having, but I been feeling like something real fucked up bout to happen and I'm not liking the looks I'm seeing on niggas faces sometimes." Plucking the blunt ashes in his almost empty pizza box he passes the blunt to Joe who in a calm tone takes the blunt and asks "Who you talking bout? Me big homie?" While hitting the blunt.

"Naw homie I view nothing but realness when I, look at you. But I can't speak for the rest of them niggas. I just been getting fucked up vibes lately and niggas been moving real crazy." Replies Big Bro leaned back in the seat and staring off into space as the weed smoke starts to cloud the truck.

"I've been viewing that shit. I'm just waiting to view who gone stick they head out that hole so I can pop they motherfucking top off!" Joe says passing the blunt back to him and looking out the window seeing some of the older homies showing a crowd of the younger homies how to B walk as they do it and stack spelling out everything with ease. Looking back at Big Bro who's staring off into space while smoking the blunt Joe says, "Fuck these niggas for real, cause if any of these niggas try something they gone have to kill me too." As Big Bro nods in agreement but remains silent as he passes the blunt back to Joe.

Pulling up in the SanSusan apartments in a stolen gold drop top banging Jay Z; Vel, who's driving finds a parking space in the crowded parking lot before letting the black rag top up on the car while J.V and Trigger hold a conversation. Cutting the car off with the screw driver, Vel and Trigger get out of the two-door car while J.V has to first push the passenger seat up and then gets out shutting the door behind him. Eye balling a Bonneville Trigger says "I gotta have that whenever we leave from out here."

Looking at the black and gold trimmed car neither J.V or Vel responds as they make their way to an apartment directly in front of them. Getting in the hallway they walk to the door on the left and Vel knocks. After a few seconds pass a female voice asks, "Who is it?"

"Vel." He replies before the door opens revealing a chubby light skin girl with her hair in a ponytail." Robin here?" asks Vel.

"I'm Robin. "she replies smiling before inviting them into the nicely decorated living room where they all have a seat in silence while Trigger and

J.V both look at Vel like "What the fuck."

"Yall ain't got to be so quiet ain't nobody here. My aunt and them at work and school." Robin says sitting down on the other side of Vel on the couch. Trying to be funny J.V asks her "So how did the two of yall meet?"

"The Chat Line." She replies still smiling. "Oh yeah, so you think he cute or what?"

"He knows he cute." She replies taking her finger and using it to turn his face directly in front of hers as she looks at him as if she expects a kiss. Not trying to disrespect her he just smiles and acts as if he's shy by putting his head back down.

"Gat damn Vel, you see she wanted a kiss. What you acting like that for? You want us to leave?" asks Trigger joining in with J.V.

Giving him a look that should tell him to shut the fuck up Vel smoothly replies "This ain't the time or place for that right now." To which J.V and Trigger start laughing.

"So, you trying to go upstairs then?" She asks seriously as J.V and Triggers jaws drop in shock. Looking at each other as to verify what was just said, they then look at Vel to see what his response would be.

After a short pause he looks at them and smiles before looking at her and saying, "I don't care." as she grabs his hand and gets up before he even finishes his sentence. Pulling him up off the couch with a huge smile on her face, she leads him to and up the steps as Trigger and J.V watch them disappear upstairs. When they get upstairs she leads him to her aunts room and shuts the door behind them.

"Take your clothes off." She says looking at him with the same smile she had on her face ever since she opened the door as he thinks to his self how much of a freak she is as he sits on her aunt's bed and starts undressing while she watches him with lust in her eyes without saying a word.

When he gets down to nothing but his black and grey Joe boxers and white socks he asks her to do the same to which she walks over and sits beside him. Grabbing his hand, she guides it under her long T-shirt until his hand feels the moistness of her hairless pussy.

"I don't have anything on under this shirt." She says sliding her tongue in his ear before she sucks on it and places her hand inside of his boxers and starts stroking his penis. "Take yo boxers off and come on." She tells him and he does what she says while she lays on her back with her T shirt still on and her legs open.

"You ain't gone take that shirt off?" Asks Vel which she declines before he crawls on top of her and slides right in while she breaths heavier and heavier with every stroke but refuses to moan as he picks up one of her legs and starts to go faster which makes her open her mouth like she is ready to scream but she only continues to breath heavily. After holding this position for a few moments and still not getting the desired effect, he stops and a bit winded he tells her to bend over.

Poking her big light skin ass directly up at him, as he goes to enter her from the back she looks back at him seductively and says, "Put it in my ass."

Shocking him for a brief moment, he takes his dick and slides it up and down her now sweaty ass crack before trying to get it inside of her tight asshole which now causes her to moan loudly into the pillow on the bed that she grips tightly with every thrust he makes to try and get deeper inside of her.

The more he gets inside of her the louder she moans. Getting half of it up in her he feels his self cumming and pulls out just in time as he busts off on her ass and the lower part of her back.

"Damn." He says looking down at her as she looks at him with an unsatisfied look and asks, "That's all?"

"Is that all?" Vel asks in a surprised tone shocked that she would ask him something like that.

"Yeah, is that all you got? Cause I ain't cum nothing but one or two times." She says with her ass still up in the air.

"I done came already, you want some more?" Asks Vel still on his knees behind her. Smiling she says, "Look I'm gone go wipe this stuff off me and when I come back I want you to eat me."

"This bitch is unbelievable." Vel thinks to his self before quickly saying "Alright, but let me go clean myself up first." As he gets up off the bed and she does as well saying "We might as well just get in the shower together."

Trying to think of a quick escape plan he says" I ain't trying to get in the shower, I'm just trying to wash myself up." But she refuses to take no for an answer as she drags both of them naked to and in the bathroom.

Colonial Heights

Climbing through his second window of that day, Hova follows Nobel from the living room to the stairs of a house where Nobel says someone named "Michael" lives at. Walking up the stairs holding empty black trash bags Nobel goes one way while Hova goes the other as they both enter separate rooms. So far Hova has went from being a look out in the car to actually breaking in these houses with him.

Even though he knows Noble had found something, he constantly pretended he found nothing, but took what Hova found. Quickly sweeping the room Hova, who from the look of the room is in a teenage boys room so he leaves out to the next room which is a girls room that he doesn't even bother to enter after seeing the stuffed teddy bears all lined neatly on the wall, so he decides to try his hand down stairs.

Walking past the room Nobel is in he sees him with a bag full of something and opening his second bag, but he doesn't say anything he just makes his way down stairs.

Sunny Drive Ashland, VA That Evening

As "Get Money" blasts from the house speakers everyone looks to be having a good time while they either dance or converse with one another. With a group of at least Thirty Bloods and Crips together, Big Bro and Quarter speak with each other as they stand on the wall with plastic cups of Absolute while some of their homies stand post in front of them stopping any and every one from approaching either of them.

"Speaking of the devil." Big Bro says seeing Nobel walk through the front door and not seeing them so he walks in the opposite direction of where they are.

"I wonder where the fuck he been at all day. He's usually right beside you." Quarter says to Big Bro.

"Yeah, that's only when shit jumping. When ain't shit popping that nigga ain't nowhere to be found." Replies Big Bro in a disgusted tone as Varsity tries to holla at him but is stopped by the dudes standing in front of them.

"Nah, Yall can let him through he straight." Big Bro says to the group before they let him through with cold stares which he ignores as he walks up to Big Bro and Quarter giving them both five with hugs and asking "Yall niggas been upstairs yet?"

"Nah, why? What's up." Asks Quarter who had noticed a lot of people going up or coming down the steps.

"It's a pretty little freak joint letting niggas run trains on her left and right. I just came from up that joint, me and some niggas I ain't never met was punishing this bitch." Replies Varsity with a huge smile on his face as Big Bro looks up toward the upstairs of the house and asks "Oh yeah. What type shit she letting niggas do?"

"Everything! She drinking nut and some more shit. Four niggas had just gone in when we was coming out and the pussy sloppy wet." Replies

Varsity holding his dick getting horny again from just thinking about it.

Looking at Quarter and smiling Big Bro says, "We might have to go up there and show that bitch something."

"The crazy part about it is this ain't no ugly bitch. This one of them bitches you'll let push the whip." Varsity says.

"Oh yeah, something ain't right bout that then." Quarter says, taking a sip from his cup.

"Yo, the bitch is high and drunk out of her-mind; I mean fucked up. She did have a friend up there too, but when so many groups of niggas started coming in there she left, cause at first she was letting niggas fuck her while she was eating the other bitch and sucking dick at the same time." Replies Varsity.

"Shit where she go?" Asks Quarter as Varsity looks around the crowded party before looking back at him and saying "Shit I don't know."

"She might have gone back in that motherfucker." Big Bro says wishful thinking.

"I don't know, but the way shorty up there fucking yall might can take some bitches up there if they trying to " Varsity is saying before both Quarter and Big Bro start to make their way toward the steps with their personal security not far behind them. Laughing to himself, Varsity watches them talk to some females as they make their way up the steps and before they get to the top they have two girls following them.

"That's right my niggas." Varsity says before walking back into the crowd. Bumping into Nobel he asks him if he had seen Big Bro and he points him in the direction he went before Noble makes his way towards upstairs as well.

Fairmount Ave.

Standing in front of Fair play convince store Drama who now has a freshly stolen white Infinity jeep stands beside it as him and G way try to get a crack head to buy them some beer out the store. "Naw young blood I don't do that." The crack head man says to him as G way who was leaning on the hood of a white and burgundy Oldsmobile stands up and asks "Why not? We got the money, it ain't like its coming out of your pockets."

"I could get in trouble for that. That's why I'm not gone do it. Yall don't need to be drinking no way if yall can't go in the store and buy it yourself." The man says smartly which upsets them both as G Way walks toward him with his fist balled up asking "Who the fuck you getting smart with?" Backing up, the man doesn't even pay attention to Drama who has crept behind him and before he knows it has snuffed him from behind as G Way three pieces him before he drops to the ground and they began stomping him and kicking him in the face, mouth and stomach until he lays defenseless on the pavement of the parking lot in between their two cars.

"I bet the next time a mother fucker asks you to get they ass something out the store you won't hesitate." Drama says as he kicks him one last time as hard as he could in his bloodied face before they both get in their whips and pull off.

When they get around Twenty Fourth street they see some dudes with Hova, Trigger and Vel shooting dice. Pulling up in front of them Drama gets out while G-Way parks behind him.

"Damn nigga, where the fuck yall been at?" Asks Trigger glancing up at them before catching the dice.

"A little bit of everywhere, where J.V at?" Asks Drama looking at the money they have piled in front of them.

"In the house." Replies Vel.

"Where yall get all that money from?" Asks Drama as G Way gets in the game.

"We won it from Hova." Replies Trigger as Drama looks at Hova but doesn't bother to ask him anything he just states "yall niggas hot as a bitch." but no one replies due to their attention on the dice game.

"I'll be back." Drama says not wanting to sit around watching them shoot dice so he walks back to the jeep which he left running, gets in and pulls off. Bored, he drives to his crib and parks the car a block down from his. Cutting the car off he walks to and in his house.

Going straight to the kitchen once he's inside, he opens the oak cabinets and looks at the can goods they have stacked inside. Grabbing a can of ravioli, he sits it on the counter and gets the pot out to cook it as he decides to stay in the house the rest of the night.

CHAPTER 6

Venable St East End
Next Day (Friday) September 27, 1999

Knocking on Dramas Door G Way waits awhile before Big Bro opens the door and lets him in and he goes to Drama's room where he is laying on the bed looking at TV

"What's up my nigga?" G Way asks before sitting on the small couch he has in his room.

"Ain't shit." Replies Drama not taking his eyes off the TV as he silently debates with himself if he is going to go to Pooh, Yummy and Tyrone's funeral before as if G Way is reading his mind asks, "are you going to the funeral home to see Yummy and them?"

After a short pause Drama replies "Nah, I ain't trying to see them niggas like that. J.V called me this morning and asked me the same thing before him and Varsity left to go up there."

"Well I just came from all them joints and I saw everybody but you and Hova. That's why I came over here to make sure you was alright. You is going to their funerals though ain't it?" Asks G Way but Drama tries to avoid the question by asking "you trying to play Madden?"

Noticing the avoidance of the question as he watches Drama walk to the Nintendo 64, he figures he isn't going, so he doesn't bother to ask him again as he catches the controller Drama tosses him as the video game now plays on the TV and he walks back to his bed with his controller in his hand.

"I don't know." Drama finally says and G Way silently nods as they both choose their football teams. Knocking on the door Big Bro waits for a response before sticking his head in Drama's room and saying, "I'm bout to bounce, you need anything?"

"You got some trees?" Asks Drama before Big Bro goes in his pocket and tosses him at least a quarter of weed that's tied inside of a plastic bag.

"You straight?" Asks Big Bro.

"Yeah." Replies Drama before Big Bro shuts his room door.

"I fuck with your brother." G Way says with a smile as Drama pauses the game and gets a half empty box of Dutch Masters off the dresser and passes him one out of the box as they both get ready to roll up.

Twenty Fourth St.

Sitting in Nobel's living room with a few others who are talking loudly as they smoke and drink while watching ESPN on the big screen TV, Hova with a razor blade in his hand cuts up the crack, one of the others showed him how to cook a few minutes ago as he now sits at the living room table currently bagging up the crack by himself due to them constantly stopping and arguing about everything from Hockey to Base Ball. He doesn't mind though, cause in his mind he's getting free money.

"Ask shawty." Hova hears one of the dudes say before one of them try to get him to agree with him about a sports question, but Hova knowing nothing about sports can only truthfully respond

"I don't watch sports."

"What?" Dude asks in disbelief as the room seems to get quiet and everyone stares at him.

"Nah, I just ain't into that shit." Replies Hova feeling a bit uneasy. "Don't worry about it, when I'm finished with you, you gone know more than these niggas in here." Nobel says before they all get loudly back into their sports disagreements and Hova continues to bag up the cut-up crack.

Willow Lawn, Shopping Center Later That Afternoon

Walking through the mall into the food court with two hands full of shopping bag's Big Bro, Tammy, Joe, his girl and a few of their homies slash body guards find some empty tables and have a seat to rest their feet.

"What you trying to eat?" Big Bro asks Tammy before she looks around the food court and says, "I want some tacos."

"Alright." Big Bro replies leaving the bags on the ground as he gets up and makes his way toward the mini Taco Bell restaurant with one of his homies not far behind him.

"Why you' buy them ugly ass Jordan's for?" Big Bro looks back and asks him.

"Cause, they was Jordan's. I gotta have every shoe he put out." He replies as they walk over to the small line and look at the brightly lit menu.

"Fuck that shit. He can't get my money like that." Big Bro continues before his phone rings and he pulls it from his waist and turn it on.

"Hello?" He asks as he hears huffing and puffing on the other end before Kreep blurts out "A yo big homie, the FEDS just did a sweep and locked everybody up."

"What? Where?" Asks Big Bro as shock and fear shoots through his body.

"Round Pennsylvania. They jumped out of a UPS truck and then started coming from everywhere. So, whatever you do stay from round there." Replies an out of breath Kreep.

"Alright, where Nobel at?" Asks Big Bro. "I don't know I thought he was with you."

"Naw, and I don't know if this phone tapped so I'm gone get at you later." Big Bro replies before they both disconnect, and he looks at his homie and says, "The FEDS just hit around the West end." Before they both quickly walk back toward where they were sitting.

Venable St East End

As slow music makes its way out of the stereo speakers at an even tone, two different moans and screams that are coming from the living room and Dramas room can be heard clearly over top of the music.

"Don't stop! AWH." The chubby brown skin girl moans while she lays on the couch and G Way stands leaning over her with both of her legs pent back in the air fucking her as fast and hard as he can.

Balling her face up, her leg starts to shake as she cums hard and lets out a loud "AWWWH! AWWWWH! OH GOD!" While G Way continues to pound away. In Dramas room a pretty petite light skin girl with sweat pouring down her face rides Drama backwards and he holds on to her waist while with her titties jiggling she bounces up and down on top of him saying "That's it baby. OOH YEAH. I feel you. cum for me . cum for me." Grunting as the wetness of her pussy makes all kinds of sounds he tries to stop his orgasm as she continues "Take this pussy. AWH, FUCK ME!"

"Mmmmmmmmmhhh! OOOOO, get it baby that's it, get it. OOH yeah AWH." She screams before he cums all over her ass while sweating and breathing heavily before she turns over and lays on top of him with her huge erect nipples pressing against his chest.

Six Street Market Place, Broad Street

Trying on a pair of wheat Timberland boots, Jasmine talks to J.V as he stands a few feet in front of her looking at a pair of Air Max's on the display case.

"I don't see why you ain't at least call the people back. I heard they pay good money up there."

"Them people ain't looking for nothing but a janitor and I ain't bout to be cleaning up no big ass bank unless I'm cleaning that bitch out. Fuck that, I got money saved up. It ain't like I'm hurting or nothing." Replies J.V before looking for one of the floor workers.

"I'm just saying, you ain't had a job in three weeks and in them three weeks you been running the streets with them crazy ass niggas and with all this crazy shit that's been going on lately I'm not trying to have you caught up in the middle of that." Jasmine says before putting the boot back in the box as one of the other floor workers picks the box up and walks toward the counter with it as she follows behind him. Standing in line waiting for a response from J.V who talks to one of the employees about something concerning the shoe he's holding, she can't hear what their saying over top of the other conversations going on in the store. When they finish their conversation the floor man takes the display shoe and walks toward the stock room in the back of the store and J.V gets in line a few people behind Jasmine who is standing at the counter paying for her boots and a matching skull cap with her credit card.

"A boo, get me that black V.A New Era fitted cap and that red one." J.V says to her which she does, after placing her merchandise in her bag she takes her receipt and goes to a bench in the store and waits silently for J.V to get to the counter and pay for his three pairs of shoes that she watches the dude he was talking to bring out of the store room and sit on the counter.

After paying in cash and getting his bags, he walks out of the line and she stands up before they both walk out of Foot Locker and then Six Street Market Place on to Broad Street.

"You hungry?" J.V asks her.

"I can wait until we get home." She replies as they walk to the bus stop. Grabbing his stomach J.V says "I'm hungry now. We can catch another bus. Let's go to the food court and get something to eat."

Looking at her watch she decides they won't have to wait long for another bus, so she agrees, and they make their way to the food court on the other side of the street inside Six Street Market Place on the Westside.

Mosby Court, East End

Handing a brown paper bag full of undisclosed contents to a skinny dark skin man, Varsity starts to put rolls of money in his pockets that he got from the exchange as they both sit in Varsity's car. With no more words exchanged they dap each other up before dude gets out of the car and Varsity cuts his car back on and pulls off listening to "Skies The Limit" by Biggie.

Driving up Fairmount Avenue, he sees an unfamiliar female with the face of a model and the perfect body. Beeping the horn and slowing down to a stop beside the female, he cuts the music down and calls her over to the car, but she says" Nah, if you wanna talk to me, park that car and approach me like you have some sense." Before she starts back walking as if she never saw him.

Liking her whole demeanor, he pulls off slowly while smiling to his self. Driving past her he parks a few cars in front of her before cutting his car off and stepping out into the street.

Hill Side South Side

Pulling up in the projects in a stolen black Grand Cherokee with gold trim banging "400 Degreez" by Juvenile, Trigger who's riding alone drives past lots of unfriendly faces as he takes it all in stride with his chrome nine he got from Lil One sitting on his lap as he continues driving until he sees his old friends standing out on the side walk talking to some females while selling drugs, smoking and drinking.

Stopping beside them he beeps the horn and receives hard stares from the dudes until they recognize his face.

"What's up Trig? What took you so long?" Asks the tallest in the group. "I wrecked so I had to get another car."

"You ain't getting chased or nothing is it?" asks dude backing up from the jeep and looking up and down the block.

"Naw, some old ass white lady hit the back of my shit and I conned her out of a thousand dollars talking bout I was hurt and would call the police." Trigger says which makes them all laugh.

"Shawty you crazy as a motherfucker, yall niggas come on." Dude says before walking to and getting in the passenger seat as the other dudes pile in the back and Trigger takes the Juvenile CD out and goes in his pocket and pulls out a Mobb Deep CD and puts the Juvenile CD in the Mobb Deep case after sticking the CD in the deck and skipping to the song "Shook Ones" before putting the case in his pockets and making a U-turn in the street and driving back the way he came.

Sitting on the hood of Nobel's car drinking a beer, Hova watches Nobel and two other dudes talk to a group of males about nothing as Nobel collects money from them while "Spread Love" by Mobb Deep blares through the car speakers.

Watching Nobel get on his phone, he notices a change in his demeanor as he positions his self away from the crowd and talks on the phone.

Looking behind him, he sees a tall dark skin girl, and as she walks down the street he follows her with his eyes. Looking at him she smiles but doesn't say anything as she begins to walk past.

"Hey Brittney, come here shawty. Where you going?" Hova hears one of the dudes say right as he opens his mouth to speak to her.

Walking over to the dude, she gives him a kiss and a hug before they both walk away from the dwindling crowd who are catching crack sells from passing people and a few passing cars. Watching her ass cheeks jiggle from left to right he nods to his self in approval before, taking another swig of his beer and wondering is her pussy any good.

Hanging his phone up Nobel yells "We gotta bounce." He says to his two Hench men as he stomps quickly towards the car. Looking at Hova who's getting off the hood of the car, he says "We gotta drop you off back around Church Hill. We got some serious shit we gotta take care of."

Nodding in agreement Hova throws the empty beer bottle across the street into a trash scattered field before he gets in the car and Nobel pulls off.

Twenty Fourth St. Church Hill Later that Evening

Yawning and stretching as he holds on to his bag of Dorito's, Drama leans on his stolen car as G Way, Trigger, Hova, and Vel shoot dice on the side walk.

"Is that all yall niggas ever do?" Asks Drama hearing Vel argue with Trigger about him keep catching the dice. Getting no response, he continues to eat his Dorito's and stare at the black Yukon Denali with tinted windows that his brother, Joe, Nobel, and some dudes he doesn't know sit in with "Favor for a Favor" by Nas coming out of the car speakers just loud enough to keep people from hearing the conversation they are having inside.

Seeing a police car make its way up the street, Drama looks at it and notices it's a new rookie cop, so he ignores him and continues to eat his chips knowing he can't see his friends shooting dice due to the jeep he's parked behind blocking the rookie's view.

As the officer rides past, they make eye contact, but he doesn't stop while he rides straight up the street. Seeing the police car half way up the block, now G Way stands up as they stop shooting dice and asks Drama "why you ain't tell us the police was coming?"

Not even bothering to turn around Drama plainly states "Because he couldn't even see over there."

As soon as he finishes his statement all the street lights and power go out leaving the block pitch black.

"What the fuck just happened?" Drama asks before hearing his brother yell "yall little niggas get the fuck from round here." Hearing the doors of the Yukon slam and them running before tires can be heard screeching and now what seems like thousands of head lights seem to come out of nowhere completely blocking off the block on both ends as car doors slam and screaming and yelling fill the air as some of the men in vests that read FBI try and find which way Big Bro and them ran while a few run towards them with their guns drawn screaming "GET ON THE GROUND NOW!" which they all do as they are quickly surrounded, handcuffed and snatched off the ground.

While agents search them for drugs and weapons a helicopter can be seen flying over them with a search light moving over the area.

"What the fuck is yall doing? What we do?" They all seem to ask in a scared confused tone, but they get no response as they are all thrown in and locked inside of different unmarked cars as people come outside to see what's going on and others watch from a distance and they try to scream to the agents through the rolled up glass windows but get ignored as barking dogs can be heard over top of all of the police radios that seem to all be going off simultaneously. After what seems like hours of screaming, someone finally opens Drama's door and as he steps out he's asked a series of questions before the white agent takes the handcuffs off of him and holds a flash light on him as he takes his shirt off and slowly turns around in a circle before he checks his hands with the flash light and like his body not finding any gang tattoo's or marking's he tells him he is free to go to which Drama puts his shirt back on and quickly walks away from the unmarked car and looks for his friends while the block remains dark as for all of the lights from the unmarked cars.

After constantly being told to move along by what seems like every officer he passes, he walks away from all the madness until he approaches a crowd of on lookers who look at him like he just walked away from a plane crash unharmed, but nobody says anything as he walks to and through the crowd looking around for his friends.

After not seeing them, he slowly makes his way home where he can clearly see that the street lights and power is on further down the block.

Chapter 7

Scooner Drive, Chester, VA.
The Next Day (Saturday) September 28, 1999

After hanging up the pay phony and letting Drama know their OK. Big Bro who's smoking a blunt walks away from the pay phone as the sun starts making its way in the sky. Getting back to the house he is hiding at he walks in and sees Joe eating a bowl of Lucky Charms with a plate of French toast sticks covered in syrup sitting on the table in front of him.

Coming out of one of the back rooms dressed in a suit top and matching skirt a medium height brown skin girl with her hair dyed with red streaks and pulled to the back walks out putting her purse on her shoulder and kissing Joe on the cheek before saying "yall stay out of trouble now." as he smacks her on the ass as she clips clops her way out of her house in her expensive designer shoes.

"You forgot your brief case." Joe says pointing towards her black leather brief case sitting beside the table.

"Damn thank you." She replies stopping in the door way and turning around to retrieve her brief case. Picking it up she thanks Joe again before leaving out of the house and getting in her silver Mercedes Benz.

"Where the hell did you meet her at?" Asks Big Bro watching her back out of the drive way and pull off.

"She beat that murder charge for me. Remember when I killed Roni and they gave me that boot leg ass case?" Asks Joe as a shocked Big Bro says "Get the fuck outta here, that was your lawyer? Hell naw, that's the Kelly Drumbfield everybody be talking about? I thought they was talking about a dude."

"Naw they ain't talking bout no dude, that's her. I been fucking with her ass on the low for bout a year now." Replies Joe as Big Bro still has a shocked look on his face.

"Damn." Big Bro says to his self before sitting on the sofa and leaning forward picking the ash tray off the table to pluck the ashes from his blunt in.

As Joe's beeper vibrates on the table he looks at it and says, "This nigga Quarter getting worrisome."

"I cut my shit off, he knows his line probably tapped so I don't know why the fuck he keeps trying to get niggas to call him." Replies Big Bro looking at the huge flat screen TV with no sound coming out of it as what he assumes is the movie The Bodyguard playing on the screen.

"If you hungry the fridge is flooded with food. You can do you, just clean up behind yourself." Joe is saying as Big Bro puts his blunt in the ash tray and jumps up saying "You ain't gotta tell me twice." As he disappears towards the back of the huge house.

Burma Court, Varina

Mad because Big Bro and Joe are not answering their phones or their beepers a paranoid Nobel paces back and forth in his girlfriend's apartment chain smoking Newport after Newport and running to the window every time he hears a car drive past while his girl takes a shower.

Ever since he called Quarter, his phone has been ringing non-stop as he's been getting an up to date about what's taking place in the hood by everybody who didn't get locked up. Glancing back and forth at the TV which he has tuned to the news he doesn't see anything about what transpired yesterday but from what the streets are telling him the feds are everywhere and are snatching any and everybody up left and right.

Opening the window to let some air in the apartment he then goes in the kitchen and gets a chair from the table to which he brings it back in the living room and grabs the phone before he sits the chair by the window and haves a seat as he puts the phone on the floor beside him and smokes as he looks out the window and waits to hear from Joe or Big Bro.

George Mason Square Church Hill

As Jasmine leaves for work she reminds J.V that he needs to get up and continue his job search, but he ignores her as he rolls over still half sleep and not trying to hear her mouth this early in the morning.

Just as he's ready to nod off he feels someone lightly tapping him on his face, moving his head back and opening his eyes he sees Drama standing over him smiling wearing a camouflage short sleeve shirt and matching cotton sweat pants. Glad to see that his young friend is OK and not the cause for all those agents and police storming around the streets J.V smiles and says, "What's up Rambo?"

"You need to get yo ass up out this bed and go look for a job." Drama replies in a squeaky female voice mocking Jasmine as they both laugh.

"You a funny motherfucker, is she gone?" Asks J.V.

"Yeah she got in the car with Peaches after she let me in." Replies Drama as J.V gets out of the bed wearing a black tank top and shorts.

"I know you ain't drive over here as hot as it is out there' J.V asks as Drama sits on the bed and he pulls an outfit out of his closet.

"Hell naw, I might be crazy but I ain't stupid. That ain't the regular police out there. Fuck that, I walked over here." Replies Drama cutting the TV on and flipping through the channels as J.V leaves the room and a few seconds later he hears the shower water running.

"Since yo ass sitting in there make that bed up for me shawty." J.V yells to him before shutting the bath room door

"I don't even make my own bed. You make up your own damn bed!" Drama yells back.

"We got some of them breakfast pop tarts and chocolate pop tarts in the kitchen." J.V says in a sales man type voice which makes Drama jump off the bed and ask "How you want the joint made up? With the covers folded or all the way to the head board?"

"It don't matter." Replies J.V with a smile as hot water from the shower rains down on him.

Henrico Later That Afternoon

As "Bury Me A G" by Thug Life plays loudly through the car speakers of the baby blue box caddie driven by Nobel's girlfriend, he sits in the passenger seat with the chair leaned back wearing dark Versace glasses in his own thoughts as he nods slowly along with the music with his eyes closed.

When they get to the movie theater by Regency Square mall she parks the car and they both get out and walk to the ticket booth as a couple and straight to the window and buy two tickets to see "The Sixth Sense" before entering the lobby and making their way to the theater.

Once inside the dark room, they both can see that the movie has already been playing so his girl goes to find a seat up front while Nobel has a seat in the lower right-hand corner next to two other dudes who are eating popcorn and candy while they watch the movie.

"It took yo ass long enough." Big Bro says to him through a mouth full of popcorn as Nobel sits down.

"My bad." Nobel replies before taking a hand full of popcorn out of Big Bros huge tub while Joe looks at the movie in silence.

"So, who's idea was it to meet, here?" Asks Nobel.

"Mine, it's dark and I wanted to see this movie." replies Joe not taking his eyes off the screen.

"We got every G man in the agency" Nobel is saying before his girl stops him and asks him what he wants from the concession stand to which he runs down a short list of things before deciding to go and get it himself.

"I'll be back" he says to Big Bro before getting up and walking out. "Lately every time I'm around that nigga I start to feel strange." Big Bro says to Joe.

"What you mean? You think the FEDS done got to him?" He asks still watching the movie as he takes a sip of his soda through a straw.

"Naw, it's just He been acting real strange lately, but it's like don't nobody else view the shit but me." Replies Big Bro.

"You want me to smoke him?" Asks Joe seriously as he takes his eyes off the screen and looks directly at Big Bro to help him understand how serious he is about his question, but Big Bro just brushes it off by stating "Naw, just keep an eye on him." before they both get silent until Nobel comes back with a whole card board tray full of junk food and two sodas that he carefully sits down so he won't spill them.

As he opens up his candy bar he takes a bite and asks "So do yall know how many people got knocked off cause" Nobel is saying, before Big Bro cuts him off by saying "They got damn near everybody and we got to get lawyers for those who couldn't get them for themselves so that's like two hundred thousand we bout to kick out." Big Bro is saying before Nobel blurts out!

"TWO HUNDRED THOUSAND?! That's damn near everything." as people look to the back toward the outburst and Big Bro says "Nigga will you shut the hell up and lower your voice. We don't need everybody in this conversation, damn! Now look, we a lock to get that shit on Thursday, but it's too hot to do anything around here so we gone go out somewhere like Atlanta after we hit off our regulars.

We took a big blow so we gotta go get this money and by this time Thursday everybody's going to have a lawyer and I'm taking care of that myself cause it ain't right to leave none of the little homies out there like that, not in this set. We can always get the money back, but real niggas are hard to find shawty. And everybody up under this set done walked through the fire to prove their loyalty, so I'd be damned if I'm gone turn my back on them."

Listening to what Big Bro is saying Nobel shakes his head in disbelief as he thinks about all the money Big Bro is ready to give away, but he doesn't say anything while he eats and looks at the movie but not able to pay attention to it.

17th Street, South Side

"So, you talked to your brother yet?" Lil One asks Drama as him, J.V and Varsity play Mario Kart on the Nintendo 64.

"Yeah, he called me this morning to let me know about everything that's happening." Replies Drama.

"Yeah, that shit like that round the West End too. Them motherfuckers is not playing shawty." Lil One says getting a lighter out of his pocket and trying to navigate the controller at the same time.

Getting the lighter, he pulls a rolled up blunt from behind his ear and sparks it up.

"You know Yummy and Tyrone's funeral tomorrow and Pooh joint after that?" Varsity asks out loud to no one in particular in which only J.V and Lil One responds.

"What's up Drama? You ain't going to they funerals?" asks Varsity getting the blunt from Lil One.

"I ain't decided yet, cause that shit gone be crazy having to go back and forth to two funerals in one day and then have to turn around and go to another one the next day." Replies Drama not really wanting to keep the conversation going so he says, "You be cheating too" but J.V says

"I don't think Pooh having a funeral service. I talked to his mama when we went to view the body in the church and she said she gone have him cremated."

"Can we talk about something else?" Drama asks loudly before Varsity passes him the blunt.

"Damn, my bad shawty you right. I just wanted to let niggas know what's going on." Replies J.V.

"I wasn't talking to just you. I don't feel like hearing about that shit right now. I done dealt with that death shit enough." Replies Drama before hitting the blunt as Lil One wins and they start a new game.

Church Hill

"She is the baddest bitch I've ever seen before, she could wipe her ass on my face if she wanted to." Trigger says as him, G Way and Vel sits in Hova's living room looking at his oldest sister who is in the door way with her back to them talking on the telephone while they wait for Hova to come out of his room.

"And she ain't got no drawers on. I bet her pussy be wet as a motherfucker. Damn shawty." Trigger says a bit too loud at the end as she turns around and glances at them before ignoring them and finishing her conversation. Chuckling at the way Trigger sounds Vel says "You sound like some perverted ass rapist."

"Call it what you wanna call it, but the first fiend bitch I catch I'm gone take her in the alley, pretend it's her and punish her ass." Trigger says and they all start laughing.

"Who you think she look like?" Asks G Way.

"Shit, that's easy. She looks just like that girl that was in that Tyreese Sweet Lady Video." Replies Trigger.

"Yup, what was her motherfucking name?" G Way tries to remember before Vel says "Maiya Campbell." and both G Way and Trigger laugh and say "Hell yeah, that's her name. They can be twins shawty." Replies Trigger before Vel tries to boost him up to go talk to her.

"Gone over there and talk to her and see what she says."

"Naw shawty, I ain't fucking with that Maine sister." Replies Trigger. "What? You scared?" Asks Vel before Hova comes in the living room holding a fitted cap in his hand.

"My bad, yall niggas ready?" He asks them before looking at his sister and saying, "Get the hell off the phone."

Looking at him she rolls her eyes before walking out on the porch still on the phone as G Way, Vel and Trigger all stand up and make their way to the front porch.

Walking out on the porch and passing her Trigger smiles and nods at her to which she smiles, waves and says "Bye yall." Which puts an even bigger smile on Triggers face as G Way and Vel speak as they get down the steps and to the sidewalk.

Looking at the big grin on Triggers face, Hova asks "What the hell you smiling like that for?"

"Ain't nothing." Replies Trigger.

"That nigga like yo sister shawty." Vel butts in and says which makes Hova smile as he says "Oh yeah? A Gabrielle, my friend trying to holla at you."

"Gone with that shit shawty." Trigger says embarrassed. Smiling at them she says, "Which one?" Which catches Trigger off guard.

"Him." Hova says pointing at Trigger which makes her smile as she looks him up and down noticing everything he has on is Jordan.

"What's your name?" She asks, and he tells her his real name "Christian."

Laughing, Hova repeats what he said trying to figure out how he got Trigger out of Christian.

"OK Christian your cute. You got a job?" She asks. "Naw." He replies shaking his head.

"A car?" She asks which makes him smile so Hova says "A car that's yours."

"Stop hating shawty." Trigger says playfully pushing him before saying "I can get a car."

"What you mean you can get a car?" She asks.

"To be completely honest my nigga got so many cars he'd give me one of them if I asked for it." Replies Trigger as she smiles and shakes her head before asking, "How old are you?"

"Twenty-one." Trigger says which makes G Way, Vel and Hova laugh.

Smiling she shakes her head before saying, "Come back and holla at me when your twenty-one with a car and a job and we'll finish this conversation then, until then you have a good day Christian." Waving at him before he says "Alright." As he watches her walk in the house and shuts the door.

Turning to Hova, Vel and G Way he smiles and says "Yall niggas some haters." As they all laugh and playfully push and wrestle with him as they all start to walk down the street.

"So what yall niggas trying to do today?" Asks Hova "You trying to go to the playground and ball?" Asks Vel.

"Shawty I'm not balling today, I ain't dressed for that Shit." Trigger says as if the question was directed at him.

"Am I talking to you? Take that pretty boy shit somewhere else." Vel says as Trigger puts his hands up and playfully throws a jab at Vel and says, "Shut up nigga." to which Vel does the same and they spar back and forth with each other until Vel gets up on him and Trigger runs away laughing.

Smiling Vel says "You better run."

"A yo lets go over Dollicia house. You know it's always some shit of girls over there." Hova suggests.

"Come on, it ain't like we got shit else to do." Replies Vel as they walk, talk and laugh with each other.

CHAPTER 8

Chesterfield
Five Days Later Thursday October 2, 1999

With Big Bro talking on a gas station pay phone out in Chesterfield, Tammy sits patiently in her red Bonneville with "Kissing you" by Total playing lowly as she waits for him to get off the phone.

"So, you positive, shit done calmed down around there?" Big Bro asks into the receiver.

"Yeah, I'm telling you outside of that day they jumped out on yall we ain't been seeing nothing but the regular police. And we been out this bitch everyday fucking around, doing a little something here and there." Replies Quarter as Big Bro gets quiet and thinks for a moment while on the other end Quarter stands alone on somebody's porch using their phone.

After a short pause Big Bro says call Noble and them and tell them to be at the Palace this afternoon cause I'm going to get that shit and I don't want to see nobody in that back room but yall three alright." To which Quarter responds before they both hang up.

Walking back toward the car where Tammy is waiting for him an unexplained strange feeling comes over him that makes his body shake and stops him in his tracks, seeing the weird look on his face Tammy looks up at him from the driver side window and asks "Are you OK?"

Looking up at her he tries to brush it off by replying "I'm straight." Before he continues over to the passenger side and gets in laying back in the seat which he has leaning all the way back.

Looking over at him, Tammy wants to say something, but she doesn't as she puts the car in drive and pulls off.

Willow Lawn shopping mall

Walking through the mall in a loose huddle Drama, J.V, Trigger, Varsity, G Way, Vel and Hova all have at least one shopping bag in their hand as they all engage in various conversations.

"I don't care what Trigger say, that shit was wack." G-Way says about Vel going into the bathroom and changing into the new Polo shirt, sweat pants and matching colored Jordan's he just brought.

"What's wack about it? Nigga, stop hating. You just mad cause I look better than you." Vel replies in an irritated tone.

"What? Get the fuck outta here, and for real it don't matter, cause it ain't even no bitches in here." G-way says over dramatically.

"See how small minded you is. I ain't looking for no bitches walking around here looking for a nigga like me to take care of them. I'm looking at the bitches that work here so I ain't gotta keep paying for shit when I come in here."

Vel says slickly as Drama blurts out" preach pimp, teach this young nigga something." As everyone laughs.

Jokingly G-way looks at Drama and says "shut the fuck up." Which Drama doesn't reply as he now talks to Vel while they make their way into Sun Coast video store.

"Why we going in here?" Asks Hova.

"I'm trying to step my VCR game up." J.V says as Vel instantly makes a bee line toward the young cute white girl behind the counter as everyone else goes their separate ways in the store while Hova stands at the front of the store looking at the movie that is playing on several of the monitors.

30th St. Church Hill

Standing on the corner in front of the corner store eating a Philly steak and cheese sandwich with the hood of his Nike wind breaker Jacket covering his head, Joe kicks it with a few of his outside associates while they stand around smoking, drinking and selling drugs as they try to holla at every female that makes their way past or into the store there in front of.

As Joe chews his sandwich his beeper starts to vibrate on his waist, pulling it off he looks at the number on the screen before sliding the beeper back into its holster and nodding to his self.

Henrico (Food Lion) Later That Afternoon

Sitting in his car in the parking lot of Food Lion listening to "If I Die" by Jay Z play slowly through his speakers, Big Bro keeps his eyes on his rear-view mirror while he sits leaned back in his driver seat.

After a few minutes pass, a gold Lexus pulls up slowly behind his car and stops. Popping his trunk Big Bro keeps an eye on his rear-view mirror as he watches a female get out of the passenger seat of the Lexus holding two long black gym bags and walk to his trunk.

As she opens his trunk, she pulls out three baby bags and drops the two gym bags in his trunk. Shutting his trunk, she walks back to and gets in the Lexus which pulls off. Starting his car up he puts his CD on "Originators" by Jay Z and turns it up before backing out of the parking space and driving off nodding to the music and checking his mirrors to make sure no one was watching or is following him.

Willow Lawn Henrico

Sitting in the food court with empty food wrappers sitting in front of them, patting his stomach J.V asks "Is yall ready to bounce yet?"

"Hell naw, let's go sneak in the movies." Replies Drama.

"Hell yeah, I ain't been to the movies in a minute. We should try to look at all them shits." G Way says playing with a half-eaten cheese burger.

Sucking his teeth J.V says "I ain't trying to be sitting up here all day."

"It ain't like you got a job. You ain't got shit to do." Replies Drama.

"It don't matter. I got a girl nigga, so I ain't trying to be sitting up in here all day." J.V says a bit irritated as Drama quickly retorts "Nigga yo girl at work so that shit you talking is irrelevant."

"OOH, look who learned how to use a big word." J.V says sarcastically which makes Varsity, Hova and Trigger laugh.

"Oh yeah, well here's an even bigger word, shut the fuck up." Replies Drama making everyone laugh even more.

"Shawty yall two niggas is crazy." Varsity says sipping his soda through a straw and then saying "I ain't trying to sit through no movies either, cause I really got some shit I gotta do, so if you trying to roll with me I'll give you a ride back around the way."

"I got some shit I gotta take care of too." Hova says as Drama sucks his teeth and blurts out "THAT"S BULLSHIT!" but Hova doesn't respond he just gets up holding his bags along with Varsity and J.V.

"Shawty that's fucked up yall niggas bout to bounce on us like, that." Drama says a little upset as he gives them five but not really wanting to and not getting up before the three of them walk off while Drama, G Way, Trigger and Vel remain sitting at the two tables.

George Mason Square East End Getting around the way

Stopping the car in front of J. V's crib, J.V and Hova get out of the car before Varsity beeps the horn and pulls off.

"You trying to leave yo bags in my crib?" Asks J.V

"Naw, I'm bout to go to that bitch New York crib." Replies Hova holding bags in both hands.

"New York? You talking bout the bitch that live behind me?" Asks J.V a bit confused.

"Yeah." Replies Hova with a smile.

"When the hell you hook up with her?" Asks J.V

"Last week." Replies Hova looking like he's trying to end the conversation which J.V catches onto and says "Well don't let me hold you up.

I'll get at you later than."

"Alright my nigga." They both say to each other before walking off in their own separate ways.

Getting into his apartment J.V hears some female laughter, so he walks to his living room and sees Jasmine, Terry, and New York sitting around looking at a boot leg movie and getting tipsy.

"Hey boo, what the hell you doing off work so early?" asks J.V.

"I didn't go to work today I had a dentist appointment, and what you got for me in those bags?"

"Just a couple of outfits. What's up Terry and New York, my nigga Hova looking for you

"Looking for me for what?" Asks New York.

"I don't know, he just went to your apartment just now though." Replies

J.V as Jasmine and Terry both look at New York with a crazy silent stare causing her to giggle and shake her head while saying "I don't know what that boy looking for me for.

I barely even know who he is outside of seeing him over here."

"Whatever," J.V says before turning and walking out of the living room hearing them start to question her about Hova, but she plays dumb.

Getting in his room he shuts the door behind him and puts the bags on the floor beside him on the side of the bed before sitting down and cutting the TV on with the remote.

Yawning, he flips through a few channels before kicking his shoes off and crawling to the top of his bed before noticing the phone on the bed which seems to ring as soon as he picks it up.

Answering it he hears the automated voice mail electronical voice tell him he has a message, so he pushes in his code and listens to a message left by his father.

Z St. East End

"OK! Now we in business!" Nobel says excitedly looking up and seeing Big Bro who is still clearly tired from running around the past five days come into the back room of their crack house holding two long black gym bags and shuts the door behind him.

Throwing both the bags down before he has a seat on the couch he sits down and says "Look, we gotta call in the workers to cook that powder coke, break down and weigh them trees and weigh that heroine cause I'm tired as shit and it's hot, so this my last trip with the connect. After this I'm done."

"What?! What you mean you done?" Asks a shocked Nobel.

"I mean, I ain't fucking with this shit no more. We strapped after this, plus the news said the Feds ready to lock this bitch down anyway, so don't think cause you don't see them they gone." Replies Big Bro.

"Maine them people ain't thinking about us and you know the connect don't fuck with nobody but you. Shit you the only person who know who the nigga is." Replies Nobel.

"I thought you said you was looking for a connect anyway?"

Big Bro says smartly as Nobel shuts up and Quarter comes in the room "Where everybody at?" Asks Quarter not seeing any of the niggas who usually be on post.

"When we shut down yesterday it won't no reason for nobody to be here so when my shift came on I told them they could leave cause I was leaving and didn't nobody need to know what we was bringing in here." Replies Noble as Quarter looks at Big Bro who is visibly too tired to get upset.

Rubbing his eyes Big Bro says "don't even worry about it in a few hours everybody will be here and shit will be up and running again." As he gets that strange feeling again and starts thinking about Drama and all they went through.

"Homie you look sick are you OK?" Asks Quarter.

"Yeah, I'm alright I was just up all night." He says sorting the coke, heroine, and bags of weed as Quarter rips one of the bags and tests the heroine sniffing it off his finger nail "OK." He says swallowing the drain he instantly gets.

"What the fuck is you doing, why the fuck did you just do that?" Asks Big Bro. BOOM"""" Someone kicks the door open and before anybody can reach for anything there's at least fifteen people in the small room wearing ski masks holding every type of gun you can think of.

"A nigga bet not move in this motherfucker!!" One of the masked man says holding a Tec with an extended clip.

"Put everything in the fucking bag!" He demands but nobody moves so he grabs Big Bro who was sitting closet to the door and puts the gun to him.

"I said put da shit in da fucking bag!!" He demands again as they do as their told. When everything's in the bag they back out while dude still holds Big Bro.

"You coming wit us." Dude says as Big Bro braces his self.

"Nigga you better move before I kill yo dumb ass." Dude says to Big Bro who's mind is somewhere else as everything looks as if it's going in slow motion.

"Maine yall got what yall want so let my nigga go." Nobel pleads with the gun man who's holding Big Bro before dude smiles at Nobel and blows Big Bro's brains out right in front of them before pointing the gun back at them and backing out of the crib.

CHAPTER 9

**Venable St' East End
A Few Weeks Later (Saturday) October 15, 1999**

Laying in the bed staring at the ceiling, Drama's eyes are blood shot red as tears still roll down the side of his face while he thinks about his big brother. For two weeks he has ignored the knocks on the door and the constant ringing of the telephone while he lays in bed thinking about his brothers funeral as it constantly flashes in his mind.

Seeing the block, people he knew, people he's never seen before, and people who he was told was the FEDS all sit around crying or in silence as the preacher speaks verses from the Bible while standing over top of his brothers closed casket, he stares at the pictures of him that are placed around the casket as well as on top of the casket. Sitting right beside him, Nobel and Joe who smell just like liquor constantly tells him he has nothing to worry about and they will take care of him while Tammy screams and cries in his ear on the other side of him while he himself just feels numb as he watches the Bloods who weren't picked up in the raid off and on walk up to the closed casket clearly emotional as they pay their final respects.

Regardless of how emotional anyone appears Drama knows nobody truly feels like he does as he sits there all alone not being able to cry, not being able to talk and feeling like there's nothing, he can do because no one is telling him anything. Since the funeral he has been laying in the same spot unable to sleep as he just stares at the ceiling, thinking, not moving and not saying a word.

"Look we need to just kick the door open, snatch the nigga out the bed and bring his ass back to reality cause we don't know if the nigga even eating." JV says as him, G-Way, Hova, Vel, Varsity and Trigger sit in a stolen Suburban in front of Drama's crib.

Getting out and walking to the door G Way says "Maine, I hope he alright in there." Before Varsity knocks but as usual gets no answer so he snaps "MAINE SITTING IN THE MOTHERFUCKING HOUSE ALL DAY AIN"T GONE CHANGE SHIT! NOW STOP ACTING FUCKING STUPID AND OPEN THE FUCKING DOOR FOR WE KICK THE DAMN DOOR OPEN! COME ON NOW! NIGGAS WORRIED ABOUT YOU OUT HERE!!!" Before he starts pacing back and forth as warm tears of anger form in his eyes out of worry of his nigga and what he's going through.

"Come on man, lets bounce and try back tomorrow." Hova says getting in the green Suburban leaving them behind before they all walk to and get in as Varsity gets in and starts it up with a screw driver and they pull off blasting Master P's "Ghetto D" as they all sit in silence.

"You know what, maybe the nigga ain't even in the crib." G-Way says.

"Come on now where the fuck he at then?" Asks Trigger.

"Shitttt, he might be in that bitch dead." Hova says as Varsity stops the Suburban.

"Look Maine don't say no shit like that." Varsity says in a serious tone looking at Hova.

"I mean shit we ain't seen the nigga in weeks, he ain't answering the phone or nothing, shit, Nobel ain't even talked to him." Replies Hova as a car behind them beeps the horn trying to get them to move.

"Maine, we gotta get that nigga out that fucking house shawty." J.V' says again as they still sit in the street ignoring the car blowing the horn behind them before the driver starts yelling profanities at them.

"Yall think that nigga suicidal on some real shit?" Asks Vel.

"I don't know maine, I can't even say." Replies J.V as dude behind them holds down the horn.

"Maine fuck this shit!" Varsity says in an angry tone getting out the car as they follow him to the car behind them. Snatching the car door open, Varsity punches the young dude in the face and snatches him out the car as they all jump him.

"What I do?" Dude screams repeatedly while they whip his ass before

Varsity pulls out a three eighty and puts it in his face.

"Look nigga we fucking talking bout some serious shit. So, it will be in your best interest to shut the fuck up and wait until we finish, alright!!" Varsity yells at him.

"Alright maine, I didn't know." Dude says through a busted lip and bloody nose before they all walk off to the Suburban, get in, and pull off.

"Fuck this shit! Fuck this shit!" Varsity says hitting the steering wheel. "We going to the house right now and kick the door open." Varsity says driving back to Drama's crib.

When they get there, they see someone going in and shutting the door behind them. So, while the truck is still moving, J.V jumps out and almost falls as he runs to the door and starts banging before Joe with a look of murder in his eyes opens the door and screams "What's up! Why you beating on the fucking door like that?!"

"Maine Joe my bad but we been coming over here for weeks and this is the first time we have seen this door come open, so we thought it was Drama." Replies J.V.

"I don't know what's up with Drama. He don't come out the room, but I got a key to the house, so I just come over here and make sure he straight cause I promised his brother if ever something should happen to him I'd take care of Drama like he was my brother." Joe says with a serious look on his face.

"I mean, can we at least try and go talk to him? Asks Varsity.

"He won't talk to me so I know he won't talk to yall." Replies Joe standing in the door way and stepping to the side letting them in. As soon as they are all in the crib and the door shuts Dramas room door comes open and out he walks with a sleep deprived look, his hair in small dreads and still wearing the same clothes he wore to the funeral as he goes in the bathroom.

"A yo Drama, what's up my nigga?" J.V asks as they all smile happy to see he's alive, but Drama ignores them like they're not even there.

"I told yall he ain't talking." Joe says proving his point as he walks over to the couch and has a seat, cutting the t.v. on and flipping through the channels.

Looking down at him G-Way asks a question he's been dying to know "A Joe if you don't mind me asking how come Quarter won't at the funeral and why you don't be around Noble no more?"

"That's confidential young nigga so I couldn't answer that if I wanted too." Replies Joe as simply as possible as they hear the shower water running and Joe smiles and says "At least he taking showers now."

"Hopefully he ready to bring his ass out of this house and get some of this money out here." Hova says to no one in particular.

"So Noble hitting all yall off now huh?" Asks Joe.

"Yeah, he got some shit for Drama too, but we told him to put it to the side for him." Replies Hova.

"Well at least that's true." Joe mumbles to his self before cutting the T.V off and getting up saying" Look let's give young blood some privacy, he know where we be and how to reach us."

Hesitating they don't want to leave but they don't want to piss off Joe either so they comply and follow Joe out of the crib.

Locking the door behind him Joe looks at them and says "yall be safe." before walking to his car.

Getting back in the Suburban they wonder what's up with Joe, but they feel a little better knowing Drama's OK. Rolling a blunt as Varsity pulls off

J.V asks, "Can you drop me off at the crib, so I can finish cleaning the crib up before Jasmine gets home from work and curse my ass out."

"You old sucka for love ass nigga." Varsity says with a laugh.

"I ain't got shit to do so I might as well hit the block and grind with Hova." Replies Vel.

"So, what you and Trig trying to do G-Way?" Asks Varsity.

"I'm hungry I don't know what G-Way trying to do but I'm trying to go get something to eat." Replies Trigger.

"Alright well let me drop des niggas off and well go to Pizza Hut somewhere." Varsity says stopping at a stop sign as the police slowly turns the corner but keeps driving past them.

"I'm glad they kept going cause I do not feel like getting chased right now." Varsity says pulling off. When he drops off everyone and they get to Pizza Hut they get out and walk inside of the restaurant to the counter and stand in line to order food.

"Man, I am hungry as a motherfucker." Trigger says to no one in particular as the girl in front of him turns around and smiles "How you doing?" Asks Trigger.

"I'm alright." She replies.

"Oh yeah, well my name is Trigger what's yo name?" He asks her. "You ghetto and that was weak but since you cute my name Jovanda."

She replies with a smile.

"Well since I'm cute can you buy me something to eat?" Trigger asks jokingly as she giggles.

"Is that right?" She replies still smiling.

"I'm dead serious. I'm just in line for a courtesy cup of water and a job application." Trigger says with a straight face.

"Boy stop playing." She replies as she gets to the cashier and makes her order as she pays for her food, gets her ticket and goes to a seat.

"Yall get in front of me I'm bout to go holla at this bitch. Matter fact just get me a large pepperoni and cheese pizza and I'll pay you when yall come sit down." Trigger says walking to where Jovanda is sitting.

"So, where's your cup of water?" Asks Jovanda with a smile showing her pretty white teeth. "The lady at the counter told me to get the fuck out the line." He replies with a smile as she laughs, and he admire her dark frame and the way she has her hair and nails done.

"Boy, you a trip and I just ordered a large pepperoni and cheese pizza to

take home but if it's like that I'll share it with you' she says as Trigger smiles while G-Way and Varsity sit behind them.

"Those your friends?" She asks looking in their direction. "Naw I don't know who the fuck dem niggas is. "He replies. "But I saw you talking to them." She says.

"I had stepped on dude shoe and apologized." Replies Trigger,

"Boy stop lying so much." She says still smiling as they talk until their food comes.

Venable, East End LATER THAT NIGHT

Putting on some black jeans and a black shirt Drama puts on his brand new black Timberland boots and skull cap, grabs his brothers glock a den puller and a screw driver and gets up and walks out of the house. While walking down the street he sees a few people he knows but he walks past them without saying a word. Turning down a back street that is quiet with no one on it he sees an Oldsmobile jeep, so he pulls the driver door and it comes open, so he quickly jumps inside. Screwing the den puller, a lil into the ignition he slams the screw in and yanks the ignition out. Putting the screw driver in where the ignition use to be he starts the jeep up and pulls off.

Looking through the tapes which are all rap he finds "Tru to the Game" by Tru puts it in and turns it up as he drives.

Watching every face, he drives by, he mean mugs everybody on the streets as well as the occupants of the cars. Stopping at a stop sign an old man crosses the street right before he hits the horn scaring the shit out of the old man who grabs his heart.

Laughing Drama drives around him and keeps going toward his destination. Driving through an apartment complex he sees a few people that hang with Rell and Rah-Rah. As they stand in front of an apartment that looks like a party is being thrown inside he pulls up directly in front of the apartment where the dudes are talking to a couple of girls looking like they are enjoying their selves before he cuts the high beams of the jeep on blinding them with the light before he gets out walks directly over to them and starts shooting POP POP POP POP POP POP POP POP POP.

Hearing the music stop in the house some people come to the door and then he starts shooting at them POP POP POP POP POP POP POP, click.

Noticing the clip is empty he walks back to the jeep and drives up on the curb making a wild U turn as he drives back on the street and out of the apartment complex as he cuts the high beams off.

"Easy!" he says out loud to his self as the music blares through the speakers thinking bout when his brother told him it wasn't as easy as he thinks.

Getting a few blocks away he parks the jeep takes the tape out the deck and a few other tapes, cuts the jeep off and searches it finding a thirty-two- hand gun under the seat before wiping down everything he touched in the jeep and doing the same thing to the outside of the jeep before he walks off up the block.

"EASY." He says again to his self as he walks.

Standing on the corner hustling two dudes see him walking in their direction.

"We got one." One of the dark skin dudes says to the other as they look around to make sure no one is watching them.

"What's up cuz." One of the dudes says as they stand in front of Drama who stops but doesn't reply as he tries to walk around them, but they block him.

"How much money you got on you?" Asks the dude with his hand under the front of his shirt as Drama stares him in the eyes without saying anything.

"Is you deaf, I said give me yo mother fucking money, don't make me kill you out dis bitch." Dude says as Drama takes a step back not taking his eyes off him.

"Look shawty we don't wanna hurt you just give us the damn money." The other one says smiling. Drama says "EASY." Before he pulls out the thirty-two and shoots dude in the face.

Seeing his friend drop the other one takes off running as Drama chases him.

"Naw motherfucker don't run now." He yells at dude shooting before he sees him stumble and falling into an alley.

"Alright man we was just joking." Dude says pleading with Drama. "Open your motherfucking mouth." Replies Drama with the gun in his face.

"What? Come on I." Dude is saying before Drama shoves the little gun in his mouth knocking two of his teeth out and smiling before he shoots him and starts walking down the alley.

Getting out the alley he sees his favorite car, a drop top with the top already down. Getting in the car like it's his. He den pulls the ignition, starts the car and pulls off while he takes the TRU tape back out of his pocket and puts it in the tape deck and turns the volume all the way up as he drives.

When he gets to his strip he pulls up right beside Hova and Vel who are talking to each other as they serve fiends. Turning around to see who just pulled up Vel says "Oh shit, my motherfucking nigga." As Drama leaves the music blasting while he gets out of the car and daps up Hova and Vel.

"What's up nigga, bout time you done came out the house." Hova says as Drama gives him a fake smile.

"Where everybody else at?" Asks Drama before smiling to his self-thinking that's the second whole sentence he's said in weeks not even paying attention to what Vel had just said.

"Did you hear me?" Vel asks seeing Drama smiling in his own lil world. "What did you say?" Drama asks as police cars fly down the block and

Vel just stares at him seeing something a bit different in the Drama he knew before and the Drama standing in front of him.

"You alright?" Asks Vel.

"Yeah I'm straight." He replies with a smile.

"What's so funny? What are you smiling at?" Asks Vel.

"You know some niggas just tried to rob me and I killed both they ass." Drama says without a smile as Hova turns around from the remark.

"Who tried to rob you?" Asks Vel.

"It don't even matter, they dead now, anyway." Replies Drama, as Vel and Hova look at each and then back at Drama who's nodding to the music blaring from the car.

"This nigga done snapped." Hova says under his breath.

"A look, Noble been hitting us off wit some coke lately and he got something for you." Vel says to Drama.

"So, we drug dealers now?" Asks Drama.

"Nigga's trying to get some money cause doing all dat wilding getting played out and it ain't paying for nothing." Replies Hova in a serious tone.

"Whatever." Drama replies brushing him off.

"Look we can go get the shit from Noble now and you can get on your feet tonight cause its jumping out here." Vel says trying to grab Dramas attention.

"Come on then, I wanna see Noble anyway." Drama says stepping over the passenger side door and getting in the driver seat of the drop top.

"You riding?" Vel ask Hova.

"Naw, I'm gone hold down the block till yall get back." replies Hova as Vel gets in and Drama pulls off.

CHAPTER 10

Thirty fifth East End
DA NEXT DAY Sunday October 16, 1999

"Beat dat bitch motherfucking ass!!" Varsity yells leaning on his car while two girls fight over some dude in front of his house.

"I want to see her titties rip her shirt off." G-Way says as him and Varsity watch as the skinny girl grabs the taller thicker girl's hair and starts punching her in the side of the face while the other girl swings wildly as their friends look on talking shit to each other waiting for either side to try and jump in it.

"Oh yeah! I see her tittles." G-Way says as the skinny girl gets her shirt and bra ripped off and dumped to the ground trying to cover them up before both sides run to jump in and a all out royal rumble breaks out between the eleven to twelve girls.

"All man, I never thought I'd wake up in the afternoon and see no shit like dis." G-Way say.

"Dat bitch got a brick. "OH!" Varsity says balling his fist up as one of the girls gets their face split open wit a brick while the whole neighborhood stares on.

"Gat damn." They both say as knives are pulled, sticks are swung and blood covers titties and T-shirts before police cars arrive and the officers try to break up the scuffle.

"That was the fastest I've ever seen the police come when someone calls them." G-Way says watching the group over power the police and continue to fight as more police come.

"Damn I should've brought the camera out here." G-Way says as his grandma watches from the porch.

"George yall come in this house before yall get in some trouble!" She says to G-Way.

"It's alright grandma I'm ready to leave anyway." Replies G-Way before getting in the passenger seat of Varsity's own Cadillac Deville as he gets in and pulls off playing B.G

"Trigger sill wit dat bitch?" Asks Varsity.

"I think so, he won't in da crib when I called dis morning." Replies G- Way.

"He just met da bitch and done fell in love with her." Varsity says as the

B.G tape plays low in da ride.

"Vel said Drama was wit them last night." G-Way says.

"Word, bout time dat nigga done brought his ass out da house." Replies Varsity as he drives.

Q ST East End

Sitting in his crib playing a video game with Vel, while Jovanda sits on the couch talking on the phone, Trigger talks to Vel and tries to concentrate on the game.

"It's a small world for real, me and Jovanda went to elementary and middle school together and I thought she moved from around here." Vel says to Trigger.

"You got some pictures of her in a year book? Cause back then everybody use to look crazy as a motherfucker." replies Trigger

"I don't know, I should though. I'll look when I get back to the crib." Vel says.

"Don't do that, don't be showing that boy them pictures." Jovanda says with a smile as she Continues to talk on the phone before it beep. "Yo line beeping you want me to click over?" She asks.

"Yeah see who it is." Replies Vel not taking his eyes off the TV. "Hello?" She says clicking over.

"Hello? Who is this?" Asks the male voice on the other end of the phone.

"Dis Jovanda who is this?" She asks.

"Dis Drama, shawty where Trigger at? Asks Drama.

"Hold up." She says clicking back over and hanging her call up before clicking back over.

"Hello?"

"Yeah, I'm still here." He says as she hands him the phone and says," it's some boy name Drama." Pausing the game and getting the phone, he says, "what's up my nigga?"

"Ain't shit, Noble took me to the dealership, so I could trade my brother's car in, I ain't even wanna drive that shit so he took me to get a ninety-eight Infiniti 130, so I got my own whip now but I'm still in da game of driving other people's shit." Replies Drama.

"Doing big things ain't it." Tigger says happy to hear his nigga on the phone but can barely hear him through the static.

"What's wrong wit ya phone?" Asks Trigger.

"It's dis dumb ass phone I just brought, I had da shit charging in da car, but I don't think the motherfucker charged all the way up or something." Replies Drama.

"Where you at? On da block?" Asks Trigger as Vel talks to Jovanda. "Yeah." Replies Drama.

"Where everybody else at?" Asks Trigger.

"I guess they on the other strip by Noble crib, I'm out here by Joe joint by myself." Replies Drama.

"Me and Vel be through there later on." Trigger says.

"Alright and tell Vel I said what's up. Alright One." Drama says hanging the phone up and leaning on the stop sign smoking a cigarette.

Twenty Fourth East End

"You got a nick?" A fiend asks Drama holding out five dollars. Taking the money, he gives him the crack and then stares in the sky wondering what his brother would think of what he's doing.

Smiling he says to his self" I gotta step it up, I'm trying to walk in a great man's shoes." staring in the sky. "Excuse me, you got a twenty rock?" Asks a fiend as he hands him four nicks and says, "just getting the hang of it." as the fiend hands him two ten-dollar bills and walks off. Sitting on the porch drinking a bottle of Night train Joe smiles as he watches Drama stand on the corner by himself serving fiends like his brother use to do when they first started. Wanting to call him and talk to him he decides not to cause he can clearly see that Drama is striving to step it up and fill a position he feels he's destine to have.

Twenty Fifth St East End

Putting some milk, cereal, bread, some potato chips and a few other items on the counter J.V gives the clerk a fifty-dollar bill and says "keep the change." As the clerk bags his groceries and gives them to him with a smile, before J.V walks out of Community Pride back to his crib.

"It's hot as a motherfucker out here." He says to his self as the sun beams down on him while he walks eating an ice cream sandwich.

"What's up J.V?" A few people say to him as he walks by and he replies with a nod.

"A look yo, watch yourself cause I heard Tragedy and Lil J looking for yall." A fat dude with a small afro says to J.V.

"Looking for us for what? We ain't beefing wit Rah Rah and them no more. " Replies J.V.

"I don't know I'm just telling you what I heard, and I saw the nigga Marco they fucked up trying to get yall address, but I don't think he gave it to them." says the fat dude looking around as he talks to J.V.

"Alright, good look shawty." J.V says before they go their separate ways and J.V walks a little faster.

Turning down a side street he runs right into them. "Well speak of the devil." Tragedy says to Lil J.

"What's up Tragedy?" J.V says trying not to show he's scared.

"Nigga you know what's up, where that punk ass nigga Drama at?" Asks

Lil J.

"I don't know, what's up I thought we squashed that shit?" Asks J.V.

"I thought we squashed it too until that nigga came down the apartments

shooting at my homies yesterday." Replies Tragedy seeing J.V is scared. "How you figure it was him?" Asks J.V.

"Nigga don't play stupid with me, where the fuck that nigga live at?!" Tragedy says bucking at him like he's about to hit him which makes him jump back.

"Nigga You's a pussy." Tragedy says as him and Lil J laugh. "Look maine I ain't do nothing to nobody, so why yall fucking with me?" Asks J.V.

"Nigga shut the fuck up and give me that. And what you got in yo motherfucking pockets? " Lil J says snatching his chain off before they both rush him and go through his pockets taking his money and beeper as he just stands there in fear.

"What you got in this motherfucking bag?" Lil J says taking the grocery bag from him and looking inside as tears of anger and fear start to roll down his eyes.

"What you crying? I know yo pussy ass ain't crying. Get yo pussy ass from round here before we beat the shit out of yo ass." Tragedy says mushing him in the face and kicking him in the ass as he runs away from them while they laugh.

When he gets a distance away from them he stops running and starts crying "I'm tired of these pussy ass niggas yo! Watch wait till I call my niggas, we gone kill all them Niggas watch." He says to his self through sobs as he looks back and see Tragedy's black Tempo coming round the corner so he runs through the house beside him into the backyard jumping gate after gate going through yard after yard until he gets to his crib.

Taking his keys out of his pocket which is the only thing left in his pockets he unlocks his back door and walks in the house slamming the door behind him going straight to the telephone, where it is already ringing.

"Hello?!" He asks picking it up.

"May I speak to a Ms. Jasmine Jackson?" Asks the female voice on the phone before he hangs up the phone in the woman's face before it rings again seconds later.

"YO?!" He yells into the receiver.

"Damn dawg what da fuck wrong wit you?"

"DRAMA, main nigga's just robbed me and took my chain and asked me where you live at."

"Hold up you talking too fast, you hear this dumb ass phone got all dis static. Hold up I'm gone call you back on Hova's phone. Drama says as they both hang up. When it rings again J.V picks it up and hears Hova clearly telling Drama why his phone has static in it.

"Oh damn." He hears Drama saying before getting on the phone. "Hello?" Asks Drama.

"Yeah, look maine da niggas Tragedy and Lil J just robbed me for my chain and money and tried to make me tell them where you live at." J.V says. "What???" Drama says in an upset tone.

"They driving around in a black." POP POP POP POP J.V hears in the back ground over the phone as static fills the phone.

"Hello?? DRAMA!" He yells in the phone but just hears static.

"Man shit!" He says slamming the phone down in anger and fear. Getting up off the ground from behind a car Hova and Drama watch the Tempo speed off Banging Pac as they shake the shattered glass from the shot- out car windows off them.

"See now somebody gotta die." Drama says storming off with Hova picking up his phone behind him.

"Man, I don't know what the fuck dat shit was about I thought we been squashed that shit." Hova says as Drama gets in his Infinity and Hova gets in the passenger seat as Drama starts his car up and pulls off running the stop sign making a U turn and going in the direction that the black Tempo went.

"Maine slow this motherfucker down before we wreck." Hova says. "Fuck dat shit dem niggas just shot at me." Drama says going even faster now that he sees the car a couple of blocks up as he runs all stop signs.

Seeing the Infinity flying toward them they pick up speed as well as they both race through the small streets. With the Infinity being faster than the Tempo Drama has no problem catching up with them as he is almost behind them while they both bend corners into oncoming traffic and flying down the streets.

Losing control of the wheel, Tragedy turns a corner smacking the back of a pickup truck before spinning out of control and smashing into a Dodge Caravan. Seeing the crash Drama slows down to a stop and pulls his black bandanna off his waist and ties it around his face.

"What da fuck is you ready to do?" Asks Hova as Drama jumps out of the car with his gun out and runs toward the smashed-up Tempo.

Seeing the door already open he, yanks a bloody Tragedy out of the car "you shot at me nigga??" He says putting the gun in his face and shooting him.

Looking over at Lil J, he sees he's hanging half way out the windshield so he snatches Tragedy's chain before quickly going through his pockets pulling out money, JV's chain and some weed.

"Hey what the hell are you doing?" He hears the driver of the pickup truck says with blood leaking from a head wound.

"Get da fuck back! Matter of fact, get da fuck under your truck!" Drama demands as the old white man does what he's told as Drama points the gun at him before shooting in the air

POP POP POP POP and screaming "and you bet not say shit cause I know what you look like!" He says before running back to his Infinity and throwing it in reverse as he backs all the way back down the street.

"Yo man what the fuck is wrong with you??" Hova asks Drama in serious tone as he puts the car in drive after turning the corner.

Stopping Drama looks at Hova, spins the barrel on the three fifty-seven, puts it to the side of his own head and screams

"I DON'T GIVE A FUCK" pulling the trigger each time for dramatic affect as the gun clicks five times before he hangs the gun out the window and lets the last shot off in the air as he pulls off scaring Hova to death so he just sits quiet and stares out the window while Drama drives listening to "Untouchable" by Scarface.

George Mason Square East End LATER THAT DAY

Sitting in J. V's apartment Hova, Drama, G-Way, Trigger, Varsity and Vel stare at the TV waiting for the news to come on. Other than J.V nobody has said anything to Drama and all he said was "thank you." for him returning his chain and money. And other than that, after what Hova told them, they've been afraid that they might say the wrong thing to him, so they talk to each other while Drama sits on the lazy boy smoking a blunt.

"I hope don't nobody say shit."

"Man, fuck dat we need to get dat nigga to one of them crazy clinics." I'm telling you."

"Shut up man da news coming on." They say to each other as the late breaking report comes on and all eyes are glued to the TV, but Drama who smokes a blunts and looks to be in his own lil world.

"I'm your brother, ride for me, kill his ass" "You want me to kill him for real?

"I'm serious kill him. Ain't nobody gone say shit."

"Come on bad ass hurry up it's getting cold out here." "You right, I can be a man and admit that."

"Preach pimp, but I know you got some hoes house we can go over."

"Let me see what I can do."

"I know she ain't just fart, fuck dat she just gotta catch me in here."

"And dat shit sounded wet.".

"What da fuck!??" Drama hears as he snaps out of the trance and sees the whole room jumping wit joy.

"They just described somebody else and their car which was a jeep with different license plates and everything and they showed a picture of a dude that don't look shit like you. You a lucky ass motherfucker" J.V says with a big smile as Drama smiles and says, "Well since I'm on such a lucky streak all of a sudden who trying to roll with me down the apartments?" Before inhaling and exhaling some smoke.

"What's down, the apartments?" Asks Vel.

"You'll find out if you down to ride." Replies Drama.

"I know you ain't talking bout going to fuck with them people." Asks Trigger.

"They started it and I'm gone finish it."

"Dawg you just got away with murder, what the fuck, chill for a minute." Replies G-Way

"I was chilling and then niggas started shooting at me- so apparently I can't chill until it ain't no more of them niggas left." Replies Drama.

"Fuck that shit I'm riding with you dawg." Says J.V.

"That's right my nigga we gone make these niggas respect our motherfucking gangsta." Drama says getting up and walking to the bathroom.

"Why the fuck you gone edge the nigga on? You know the motherfucker done went crazy," Hova says to J.V.

"I mean he ain't hesitate to hold me down, so I'm gone do the same for him." Replies J.V.

"Hold you down, the nigga put a three fifty-seven to his head and pulled the trigger five times, that motherfucker is crazy." Replies Hova.

"I don't give a fuck, dat's still my nigga and if he riding, I'm riding." J.V says as Drama comes out the bathroom and walks past them out the front door saying." If you coming, come on cause I got to get some shit before I go down, there." Looking at each other the only people who get up and leaves with him are J.V and Vel.

When they get to Hill top apartments, they walk down some steps and stand on the side of an apartment down in the lower part of the complex.

"Man, where da fuck dem niggas at?" Drama says peeking from beside the apartment with a gun in his hand. "Da niggas car right there so there around here somewhere" replies Vel watching the door across the street.

"Man, somebody gone see us, fuck dis waiting shit let's rush the apartment or bounce." Says J.V.

"Nigga shut da fuck up and chill, just be patient" replies Vel. "There goes one of them niggas right there coming out da cut with a bitch." Says Drama.

"Da nigga holding a baby though." Replies J.V.

"I don't give a fuck, let's go." Drama says putting the gun up walking toward them.

"A stick man, you know where we can find some smoke at?" asks Drama as he approaches dude.

"Hold on, here boo hold mama." Dude says handing the baby to the girl. "I got some, how much you want?" Asks dude pulling out a bag of weed that's bagged up, pausing Drama rubs his face and says, "nigga just give me all dat shit." pulling out a glock and putting the beam in dude's face. "Hold on you can have da shit." Dude says with his hands up.

"Dem niggas coming out da apartment." J.V says watching the cut.

"He got a gun." The girl screams.

"Bitch, shut da fuck up?" POP POP POP POP POP Drama says shooting at her.

"Man, what the fuck??" Dude says in tears.

"Yeah nigga you right." Replies Drama before he snatches the weed from him puts the beam in his face and shoots before they run off.

Coming around the corner in the cut one of the dudes scream, "Oh shit." running toward him he says "Grim, Grim, you alright man?" But he doesn't reply. Bending down he shakes him and smacks his face. "Wake up nigga, wake up don't die on me dawg" dude says emotionally.

Opening his eyes Grim asks, "Is my daughter and baby mama OK?" Looking at them then looking back at him one of the other dudes say "the baby ain't crying and ain't neither one of them moving."

Looking up at the sky a tear leaves Grims eye as he himself stops moving and dies.

"WHO DA FUCK DID DIS SHIT?? Dude screams as he holds Grim while people come out of their apartments and start to crowd around.

Now inside the Infinity driving back pass the scene J.V says "damn maine you ain't had to shoot da girl and you damn sure ain't had to shoot the baby."

"Word shawty that was fucked up." Replies Vel.

"What?? Yall niggas got feelings for them now? Fuck them motherfuckers." Drama says as he drives out the apartment

"It ain't nothing like that but damn nigga." Replies Vel.

"Shawty fuck these dem people." Drama says turning up "Hit 'em up" and leaning back in the seat as he drives.

"Let them take it as a warning, dump and get dumped on!!!!" Drama says with a smile.

Twenty Fourth

Getting around the way and pulling up on the strip Vel steps out of the back-passenger side and takes his hat off and scratches his head. Rubbing his face and eyes he says, "I want to get down with them dice too."

"If you got some loot bring ya ass over here." Trigger replies to him shaking the dice as Vel walks to the dice game.

"Yall niggas cry to much stop acting like bitches, dem niggas killed most of our click and yall acting like the shit ain't happen." Drama says to J.V.

"I feel you, fuck it they deserved it." He replies sitting on the trunk watching the dice game.

"Four, five, six niggas I want mines and some more." Trigger says to Vel, Hova, G way and Varsity.

"You think your hot but, when them dice get around here I'm going to break your ass." Says G way.

"Don't worry nigga I'll get to you in a minute." Replies Trigger. "What time is that party shorty was talking about?" Asks Hova. "I don't know but Lil One might." Replies Varsity.

"I'm gone be rich fucking with yall niggas." Trigger says getting up and putting the money he won in his pocket as Varsity quits while a fiend walks up, and Drama walks away with him catching the sell.

"Good looking out." The fiend says walking away.

Ring, Ring, Ring, Ring, A that's me." Replies Hova as everyone checks their phones who has one.

"Damn nigga pass the motherfucking blunt where the fuck you think you at?" Vel says to J.V.

"Here nigga roll ya own." he replies throwing him a blunt.

Getting up from the dice game walking toward J.V and sitting on the curb Vel throws the blunt stuffing in the street and empties a bag of weed he pulls from his pocket into the blunt.

"A Drama!" Nobel yells to him from across the street standing in his door way as Drama turns around and walks to him to see what he wants.

When they get in his crib Nobel asks, "So how much shit you sold?"

"I ain't got nothing but a couple of nicks and dubs left." Replies Drama as they stand in his dining room.

"My little money man. You know your brother would've been proud of you." Nobel says with a smile, but Drama doesn't return it as he says "You know my brother wouldn't want me doing this shit."

"Yeah whatever, but look I'm gone hit you off with some money and some more shit later on today alright." Replies Nobel.

"Alright." Replies Drama as Nobel gives him five and a hug before Drama turns to leave out and Nobel says "yall niggas stop shooting dice on the corner, yall getting shit hot."

"Alright, I'll tell them." Drama says as he walks on the porch and sees Hova sitting on the steps and a police car parked behind Drama's Infinity with the police looking at the stolen jeep they had.

"Why yall leave that jeep out here like that?" Drama asks Hova.

"Man, that shit done been out here for a minute. The battery dead. The only reason he stopped was cause them niggas was standing right there shooting dice and smoking weed." Hova says as they watch the police man walk around the jeep.

"So, where everybody go?" Asks Drama.

"Them niggas hauled ass. I just walked over here and sat down, he ain't even pay me no mind." Replies Hova.

"Maine yall little bad ass niggas stay in some shit." Nobel says coming out of the house and seeing the police as he glances over at them before going back to his car and having a seat.

"He ain't fucking with yo car is he Drama?" Asks Nobel.

"Hell naw, he bet not be fucking with my car." Replies Drama as they watch him watch them.

"What the fuck he keeps looking over here for?" Asks Hova as he gets out of the car and shuts the door and walks toward them.

"All shit, ain't nether of yall got any guns on yall or nothing do it?" Asks Nobel.

"Hell yeah, we live in Richmond. You'd be crazy to not have one." Replies Drama as the black police man stops at Nobel's metal black gate and asks "Yall wouldn't happen to know any of those individuals who were standing on that corner just now would you?"

"What da fuck you looking at me like that for, I ain't about to tell on nobody, you get paid to find that out on your own." Drama says seriously.

"Darell I know you're a car thief and if I thought you had anything to do with that jeep over there I would've been putting you in handcuffs so don't talk to me like that cause with your record and reputation I can easily say it's yours." The officer says as Drama gets quiet sucks his teeth and looks away.

"A yo man why you bothering us we ain't doing nothing to nobody?" Asks Hova before a call comes in over his radio about the shooting down the apartments and he look at Hova with a mean stare before walking off answering his radio, getting in his car and pulling off.

"You on his radar now. I call that nigga T-one thousand cause when he out to get you, he out to get you and you are now on his radar." Says Drama watching him drive off as Hova says "fuck that motherfucker."

"Man, yall get yall bad asses off my porch, yall making me hot." Noble says to them before going back in his crib and shutting the door.

"I wonder where the fuck them niggas went?" Drama asks out loud. "Probably over Lil One's Crib You know that party is at shorty girls house tonight." Replies Hova.

"Damn, I forget all about that shit, you trying to go around there?" Asks Drama getting up.

"He'll yeah." Replies Hova as they get up and walk to Dramas Infinity and get-in with Hova asking about Rah-Rah, with Drama telling him about him while starting the car and pulling off.

"You know I been squashed that shit with Rell and Rah Rah so I don't know why the fuck they just up and started shooting at us again, but I'm gone try to holla at the nigga and see what's up though cause if it ain't no money involved then that shit in the way."

Hova says to Drama who doesn't reply and looks as if he could care less if he could squash it or not cause the point is he does not like them niggas.

Seventeenth St South Side

When they get to Lil Ones crib they see the Blazer Vel had stolen and been driving in parked in front of Lil Ones van. When they get on the porch Drama rings the door bell and they wait for someone to come and answer the door.

"Who is it?" Asks a female's voice as Drama wants to ask the same thing but says "Drama and Hova is Lil one here?" as a medium sized light skin female who looks like the singer T-Boz opens the door and lets them in.

"Who is you?" Asks Hova as they walk in and she shuts the door before replying "Mee Mee." Without even glancing at him as if she were uninterested in either one of them as she walks in front of them through the living room towards Lil Ones back room.

"Damn she phat as a bitch." Hova says looking at her ass as she opens the room door and they go in Lil Ones room where two females are sitting at a card table cutting up coke and Mee Mee rejoins them as Varsity and everyone else smoke, talk and looks at the huge flat screen TV where they are playing the video game.

"What's up nigga?" Drama says giving Lil One five and a hug and Hova does as well.

"A yo my nigga, seriously why you popping bitches?" Asks Lil One as he puts his long dreads in a rubber band.

"The bitch was screaming." Replies Drama before glancing over at Mee Mee and two other girls weighing, cutting and bagging up coke.

"So, what you a pimp slash drug dealer?" Hova asks reading Drama mind and Lil One laughs as the girls all give Hova a silently nasty look.

"They are not the ones to piss off." Lil One warns Hova seeing the looks on the girls faces.

After an hour or so passes, Mee Mee and her friends finish bagging up and cleaning up the table.

"Look I'm bout to go take them to her crib, yall can wait here till I get back." Lil One says to them as they play a video game.

Putting his controller down Drama says, "I'm bout to go change my clothes before we go to this party."

"I'm gone change my shit too." Replies Vel putting down his controller as well while J.V and Hova continues to play the game as Trigger and G Way who were watching them play pick up their controllers.

"We be back." Drama says to them as him and Vel leave and see Lil One walking to his van as they get outside. Walking to the stolen white Blazer Vel gets in the driver seat and Drama in his Infinity before they all pull off.

THIRTY MINUTES LATER

Fully dressed Drama gets on his phone and calls Vel.

"Damn let a nigga put some clothes on first." Vel says to his self-walking out of the bath room wet with just a towel around him.

By the time he picks the phone up Drama has hung up and him not knowing who it was hangs up and goes back in the bathroom.

Leaving out of his crib Drama gets in his Infinity and drives back to Lil Ones crib. When he gets there, he parks behind Lil Ones van and goes straight in the crib.

"Damn nigga you scared the shit out of me." Varsity says as Drama trying to be funny bursts in the door and sees Lil One, Varsity, G-Way, Hova,

J.V and Trigger all staring at the TV.

"What the fuck is this?" Asks Drama looking at the TV and seeing Lil One having sex with the three girls that he had left with.

"You know what it is I'm a porno star nigga, and this can be yours for twenty dollars." Replies Lil One as they watch Mee Mee eat one of the girls while another girl is riding the face of the girl Mee Mee is eating while sucking Lil Ones dick as he stands over Mee Mee.

"Nigga You's a freaky motherfucker." Drama says.

"Look I'm bout to fuck the shit out of Mee Mee from the back." Lil One says as the part comes on.

"Hold on maine yo ass all in front of the camera, who holding that shit? Maine fast forward this part." Drama says as G Way fast forwards a little bit and presses play again as Vel comes in the room.

As the flick goes off Lil One smiles as they look at the TV in shock as Drama says " You must have took some X, Viagra and Ginseng. It ain't no way in heeellll you fucked all them bitches. And who the fuck was holding the camera while yall was doing that shit?" Asks Drama smoking a blunt.

"Shorty that was holding the camera claim that she ain't no freak and she love her man and all that bullshit, but I actually did fuck all them hoes." Replies Lil One.

"Hell, naw I ain't going for that shit!" Yells Drama.

"Alright whatever, you ain't gotta hate cause I can keep it straight." Lil One says laughing.

"Whatever." Replies Drama standing up and stretching.

"What's up with the party cause I'm ready to fuck something." G-Way says still rewinding and looking at the flick.

"Ah shit, I almost forgot. Cut that shit off with yo freaky ass and come on. We going in my Astro van so we ain't gotta waste gas." Lil One says going in his room.

"Let me get some cologne."

"Me too." Drama and Hova say.

Afton, South Side

When they get to the party it's so crowded people are standing outside. "I knew this shit was gone be off the hook." G Way says as he walks excitedly in the house. Stopping Drama says "I ain't know yall had these many bitches living around here. Look I'm bout to go get on some ass and who ever come back with the least amount of numbers gotta buy the blunts and beer when we leave." As everyone agrees and they all split up.

"What's up Shawty?" A dark skin dude asks Lil One.

"Oh, what's up Moe?" Lil One says giving him five and finding a female to dance with as Reggae music plays.

"Damn shorty you throwing that ass ain't it?" Lil One asks as he slides his hands down her panties and into her drawers as he fingers her, and she moans as they continue dancing.

A FEW HOURS LATER

Meeting up with Drama, G-Way says "I got some shit of numbers and I wrote my shits on almost all the dollar bills I had in my pockets and if those hoes don't call me I hope they all suck a sick dick."

Laughing Drama takes a swig of his beer and says "Nigga you crazy and these bitches is starting to stink. I'm ready to get the fuck up outta here."

"Alright, well let me go get this bitch number first." replies G-Way. "I'm gone go find Lil One and them then." Drama says as they split up. "What's up shorty, a nigga ready to bounce so what's up with that number?" asks G-Way pulling up on a light skin girl. "You got some paper?" She asks.

"Naw, but I can write it on this dollar." G-way says going in his pocket. "Yo, excuse me cuz but is there a problem here?" Asks a skinny light skin dude wearing a blue bandanna on his head.

"Naw it ain't no problem why what's up?" Asks G-way. This my motherfucking baby mama, that's what's up cuz." dude says getting in G- Way's face as G-Way sees Drama, J.V, Varsity, Trigger, Hova, and Lil One walking toward them.

"I mean fuck that shit, what you trying to do?" G-way yells while pushing him as dude's baby's mama grabs him as he falls back into her and she tries to hold him back. Seeing what's going on Drama pushes through the crowd toward them.

Walking up behind dude Drama smashes his beer bottle across his head dropping him.

"Nigga what the fuck you doing!" His baby mama screams.

"Shut up bitch." Drama says about to back hand her as they start to stomp, spit and pour beer on dude as the whole party watches as some girls go out toward the back door to get his friends.

"Fuck this shit lets bounce!" Lil One says as they start to make their way away from dude on the ground.

"Nigga, yall ain't had to waste all that beer on my pants."

Drama says shaking his pants leg as people stare and get out of their way as they leave out of the house.

Getting to the van a group of dudes all wearing a blue bandanna somewhere on their body all come out the house with the dude they jumped.

"Their they go!" He says pointing to Lil One as he gets in the Van and start it up pulling off.

"Yeah yall bitch ass niggas better peel off!" Dude yells as they start shooting at the van. As shots hit the van and the glass, they ducked as Lil One says "I know these niggas didn't shoot at my shit." As he turns a corner and parks.

"Get them guns from under yall seat, we about to let them niggas know what time it is." Lil One says as they check under their seats and feels all types of guns and Drama whose in the front already has his gun out in his lap.

Circling the block, they slow down and see the dude they jumped getting in a car with a few others as Hova slides the minivan door open and G-way lets the AR-fifteen hang out the door as the automatic gun fire fills the small car with holes and shatters glass as Drama whose holding his glock dumps on the car from out the passenger window before Lil One pulls off and some people run out the house of the party shooting trying to save the niggas in the car who they can see are clearly shot up before they even get to the car as Lil Ones van disappears around the corner.

"That's right my niggas, yeah!" Lil One yells hyper as they all talk excitably about what just happened.

"I'm saying though, you seen how I was leaning in on that nigga." Drama says using his gun to re-enact what he did as they give each other five and J.V sits in silence staring at them from in the back corner.

"Hold on, hold on yall niggas be quiet right quick my phone ringing." Varsity yells over the top of them as he takes his phone off his hip and tries his best to talk and hear who it is on the phone as they continue talking about what they did.

"A, WHAT YALL NIGGAS GONE DO?" Lil One screams trying to sound like dude they jumped as they all laugh.

"Damn, hold up. Can yall be quiet for like two minutes?" Varsity yells trying to talk on the phone as they quiet down a little bit but continue laughing and talking as J.V looks around at them and smiles as he shakes his head watching them actually enjoy what they just did." And I love these crazy Ass niggas." He says to his self.

Seventeenth St. South side

Getting to Lil Ones crib, they get out as Lil One walks around his van to see what kinda damage is done to it as Drama and G Way talk as they walk to Drama's Infinity and leans up against it.

"I'm bout to go over these bitch's house. She got two friends, so what's up, who trying to ride?" Asks Varsity while Lil One looks at his van Drama talks to G Way by Drama's car, J.V stands on the side walk looking at the ground, Vel and Trigger sit on the hood of the Blazer and Hova is nowhere in sight.

"Shit, I'm trying to go." Vel says as Varsity looks at J.V who always looks pitiful and asks jokingly knowing he's going to bring up Jasmine.

"You trying to go get some pussy?"

"I don't care, I'll go." He replies shocking Varsity.

"Man, hell naw, I ain't forgot. One of yall niggas gotta go to the store, we bet on that shit." Drama says walking over to Varsity who's standing in the street.

"Fuck that shit, niggas bout to go get some pussy and where the fuck did Hova go?" Asks Vel from on the hood of the Blazer parked in front of Lil Ones van.

"See, that's that bullshit! That's fucked up." Drama says as Lil One says "I don't know about ya'11, but I'm decent and I'm bout to go in the crib." But no one pays him any mind as they talk, and he walks past J.V towards his crib and goes in.

Hold up, hold up, hold up, you getting mad for real cause niggas don't want to go to the store?" Varsity asks Drama who's gotten a little loud and visibly upset as he hits his fist's in his palm saying " All I'm saying, if it would've came down to me buying the shit I would have had no problem doing it." As Lil One comes back out the house, walks to his van and starts taking the guns out as he goes back and forth from the house listening to Drama and Varsity argue in the street.

"Yall niggas cut that shit out. I'm not going over the bitch's house, so I'll buy the shit. Damn yall arguing bout some dumb shit." G-Way says as J.V leans on the back of the Blazer in front of the van as they get out of the street as a car drives by and Trigger trips off of the stupid argument as he keeps saying little stuff to boost it up and J.V leans on the trunk laughing at all their drunk asses.

"Cut that shit out Trigger before them drunk ass niggas get the fighting." Vel says to him.

"All I'm saying is how come every time niggas wanna do something, Varsity always got something else to do." Trigger says laughing and

Drama says "Thank You. I know I won't the only person who saw it like that and that's all I was trying to say." in a serious tone.

"Yall niggas tripping." G-Way says laughing at Drama who doesn't seem to see Trigger is only boosting shit up.

"A maine yall drunk ass niggas get from in front of my shit with all that damn noise." Lil One yells from his porch while talking on his cordless phone.

"Shut the hell up." G-Way says picking up a rock and throwing it at him causing him to ball up even though the rock gets nowhere near him.

"Cut that shit out maine, don't be throwing nothing over here, the fuck wrong with you." Lil One replies as Drama walks to his Infinity and Vel gets in the driver seat of the stolen whip and J.V gets in the back with him with Varsity getting in the passenger seat.

"A yo where you going nigga I need a ride." Trigger says getting off the hood as Vel starts the jeep up and he walks toward Drama. "I'm bout to go to the block." Drama says sitting in his.

Infinity with the door open as Vel with Varsity and J.V in the car with him rides past them and beeps the horn. "Where the hell did Hova go?" Drama asks Trigger as they look up and down the street not seeing him. "I don't know." Replies Trigger as G-Way flips through the songs on the C.D changer while he sits in the passenger seat.

"Come on and get in unless you gone stay round here with Lil One." Drama says to Trigger before he gets in the back seat as Drama shuts his door starts the engine and pulls off.

Seminary St Northside

When Vel and them finally get around the quiet residential neighborhood where the females stay J.V says, "we don't even look like we belong around here." As Vel parks and cuts the car off.

"You sure this where she stay at?" Asks Vel as they get out the car and he looks up and down the quiet street.

"Yeah nigga, come on." Replies Varsity as they make their way toward a nice looking two story house up on the porch and Varsity rings the doorbell while Vel sparks a half a blunt and sits on the steps as J.V stands beside him.

After a few seconds pass a female voice asks "who is it?" "Varsity" he replies. Opening the door, a beautiful dark skin female with short hair smiles and says, "hey baby," as she gives him a hug.

"What's up boo." Varsity replies hugging her before stepping in the house and looking back at Vel and J.V who haven't moved and asking them "yall niggas coming in or what?"

When they get up and walk in the house the female shuts and locks the door before they follow her down the well-lit hall into a room where a dark skin Nia Long looking female and a girl who looks like she could be in the eye candy section of any magazine sit around a glass and black ivory table getting drunk and talking. Sitting down on the couch beside the Chante Moore look alike. J.V lets out a sigh as he stares down at the floor. "A boy." She looks at him and says as Varsity and everyone else sits down as well.

"Yo?" Asks J.V looking up at her. "What's wrong with you?" She asks.

"I'm alright." Replies J.V while Vel and Varsity converse with the other females.

"You look drunk." Vel says to the light skin brown eyed girl with long blond hair in front of him as she teases him by giving him a seductive look and licking her lips. "Can I get nice like that too so I can feel like you feel?" Asks Vel.

"You gotta ask her." She replies looking and nodding toward the girl who opened the door as she sits talking to Varsity. "A shorty, can a nigga please get drunk with yall?" Asks Vel.

"Meka, not shorty and yeah I'm gone bring all yall some cups in a minute." She replies before she continues her conversation with Varsity.

"Can I smoke in here?" Vel asks the girl in front of him.

"Yeah, and my name is Kim she replies with a smile. Seeing Vel blaze up J.V pulls out the rest of the blunt he had lit in the car and sparks it back up.

"Why you ain't talking to me, what you think I'm ugly or something?" The girl with the strong smell of Hennessey on her breath asks J.V who slowly looks over at her and says" It ain't nothing like that, it's just I got a lot on my mind. But what's your name though?"

Smiling she replies "Kiesha." Before they get into a conversation.

Getting up and leaving out the room Varsity watches Meka's ass jiggle in her tight blue jeans before she turns down the hall.

"Can a nigga smoke with yall?" Asks Varsity to Vel and J.V before Vel throws him an already rolled blunt and he takes out his lighter and lights it as he takes a few short pulls before inhaling and exhaling deeply.

"Where yall get this?" Varsity asks about the weed as he looks at the blunt before taking another pull.

"Noble, why?" Asks Vel.

"Dis shit some fire." Varsity says blowing smoke out of his nose and plucking the ashes in the huge clear ashtray on the table that they are all using.

"Here go yall cups." Meka says putting their Styrofoam cups on the table when she comes back in the room.

"Thank you." Vel says leaning forward and grabbing a cup out of the stack and the bottle of Hennessey on the table as he opens it and pours some in his cup before passing the bottle to J.V across the table.

"I got some E & J too if yall want some." Meka says pulling the bottle from beside the couch as she sits on Varsity's lap.

"Yeah yall in this bitch getting fucked up for real." Vel says taking a sip of his Hennessey.

"Yall getting us drunk so yall gotta have something planned for us tonight." Varsity says out loud while drinking from Meka's cup as she sits in his lap.

Looking at him Meka replies out loud "you ain't saying nothing, me and my girl bout whatever." As Kiesha and Kim say "you know that's right."

"Oh yeah, I can't tell it." Replies Vel with a smile. "boy I would drown you." Kim looks at him and says as J.V and Varsity both say "OOH." As Vel looks at them smiling before looking at Kim and saying "make me know it then." before she looks over at Meka who gives her the do your thing nod and then looking back at Vel and saying "come on then."-As she gets up and Vel does as well as they walk out the room to the steps and disappears up the stairs with Varsity and Meka not far behind them.

When Kiesha hears both doors upstairs shut she put her hand on J.V's leg looks at him and smiles and slides her hand up his pants leg before undoing his belt as he sits in silence, unbuttoning his pants and then unzipping his zipper she then goes to pull down his pants and boxers as he lifts himself up on the couch and she pulls them until they fall down around his ankles, stopping she stands up in front of him as she smiles and slowly undresses while glancing back and forth from his face to his dick.

When she's completely naked she climbs on top of him and places one hand on the top of the couch as she uses her other hand to put him inside her as she moans and bounces up and down on him until her tight wet walls allow all of him completely inside of her as she holds on to the top of the couch while arching her back and letting out loud moans of pleasure as she forces herself to go faster while feeling his mouth and tongue on her breasts and hearing how wet she actually is which turns her on even more as she gasps for air staring at the ceiling with her eyes closed and mouth open as moans of pleasure and ecstasy flow from her body as he holds on to both of her ass cheeks moaning as well.

"Yeah, yeah, ummh, ha." She moans repeatedly as she bites down on her bottom lip as she rides him faster.

"Ummh, ummh, ummh" she groans now Squeezing him and scratching his back.

"I'm bout to cum." J.V says desperately as she gets up off him and says "put it in my mouth." As she drops to her knees and opens her mouth as he stands up and strokes his dick until he busses in and on her mouth, lips and face before she starts sucking his dick like she trying to suck another nut out while he trembles as he moans holding the back of her head as she goes back and forth until he cums again and she swallows it before she starts sucking and licking his balls as he continues to tremble and moan before saying "stop." Out of desperation and feeling like he can't take any more.

"You had enough?" She asks looking up at him before licking and sucking some left over cum off of his dick as he nods yes before she stops and smiles.

Pulling his pants up as she stands up J.V drops down on the couch exhausted, amazed and in love as she bends over naked picking her clothes up and asking, "so tell me some more about this company you bout to own." trying to break the silence as she walks toward the door that leads to the hallway while holding her clothes and under garments in her hands.

"I'll finish telling you about it when you come back from where ever you going." Replies J.V fixing his clothes as she says. "the bathroom." and disappears into the hallway.

About twenty minutes later she reappears in the room fully dressed as J.V sits back smoking a blunt.

"Can I have some?" She asks. Smiling J.V goes in his pocket and pulls out a blunt and a bag of weed and says "you can roll one."

"Alright." She says taking the blunt and weed as she sits on the arm rest. "What was you saying about yo company?" She asks.

"Oh yeah, it's not gone be mines but my daddy wants me to work with him and he gone leave it to me when he retires, but the only problem is I gotta move with him way out L.A." He replies.

"You gone do it?" Asks Kiesha as she rolls her blunt.

"I don't know, that's what I been thinking about though. But still I love my niggas too much to leave them." Replies J.V pulling his blunt.

"You shouldn't put friends over something like that, cause one thing could go wrong that all yall could get mad at each other behind and the next thing you know yall beefing." says Kiesha as she finishes rolling her blunt.

"I feel you, but what me and my niggas got is way deeper than that shawty." Replies J.V pulling out his lighter and passing it to her.

"O.K." She says with a we'll see tone of voice as she lights her blunt. "This puddle of white stuff right here on this couch belongs to you, not me." J.V says pointing at the spot.

"Damn, let me get that shit up for Meka cuss my ass out." Kiesha says getting up and going back in the bathroom to get some tissue. Before they finally do go to sleep they talk, drink, smoke and eventually end up fucking again and going to sleep holding each other as they lay naked, drunk and high on the couch.

Chapter 11

Seminary North Side
The Next Morning Monday October 17, 1999

"Nigga wake yo naked ashy ass up and put some clothes on! And damn shorty you phat as a motherfucker." Vel says standing over them smacking J.V on the shoulder while looking at Kiesha's naked body.

"Damn nigga, stop hitting me." J.V says with sleep on his voice as Kiesha gets up and climbs over top of him holding her breast as she gets off the couch, picks her clothes up and runs embarrassed out into the hall toward the bathroom.

"Look at all that ass, damn I picked the wrong one, shit." Vel says staring at her the whole time until she leaves the room.

"Nigga get out here and let me put some clothes on." J.V says balled up on the couch.

"Fuck you balled up on the couch for, ain't nobody looking at you." Vel says before walking out into the hall and toward the front door going on the porch as Kim comes down the steps and watches J.V getting dressed before she goes on the porch with Vel.

"Damn." She says still thinking about what she saw. "What?" Asks Vel.

"Nothing." She replies shutting the door.

"So, is you gone call me or what?" She asks him.

"Yeah, but you got my number too, so you call me." He replies. "Whatever." She says before grabbing his dick and kissing him before going back in the house, as she's going in JV's coming out and they make eye contact before J.V hears Vel asks "you ready?"

"Yeah, but where Varsity at?" Asks J.V. "He chilling over here, but I'm ready to bounce cause I gotta shit." Vel says as they walk down the steps

toward the stolen Blazer they pulled up in and getting in. Sitting in the passenger seat as Vel starts the car up. With the screw driver he had in his pocket J.V says, "shorty girl was a freak."

"And I bet you ain't put no condom on fucking that freak!" Replies Vel pulling off.

"I pulled out when it won't in her mouth, hell naw I won't gone buss in her. I couldn't let her kiss my kids with that mouth and I was so fucked up I won't thinking about no condom." J.V says as Vel replies "if that bitch gave yo ass something you gone be wishing you put a condom on." But J.V doesn't reply as he looks out the window.

Twenty Forth East End

Walking out of his crib and up the block, when he gets to the street Nobel lives on Drama sees Trigger, G-Way and Hova standing on the corner hustling.

"What's up my nigga Noble looking for you." G-way says giving him five.

"I'm gone holla at that nigga later, I'm about to go get this car and take care of something." Replies Drama walking past them as G-way walks with him and asks, "what you gotta take care of this early in the morning?" As they turn off into an alley.

"I'm about to go back down the apartments." Replies Drama.

"For what?" Asks G-Way as they approach the drop top Drama stole.

"The fuck you think I'm going back down the apartments for! To see what's going on." Drama says getting in the car and starting it up with the screw driver he had on him as G-way gets in before he backs the car out the alley, drops the top, puts in a tape and turns "My down fall" up as he pulls off and rides right past Hova and Trigger nodding to the music.

Stopping the car at his crib he jumps out and goes to his Infinity taking his keys out of his pocket and opening the trunk taking out a AK, a ski mask and a coat before yelling to G-way to pop the trunk as he shuts his trunk and

walks to the trunk of the stolen drop top lifting it up putting the stuff in it shutting it and getting back in the car and pulling off-.

"What you just put in there?" G-way asks Drama who replies, "it won't nothing." As he drives.

"A yo if you about to do something crazy you can let me out or take me back around there with Trigger and them." G-way says as Drama sucks his teeth and says "yall niggas be acting like some bitches." As he gets to the corner and makes a U-turn.

"Come on man niggas trying to get money, we ain't trying to be wild in all day." Replies G-Way as they sit in silence the rest of the ride back to where Hova and them. are standing as they pull up the same time as Vel and J.V, getting out the car G-way walks to where Hova and them are standing and Drama pulls off but stops when he hears and sees J.V calling him and jogging toward him as he sits stopped in the street.

"What's up my nigga?" Asks a smiling J.V getting in the passenger seat as Drama pulls off, looking over at J.V Drama says "I ain't trying to be funny or nothing but you stink." As J.V smells himself before saying "No I don't, I smell like pussy, weed and Hennessey you smelling something else."

"Oh, so you and Jasmine been freaking this morning or you just coming from them bitches house?" Asks Drama.

"Them bitches house and I found a freak." Replies J.V.

"Yeah, well don't let Jasmine fine out about yo freak." Drama says as he watches the road.

"I know, that's why I need you to say I was with yall out here all night. And where we going anyway?" Asks J.V.

"Down the apartments." Replies Drama putting the top back up on the drop top. "For what?" Asks J.V.

"All shit here we go again, cause I wanna see something. What, you scared nigga?" Drama asks smartly. Sucking his teeth J.V replies "I ain't scared of shit." as Drama drives.

When they get down the apartments where Drama shot Grim and his baby mama they see a detective talking to three drug dealers out on the early morning grind.

Slowing down and looking in the cut where they are standing Drama looks in the crowd to see if he recognizes any faces.

"I think that's some of them niggas right there" Drama says to J.V as he turns a corner and stops.

"What you about to do?" JV asks Drama as he opens the glove

compartment and pushes a button opening the trunk.

"You'll see, get in the driver seat and when I say pull off, pull off and meet me at the top of the alley on the side street." Drama says getting out the car and J.V slides in the driver seat as Drama walks to the trunk and pulls out the coat and ski mask and puts it on before grabbing the AK and shutting the trunk as he walks around the corner to the other end of the cut to block them off from running past him.

"What the fuck is wrong with this nigga?" JV asks his self, watching Drama dressed in a long coat and ski mask turn the corner holding that big ass AK. Walking toward the cut Drama observes his surrounding and doesn't see anyone outside this early in the morning.

Peeking around the corner into the cut he sees them in a small circle looking at some pictures the detective is showing them.

Turning into the cut Drama screams "fuck all yall niggas!" As he AIMS toward them shooting.

Seeing the hustlers drop and the detective try to run for cover Drama starts shooting left and right picking them all apart.

After seeing the detective fall dead and making sure the dudes are dead as he shoots the one still moving and breathing, Drama takes off running out the cut and to the left screaming "Go! Go! Go!" As he runs past J.V and up the hill still holding the gun as J.V pulls off and drives around the corner and past the cut seeing people laid out before he makes a left and then a right and another right as he drives up the hill.

Stopping at the top of the alley he watches Drama run down the alley toward the car, so he opens the passenger door and Drama jumps in and he pulls off slowly making a left and driving down the next alley across from them.

"No, you didn't do what the fuck I think you just did." J.V asks Drama as they drive down the alley.

"Fuck it, ride or die nigga." Replies Drama breathing heavily taking off his ski mask and putting it in his coat pocket as J.V turns out of the alley and back on to the street making a right and looking straight as he drives.

"I got them motherfuckers." Drama says taking off the coat and throwing it into the back seat.

"Watch where you pointing that gun." J.V says looking over at the AK in Drama lap pointing at him as he drives.

"Nigga you my dawg, I'll shoot myself before I shoot you." Replies Drama grabbing the AK and putting it under the seat.

"I know that cop shit gone be all over the news, especially since niggas done got killed down there two days in a row. I was looking at the news yesterday and that's all them motherfuckers was talking about, people dying here and people dying there. We already got the murder capital, so we need to chill and be easy for a little while." J.V says stopping at a stop sign as the city bus drives past them.

"For what? Them bitch ass niggas ain't even breathing no more and ain't nobody see dat shit so what the fuck we need to chill for?" Asks Drama as

J.V pulls off from the stop sign.

"I'm just saying, I'm not trying to see nothing happen to any of us and if we keep this up something bad is bound to happen." Replies J.V.

"I ain't even worried about that, cause one thing for sure and two things for certain whenever my back is on the wall niggas gone have to kill me cause I'm gone try my best to shoot my way out whatever." Drama says seriously as he looks out the window.

"So, the thought of dying doesn't scare you?" Asks J.V.

"Scare me for what? Almost everybody I love is dead so dying is just doing me a favor, what you think I was trying to do when I locked myself in my brothers room for all them weeks?

I was wishing for the shit, but it never happened, so by chance I found one of my brother's books. I forget the name of it, but anyway I realized after reading that book that shit ain't gone happen unless it's meant to be and since I been dumping on them niggas ain't nothing bad has happen to me so the shit must be meant to be and I ain't gone stop till I kill all them niggas, like I'm the prophet of death." Replies Drama as J.V realizes he has went crazy and tries to change the subject by asking. "So, what if they want peace?"

"Fuck peace! It ain't no such thing as peace until it's war and stop asking me these dumb ass questions cause ain't nobody thinking about peace and you pissing me off with this stupid scared shit. So, since were on your block, carry yo ass in the house!" Drama says before J.V sucks his teeth but remains silent until he pulls up in front of his crib and parks.

"I don't care if you get mad, if you're scared you need to stay in the crib." Drama says as J.V gets out of the car and Drama gets in the driver seat.

"I told you, I ain't scared of shit." J.V says hiding the anger in his voice. "You ready to die?" Asks Drama scaring J.V with the question not knowing what's on Drama mind.

"Naw I ain't ready to die, it's too much to live for." Replies J.V. "Well you scared of something then and hesitation will get you killed.

Now take this and carry it in the apartment with you. I'll be back through later on." Drama says turning around and getting the coat out of the back seat and then getting the AK from under the passenger seat and wrapping the coat around it before giving it to him and pulling off as J.V stares as the car drive away before shaking his head and turning around walking to and in his apartment. When he gets inside he puts the AK wrapped in the coat under his love seat before walking to the cordless phone hanging from the wall in the kitchen and taking it off the receiver as he cuts it on and dials numbers on the phone as he walks back to his front room and sits on the couch as the phone rings.

"Powells Industrial Steel this is Cynthia how may I help you?" Asks the female secretary picking up the phone.

"May I speak to Johnathan Powells please?" "May I ask whose calling?" Asks his secretary. "His son," Replies JV.

"Hold please." She says putting him on hold. "Hello?" Asks his father moments later. "Hey daddy, how are you doing?" Asks J.V

"Hey Jerrell, I'm fine how are you doing?" Asks his father.

"I'm alright I'm just calling to tell you that I've made my choice and I've decided I'm coming out there with you." replies J.V as his father laughs from happiness.

"My boy I'm glad to hear that. I can get some plane tickets for you and Jasmine before the week is out. By the way, what is today?" Asks his father as J.V replies "Monday. But Jasmine don't wanna come cause she made manager at her job and she ain't trying to leave it after working so hard to get it, plus she ain't trying to move out this crib anyway."

"Alright, but you should be gone by Friday, so you should see if you could get her to reconsider." Says his father.

"I will. I'll talk to you later though. I love you. Bye."

J.V replies before hanging the phone up and getting up walking back to the kitchen and putting it on the receiver before going to and in the refrigerator and looking through it before taking out a sub sandwich Jasmine hadn't eaten, a big pack of Oreo's and a jug of fruit punch before kicking the refrigerator closed and going in his room.

Twenty Fourth East End

While driving around, Drama sees Nobel on the corner, so he pulls right up beside him.

"What's up nigga?" Asks Drama to Nobel who's standing with a group of Bloods.

"I know that shit is stolen so park it round the corner somewhere and come here cause I got something important to ask you so hurry up." Replies Nobel as Drama pulls off and parks around the corner.

When he gets back down the street where they are standing they all get quiet as they slowly make a circle around him and Noble.

"What yall about to do?" Asks Drama on point as he glances around at them.

"Look lil nigga this is some serious shit and if your down cool but if not don't even say nothing else about this shit to nobody and I mean nobody." Nobel says, giving him a cold stare.

"Alright, what's up?" Asks Drama still glancing to his left and right side where some of the Bloods have gotten a few steps closer to them.

"I got this lick I want you and yo niggas to pull off for me since niggas won't suspect yall of doing it and yall know how to steal cars. And if everything goes right yall can have any and everything yall find which I know gone be a lot but that's only if your down." Replies Noble.

"Hell, yeah I'm down, what's up, where the niggas at? Fuck dat shit!" Drama says seriously as they laugh.

"Calm down lil nigga, it's just one nigga and I fuck with his bitch. But anyway, she told me once in a while he makes big trips out of town and he come back with a lot of weight in coke and heroin and today is that day so I need one of yall to steal that car and don't worry about it.

I know he's gone be by himself. But this where yo boys come in at cause a couple of them gone have to break in his house as a diversion plus that's where all yall payment gone be found at and if I remember correctly he keeps all his money inside the couch cushions in the front room but anyway the other reason I need them in the house is to set that front room on fire so yall need to move fast cause I'm gone give yall the word when to set the shit on fire when I call the crib and hang up letting yall know I see him coming up or down the block. His girl gave me the number so when I call and hang up. I need that room blazing with fire so hopefully when he's pulling up he'll see his shit up in flames and jump out to-try.to come put the shit out and save his shit and while he's doing that."

"That's when one of yall steal the car plus everybody that's anybody gone be out tonight at a nigga name Melly Mel homecoming party, so the block should be empty you got me." Nobel says pulling his beeper off his hip and holding it out toward Drama.

"Alright I got you. But who we supposed to be doing this shit to anyway?" asks Drama as everyone pauses, gets quiet and looks at each other before Nobel breaks the silence by saying "Quarter."

"The OG Crip nigga Quarter? I thought that was yall nigga?" Asks Drama.

"Yeah, he was, but fuck that nigga. And he got yo nigga killed this morning." Replies Nobel.

"Who?" Asks Drama a bit shocked.

"Lil One. Niggas say he killed his cousin and shot up his homies yesterday at some party." Replies Nobel with a straight face as Drama's face drops and Nobel holds the beeper up again and Drama takes it feeling like he's dreaming before asking "you sure it was him?"

"Yeah, I seen the nigga laid out in the street and everything. The shit happened by the motel on Chamberlayne. That's one of the reasons I really want to get at this nigga anyway cause I fucked with Lil One." replies Nobel as anger and frustration can clearly be seen on Dramas face.

"Look, if that nigga cross my path I'm gone lay that nigga down man." "Chill young nigga, don't let that fuck this mission up cause when it's time to get his ass you'll get yo chance." replies Noble Patting Drama on his back as Drama wipes tears from his face.

"I got you dawg." Drama says trying to calm himself down.

"That's my Lil nigga, see I told yall he don't give a fuck." Noble says to his niggas.

"Look lil nigga, gone finish doing what you was doing and get ready to take care of that." Noble says giving him five and so does everyone else before he walks back down the street toward the car he stolen.

"Damn my nigga, I got you though. That's my word I got you."

Drama says to his self, walking down the street thinking about Lil One. When he gets around the corner he looks up and sees a police man by the car.

"Damn, at least I took the screw driver with me." He says to his self-turning around and walking back down the street.

"Police around the corner!" He yells as everybody on the block starts to walk off as well as looking to make sure they're not on their way around the corner, as he keeps straight instead of walking back down toward where Noble and them were as he glances back at the police man who is now sitting in his squad car smoking a cigarette with the driver door open, before Drama notices a car slowing down beside him.

Knowing he doesn't have a gun on him and his pride won't let him run, he stops and turns to the car ready to deal with whatever is about to go down as the car stops.

Seeing all females in the car he slightly relaxes as the back window rolls down and a light skin female with long black hair asks, "hey boy, ain't your name Drama?"

"Why? What's up?" Asks Drama still standing in his same position not smiling and glancing up and down the street.

"Don't you be with Lil One?" She asks noticing his body language. "Yeah why?" Asks Drama wondering who the hell she is.

"That's my baby's daddy and I done seen you and your friends with him a couple of times and I just wanted to tell you somebody killed him if you ain't know yet." She replies.

"Yeah, I know I just found out." Drama says looking in her face and seeing the grief and sadness.

"Well if yall know or find out who did it yall need to do something about it and not just for Lil One but for me and his daughter as well." She replies in a sad tone.

"No question. I'm gone ride for him." Drama says in a serious low tone as she stares in his face to verify if his words are real before saying "Thank You." and leaning back in the seat as her window goes back up and the driver pulls off as Drama stands there watching the car drive away knowing he has to revenge the death of his nigga no matter the cause so at least his little daughter would know that her daddy had niggas who loved him enough to kill for him and that he didn't die in vain.

Taking a deep breath, he looks back down the street and sees the police still in the squad car before he continues walking and thinking to his self about all the loved ones he's lost to death and how he feels like only he can make things better killing off all of their enemies to make his hood a safer place.

After walking a couple of blocks while talking to himself he sees an Oldsmobile Ninety eight he likes so he walks past it and breaks the small back window and keeps walking.

Walking around the block he checks to see if anyone came out the house before he goes back to the car and knocks the glass out of the back window then sticks his arm through it unlocking the back door. Getting in he climbs to the front after shutting the door.

Tilting the steering wheel up he breaks the left side of the neck of the steering wheel with the screw driver until a metal piece that looks like a doughnut is exposed.

After breaking the doughnut completely off a square metal piece is exposed so he takes the screw driver out and puts it where the tilt is and knocks the box around it off and pushes the spring out knocking pieces back with his screw driver which loosens the steering wheel and then sticks the screw driver back where the doughnut use to be and pushes the square metal starter piece up once and the radio comes on, pushing it up again the car starts and he puts it in drive and pulls off.

While Vel drives around Church hill with Trigger in the passenger seat, Trigger sees Jovanda walk out of a house so he tells Vel to pull over and he does.

"A boo, where you going?" Asks Trigger as she looks over and sees "To get my hair done." She replies walking to the car with a smile and giving him a kiss.

"You need some money?" Asks Trigger.

"Yeah, I could use it to pay for my hair and get my nails done." Replies Jovanda as Trigger goes in his pocket while asking

"How much you need?"

"Like, three hundred." Replies Jovanda as Vel makes a face that says yeah right but doesn't say anything as Trigger counts out the money and gives it to her saying "that's four, so get ya feet done too."

Smiling she kisses him again and says, "thank you boo." "It ain't no problem, you want a ride?" He asks.

"Naw I'm alright, Jennifer and Sasha in the house waiting on me to come back with the weave and the store just right there plus she got a car and were all going together but where was you on your way out to?" She asks. "around the strip, we just came from taking care of something around Raven street." replies Trigger. "you do remember this is a stolen car." Vel says interrupting them.

"Well look, I'm gone call you when I get home." Jovanda says after hearing Vel. Looking over at him Trigger doesn't say anything before turning back to Jovanda and saying, "alright then boo." and giving her another kiss before she walks off and Vel pulls off.

When they get around the strip Vel pulls up to where Varsity is standing selling drugs and they get out of the car.

"What's up niggas?" Asks Varsity giving them five as they walk toward him and stand beside them.

"Yall niggas seen Drama?" Asks Varsity.

"Naw, I don't know where the fuck dat niggas at." replies Vel.

"Fuck all that, I'm trying to get drunk, who's trying to role with me to the liquor store." Trigger say as he leans on the stop sign.

"I got some Gin in my car, you can get the shit." replies Varsity as Trigger makes his way toward the car.

Beep Beep Beep Beep! "A yall, come here." Drama says out the window as he pulls up beeping the horn and Trigger walks over to the car as Varsity continues to serve friends.

"Serious business, yall niggas come here man and get in the car." Drama says with a serious tone as they all walk over to the car.

"What's up? What the fuck is wrong with you?" Asks Trigger.

"Fuck all that, get in the car and come on." Drama says before they all pile in the car and he pulls off.

"What's up? Why you looking all crazy for? And where we going?" Asks Vel.

"To find Hova and them." Replies Drama with a serious look on his face.

"What the hell is going on?" Asks Varsity as Drama sucks his teeth and says, "Man Quarter's homies killed Lil One this morning behind that shit at the party yesterday."

"Get the fuck outta here." Trigger says in disbelief.

"Dats my word yo, I just talked to that niggas baby's mama and everything." Replies Drama as sadness darkens all of their faces and the only noise is the music playing from the car stereo as Drama drives.

"We gotta get at them niggas, I don't give a fuck if their Crips or not it's going down." Vel says as Drama nods in agreement turning the corner and seeing Hova and G-way talking to some females.

Pulling up beside them Hova looks back and sees them and says, "What the fuck is going on today?" Niggas out this bitch riding around shooting at."

Before Drama cuts him off yelling over the top of Vel out the passenger window "Shut the fuck up! Damn nigga you don't know them females right there!" As they all stand looking at them in the car in shock and confusion before Hova turns around and walks toward the car saying "Damn nigga!

What's up?"

"Just get in the car." Vel says before Hova looks at G-way and they both crowd in the back seat.

Dreaming J.V sees his self the owner of his father's company happy with a family but in away very sad because off and on he goes to Drama's grave, site and only if I was there." Keeps echoing through his mind before he's awaken by loud knocks on his door.

By the time he gets to the door Jasmine is walking in with everyone behind her."

"Damn, you just getting off work? I know I wasn't asleep that long." J.V says as Jasmine walks to the bathroom and they sit down.

"What's wrong with yall?" Asks J.V as they all remain silent.

"Yall heard about all them people that got shot yesterday and today?" Jasmine yells asking from behind the bathroom door. "Today?" "What happened today?" Asks Varsity to her as J.V turns and walks to the bathroom.

"Some people and police got shot and killed down the apartments."

Replies Jasmine.

"How you know that?" Asks Drama.

"It was on the radio all day, it might even be on the news too." She replies with J.V in there with her running the shower.

Thinking about it, Vel looks at Varsity who looks at Trigger who looks at Hova who looks at G-way who looks at Drama along with everyone else.

"What?" Asks Drama with a devilish grin but nobody says anything to him and Varsity looks away. Laughing Drama says "Niggas is crazy."

"I'm telling you." Varsity says looking at the ground.

"Yall want anything to drink?" Asks Jasmine coming out of the bathroom.

"What yall got?" Asks Trigger dialing numbers on his phone. "Anything you could think of." She replies walking to the kitchen.

"Well in that case, it don't matter." Replies Trigger now with the phone to his ear. "and yall?" Asks Jasmine from the kitchen."

"Same." replies Hova for everyone.

"You're a wild ass dude." Varsity says to Drama. "What? you think I did that shit?" Asks Drama.

"Nigga the AK's right here by my foot, and why would it be over here?" Replies Varsity.

Laughing Drama says "it ain't nobody fault but they own."

"I respect that. And since you seem like you feel like wilding I got this girl who works at a jewelry store who done set it up so I can hit the joint and all she wants out of the shit is a little bit of jewelry, so what's up?" Asks Varsity as Jasmine walks back and forth putting cups and a bottle of Tanqueray on the table before going in her room with a bottle of Remy Martin.

"When this supposed to jump off?" Asks Drama.

"I can make it happen tomorrow if you trying to do it." Replies Varsity as the beeper Noble gave him starts beeping and he pulls it out of his pocket not remembering if Noble told him why he gave him the beeper that hasn't beeped since he had it with him as he now stares at the number on the screen.

Getting up he walks to the phone in the kitchen and picks it up and starts dialing the number on the screen of the beeper.

After a few rings Noble picks, up and says "Drama?" "Yeah dis me." Replies Drama.

"It's going down in a few, so go set up and when I beep you again that's the green light to rush the joint, one."

Noble says hanging up and Drama does as well before saying "A look we gotta get ready to take care of that thing I told yall about, so it's gone be me, Varsity, G-way and Trigger." "Naw, I can't go dawg me, my girl and her friends supposed to go to the movies." Replies Trigger still on the phone.

"Nigga, money over bitches, fuck dat shit. You trying to go Vel?" Asks Drama.

"Naw, I wanna go to the movies too now. Since you left me out the starting line-up." Replies Vel as Drama sucks his teeth and says "yall niggas trippin, so don't ask for shit when we come back with all types of shit."

"I mean I wanna go, what happened to me?" Asks Hova.

"Alright come on then, that's why yall niggas ain't got no ride." Drama says as him, Varsity, and G-Way get up and leave out laughing.

"It ain't like she can't pick us up." Trigger yells to them as they leave out.

"A J.V, you trying to go to the movies?" Trigger yells to him.

"Yeah! A boo you trying." J. V's yelling from the shower before she cuts him off by yelling "I'm trying to go to bed if yall shut the hell up!" As Trigger and them laughs.

"Fuck it! I'm coming." J.V says from the shower.

Twenty First East End

Later that evening as Drama and them slowly cruise the block as it starts to get darker outside Hova asks "why we just driving around the same blocks, we should've just parked."

"I ain't want nobody to see us just sitting parked around here, that shit looks suspicious." Replies Drama before the beeper Noble gave him goes off and he turns on to the block where Quarter lives saying, "There it go, look I'm gone get the car and yall get the house." Drama says parking the car and getting out as they make their way up the side street and turn on to the street where Quarter stays. Other than the usual drunks and crack heads wondering the street the block is damn near empty.

Stopping on the corner across from where Quarters house is Drama posts on the corner as Hova, Varsity and G-way who's holding a gas can keeps walking as they cross the street and walk straight until they turn off into the alley behind quarters house and Drama turns back around and walks toward the car.

Jumping Quarters gate, they creep through his big empty back yard and make their way to the back porch where the only thing they hear is the wind blowing around them.

"Yall niggas ready?" Asks Varsity as adrenaline runs through them. "Not really but fuck it." Replies G-way.

"I'm ready, fuck this shit we already over here now." Hova says backing up to get some speed before he runs and kicks the door which makes a loud thud but doesn't move.

"Why you ain't waiting for all of us, now if a nigga is their they are probably laying on us." Varsity says looking at Hova with a bit of disgust in his eyes.

"Man, fuck dat shit I'm trying to get this money." Replies Hova backing up again as this time Varsity and G-way follow and they all rush and kick the door as it rips off of its hinges as it hangs barely by a nail as they kick it again and it falls to the ground as they all slowly walk into the dark kitchen with their guns out.

"Man, ain't nobody in here." Hova says as G-Way peeks into the dining room and he walks right past him.

"Yall check upstairs and I'm gone look around down here." Hova says as they make their way toward the steps and go upstairs.

Looking around the neatly kept dining room Hova turns back around and starts checking the kitchen first, after almost flipping the kitchen upside down he doesn't find anything but a few eight balls of cocaine inside a sugar bag which he places in his pockets and goes to search the dining and living rooms as G-Way comes running back down the steps still holding the gas can.

"We done struck gold, you seen some trash bags down here?" Asks G- Way placing the gas can on the living room floor.

"Yeah they in the kitchen." Hova says mad at his self for not picking upstairs instead of downstairs as he goes through a dresser as G-Way goes in the kitchen.

"Oh shit." Hova says to his self as he remembers what Drama said and he runs to the couches in the front room as G-way runs back upstairs with several trash bags.

Yanking the cushion off one of the couches he sees a false wooden bottom, so he removes it and says, "Oh shit." as he sees neatly stacked ten and twenties covered in a plastic wrapping before he runs toward the kitchen and almost trips over the gas can G-Way left on the floor as he runs in the kitchen and grabs some trash bags before jogging back toward the couch and dumping what he guesses is at least ten G's into the bag as he checks the next one that has one's and fives stacked the same way in the same plastic wrap.

Checking the rest of the couches he sees they are empty before he walks towards the gas can and the phone starts ringing.

Pausing and looking at the phone he wonders if that is the Q telling him that Quarter is coming and he also can't remember if he was supposed to pick it up since he wasn't really paying attention when Drama was talking.

Ignoring the phone, he picks up the gas can, opens it and with the trash bag of money in his hand he starts throwing gas all over the living room, when the phone stops ringing he walks to the front window and peeks out the blinds but doesn't see any cars other than the one Drama is sitting in parked across the street waiting for Quarter.

"Yes, fucking sir!" Varsity says running down the steps with several full trash bags in each hand with G-Way a few paces behind him with a few full bags his self.

"Nigga we hit up!" Varsity says with a huge smile on his face. "Watch the window." Hova tells him as he starts throwing more gas everywhere while making his way over to the front door which he unlocks and opens all the way like he was told as the phone ring again.

"Pick it up, it might be Noble." Varsity says as he watches the window.

"I ain't touching that motherfucking phone." Replies Hova still throwing gas everywhere.

After a few rings G-way picks the phone up but doesn't say anything. "Hello?" Asks an unfamiliar male voice on the phone.

"Hello Quarter?" Asks dude again before G-way hangs the phone up in his face.

"Why the fuck you pick the phone up?" Screams Hova.

"I thought it was Noble cause the phone started ringing after you opened the door and Drama said he was suppose to call!" Replies G-Way matching Hova's tone of voice.

"You fucking up." Varsity says glancing back at him as he continues to watch the window before the phone starts ringing again. "So now what!" G- way asks them as Varsity sees Drama quickly duck down in the car and sees Quarters car coming down the street.

"OH SHIT! The nigga pulling up now." Varsity says quickly getting away from the window as they run toward the back door.

"Hold up right quick." Hova says before turning back around and pulling out a book of matches.

Striking one he sets the whole book on fire and throws it in a puddle of gas. Instantly the whole room goes up in flames as they run out the back of the house.

"What the fuck my shit!" Screams Quarter seeing his door open, and house on fire as he leaves his car in park with the keys still in it as he jumps out of the Delta 88 and runs to his crib while pulling his gun off his waist.

"I should run up on his pussy ass." Drama says jumping out of the stolen car with a screw driver and running to the Delta, jumping in and pulling off listening to "Young G's" by Puff Daddy and Jay Z as he bends the corner.

Meeting Hova, G-Way and Varsity a couple of blocks up they get in the car and Drama makes his way to the spot Nobel said he'll meet them at.

Clover Leaf Mall, Movie Theater (South Side)

"Bout time this bullshit ass movie starting." J.V says to the female he's with.

"Shhh, it's coming on." She replies.

"You Shhh." J.V says back to her smiling.

"Why yall pick this wack movie for?" Vel asks Trigger. "Cause I ain't seen it yet." Replies Jovanda.

"But I didn't ask you." Vel says to Jovanda.

"Why is yall complaining" Asks the girl with Vel.

"Cause I done seen dis shit." Replies Vel as the girl looks away and stares at the screen.

"Can yall quiet down some?" Asks a guy behind them.

"It would be quiet in this bitch if you sit back and shut the fuck up." Replies J.V turning around to dude as he sits back with a stupid face.

"Deja and Neka don't yall wanna see the movie." Replies Jovanda. "I mean, I'd rather see the other movie." Replies Deja

"Well good let's go." Replies J.V as they get up and go in the other movie.

"You gone go to." Neka asks Vel.

"Naw I'll watch this shit." He says throwing skittles in the crowd as people look around to see who it is.

"Boy stop" Jovanda whispers to Vel hitting him in the arm while Trigger watches the movie.

"Alright I ran out of candy anyway." Replies Vel getting up.

"Yall want anything while I'm out dis bitch" ask Vel but nobody replies as he walks out.

"I gotta piss" Jovanda whispers in Trigger ear.

"Do you want me to hold your hand walk and watch you use the bathroom." He whispers back still looking at the movie before she gets up and goes to the bathroom. Out in the snack area Jovanda walks up behind Vel and kisses him on the ear.

"Girl you better chill with dat shit in public for somebody see us." Replies Vel.

"Well come in the bathroom with me then" says Jovanda as

Vel walks out of the line and she pulls him toward the bathroom.

When they get in the bathroom they start kissing and almost get to the point of fucking before they hear someone in the stall next to them, so they sneak out and Jovanda goes back in the movie while Vel gets back in the line.

"Damn shorty what you was doing shitting." Asks Trigger as she sits back down looks at him and starts drinking her soda.

"Where the fuck Vel at?" Trigger asks Jovanda.

"Still standing in the line." She replies while looking at the movie. "I'll be back." Trigger says getting up and leaving out the theater.

Seeing Vel and J.V standing in the line he says" why yall niggas standing out here for."

"Cause, I want something to eat." Replies J.V.

"Man, Vel you ain't been in this line for that long ass time." Says Trigger. "Where da fuck I been at then?" Asks Vel.

"I don't know, but you wasn't right here." Replies Trigger.

"Yeah whatever, what the fuck you doing out here?" Vel asks Trigger. "I don't want to look at that boring ass movie." Replies Trigger as the girl J.V is with walks toward them.

"What yall ready to leave?" Asks Deja. "Naw why you ready to go?" Asks J.V.

"I wanna do whatever you wanna do" says Deja.

"For real." J.V says smiling before whispering something in her ear. Giggling she grabs his hand and says, "come on."

"I'll be back" J.V says smiling as she pulls him toward the bathroom.

"Damn shorty." Vel says watching them go toward the bathroom. "I wonder if Neka got down like that?" Vel says to Trigger.

"Go find out then." Replies Trigger.

"I'm gone do that." Replies Vel before Trigger turns around and walks back in the theater.

Paying for his stuff Vel comes in behind him. Sitting down. Jovanda looks at him grins and turns to Trigger and starts talking.

"I think my friend likes you." Neka whispers in Vel ear. "Why you say that?" Asks Vel.

"Come on I see the way she keeps looking at you." whispers the girl.

"That's just my friend and that's how friends sometimes look at each other." replies Vel as Trigger says "people be getting real wild in them bathrooms." laughing as Jovanda looks at him surprised and then looks at Vel.

"What I ain't saying nothing." Vel says looking back at her.

Taking some candy out his lap she rolls her eyes at him before turning back toward the screen."Where the fuck they at matter of fact call that nigga." Says G-Way. "chill." Replies Hova getting out the car with Drama.

"So, where they at." G-way asks Drama. "I have the slightest idea." He replies.

"Well at least we got something to smoke." Replies G-way digging through the bags and finally pulling out a hand full of blunts and an ounce.

After two blunts go around they finally pull up. Getting out the car tripping Noble says, "I said the room not the whole house." "Where the hell yall been." Asks Drama.

"I had to sit out there and trip off dat shit, da nigga was outside going crazy." Replies Noble.

"Damn yall." Says Drama to his boys who are tripping off Noble and them while Joe looks on silently.

"I told that nigga stop throwing dat shit everywhere." Replies Varsity laughing.

"You came through for me lil homeboy." Noble says to Drama who's watching Joe silently watch Nobel.

"You know how I get down." Replies Drama giving him five then giving him the keys to the car.

"Damn you got da keys too, you really a bad motherfucker."

Noble says laughing. "You found the money and shit didn't it." Asks Noble.

"I guess, we got some shit of bags over there." Replies Drama "alright you straight then." Noble says getting in the car.

"Look yall catch a ride with Joe so nobody thinks yall had shit to do with this." Noble says out the window before pulling off.

After they get back around the way the fire department is still trying to put the fire out so after they park they stand on the corner and watch.

Laughing Drama asks Joe could he give him a ride home so he could put his cut of profit up. When they get in the car and pull off Joe asks, "I mean why you ain't trying to bum home?"

"I ain't got no problem with being a blood but, I got a little something of my own I've been plotting on doing." replies Drama as Joe says, "I can respect that, but whenever you're ready to bum home you know I'll vouch for you."

When they get to Dramas block Joe stops at the corner.

"Go from here, cause the streets is watching and I don't want all eyes on me." Joe says giving him five as him Hova, G-way and Varsity get out of the car and walk to his crib.

When they get in his room Varsity asks," why you don't wanna be no blood?"

"Cause, like I said I got other plans." Replies Drama dumping the money, guns, and drugs on the bed.

"Damn, we hit up." Drama says picking up blocks of compressed weed and big rocks of bagged up coke.

"Look at all this shit, I wonder what the fuck was in that car that was worth letting us get all this." Hova says picking up one of the compressed blocks of weed.

"I wonder what the fuck was in that car too." Replies G-Way as well as he holds two twin chrome three fifty-seven.

"I don't know and don't give a fuck, cause right now we good." Drama says still dumping money and drugs out of bags onto the bed.

"We about to make history and now that we got finances the Lost Souls is about to show niggas what it is." Drama says as they all look at him confused.

"Who da fuck is the Lost Soul's?" Asks Varsity.

"Us nigga. Me, you, G-Way, Hova, Trigger, Vel, and J.V.

That's the plan I've been putting together and now that we got the clientele to support it, I'm putting it in effect." Replies Drama.

"Oh, so now we a gang? How the fuck this small ass click gone be a gang, ain't nobody going for that shit." Hova says.

"Were taking respect by force and niggas can respect it or run from it!" Replies Drama in a serious tone. Laughing and nodding with approval Hova says "alright my nigga I'm feeling that, but you a crazy ass motherfucker."

"We riding too yo." Varsity says speaking for him and G-Way.

"It's official then, the Lost Souls and we gone make it be known tonight in memory of Lil One." Drama says taking his black bandanna off tying it around his head.

"And how you suppose we do that?" Asks Hova.

"Get the guns and follow me." Drama says as he goes under his bed and pulls out two AK's .

South Side

"Lost Souls Motherfucker!!" TAT TAT TAT TAT TAT TAT TAT TAT G- Way yells hanging out of the passenger window dumping the AK as Varsity shoot's both of the three fifty sevens at two older people and a teenage girl who are on the porch of the house that held the party where the girls baby daddy was killed by them at, while Drama and Hova who are a few blocks away opened fire from another stolen car wearing black bandanna's on their face's shooting up a corner store they saw one of the dudes who was with the dude they shot and killed at the party posted with some others smoking, selling drugs and talking.

"When the shooting stops and Hova has peeled off bodies laid scattered and crawling on the side walk, street and in front of the store while a few lay dead and the others return fire at the car.

Chapter 12

Dale Rd Henrico
Da Next Day Tuesday October 18, 1999.

"What's up Hova?" One of the first young drug dealers says to Hova as he just gets on the block and sees him and J.V standing around inhaling weed smoke in the early morning air. As Hova looks at him with a serious mean mug the young dealer is instantly frightened.

"Look yo I'm gone tell you like I told everybody else from the top to the bottom of this whole strip, were taking this block and if a nigga wanna sell or buy anything on this block you need to holla at me and mines. We also taking half."

Hova is saying before dude cuts him off and says" come on Hova man we cool, we don't want no problems with yall and you know Butter, runs dis strip. Yall don't even live out here, niggas ain't going." dude is saying before Hova and J.V pull out and Hova says "nigga I know you hear them sirens, that's the ambulance scraping Butter ass up off the ground so if you ready to die for a block you don't own you can join him!"

"Naw man I was just saying, I don't care for real. I'm cool with it." Dude replies scared to death.

"Alright, well spread the word. And if niggas wanna act stupid we can get it poppin out dis bitch and we gone be up in this area when you get back so gone tell them niggas da Lost Souls staking claim on this right here and I know you don't want me to call Drama and them so if yall thinking about coming back with pistols you already know what it's gone be."

J.V chips in and says as dude nods with understanding before quickly walking away and they get in their stolen whip and drive down the other end of the strip.

Twenty Fourth ' East End

While driving in his stolen caddie G-Way sees some shit of police parked around the block by Nobel's crib so he quickly parks and gets out as he walks to see what's going on. Seeing some shit of Crips and Bloods as well as nosey by standers staring at Nobel's crib. G-Way slows down when he notices he's closer to the Crip's then he is the Bloods and he doesn't know if they know about last night.

Seeing a pregnant girl walking away from the scene he quickly approaches her and asks her, "What the hell going on?"

"Some people ran up in the Blood dudes house and did something to him, I don't really know what, I just know the way them boys looking at each other it's about to be some shit out here and I'm not trying to get caught in the middle of it." She replies before walking away from him trying to get far away from the tension that's in the crowd a few feet away from them as quickly as possible.

"Taking in what she said G-way looks back at the crowd and doesn't see anyone he's cool with so he walks back toward the car.

As he opens the door he notices a police man watching him and getting on his walkie talkie so he slams the car door and takes off running just as the police man is starting to get out of the police car and stops when he takes off running.

"I see you staring at the bitch, gone holla at her with yo scared ass." Lil One says to Drama as Big Bro laughs while the three of them stand on the block leaned against Big Bro's car as the sun gleams off the fresh paint while they watch some females standing in front of one of the girl's house.

"Scared of what, and what da fuck you laughing at." Drama replies pushing his brother before a loud knocking snatches him from his dream.

Waking up holding his fourty-five with a detachable infrared beam he continues to hear the constant loud knock, knock, knock, knock.

Getting out the bed in the same clothes from last night he walks to the door gun in hand and yells "who is it?"

"It's G-Way man hurry up." He replies as Drama opens the door seeing G-Way breathing hard.

"A yo a nigga ran up in Nobel's crib." G-Way says standing trying to catch his breath.

"Where Noble at?" Asks Drama coming out the crib and closing the door behind him.

"I don't know." Replies G-Way.

Running to Noble crib it looks like Quarters crib with all the people standing around but the crib was not on fire. Seeing Joe, they both walk to him and ask him "what's happen?"

"I don't know, we was sitting in the crib and a nigga came to the door to get some coke and when I want to serve; him, some shit of niggas rushed the door wit pistols. So' they got everybody on the wall and they kept asking where da shit at? Ain't nobody telling so some of the niggas started pistol whipping Noble while some of the other ones started flipping da crib upside down. Noble finally told them where the shit was at and after they got it they kidnaped him." Says Joe.

"Who you think did da shit?" Asks Drama.

"It might've been Quarter and them cause that's the same way your brother got killed." Replies Joe looking in the sky.

"So, what you saying Quarter killed my brother?" Asks Drama.

"I don't know for sure but damn, the shit happened just like this." Joe says as the Crip dude Vega approaches them.

"I ain't came over here for no problems I just wanna know who keeps shooting at us and running up in niggas cribs." He says. "Nigga, yall should know. Don't front like yall ain't do this shit." Joe says getting in his face.

Backing up Vega says "word on my flag we ain't had nothing to do with this shit."

"Whatever nigga, then who?" Replies Joe.

"I don't know, that's why I came to holla at you cause me and you go back like that." Vega says.

"Well I don't know who did that or this but when I find out I'm gone smoke they ass." Replies Joe.

"Alright." Vega says before he turns around and walks back through the crowd.

"If they ain't do the shit then who?" Joe asks himself before looking at Drama.

"I ain't do the shit, I ain't even know about it until G-Way came and told me." Drama says looking at G-Way.

"Stop playing, dawg don't even look at me like that." Replies G-Way. "Well look, I'm gone go see what the word is on the block and you know ya homie funeral got pushed to Sunday." Joe says giving them five.

"Yeah, I know and I'm gone holla at cha." Drama says as they go their separate ways.

When Drama and G-Way get back to Dramas Crib Drama picks his phone up and call's J.V. After a few rings J.V answers as he stands on the block with Hova.

"What's up my nigga?" Asks Drama.

"Ain't shit, A yo that cop shit was on TV all day." J.V replies. "So" Drama says with a I don't give a fuck tone.

"Yall know where I can get some coke?" A young nigga walk's up to J.V and Hova and asks.

"I ain't got nothing but nicks and dubs on me, unless that's what you trying to get." Hova says smoking a blunt as him and dude walk and talk.

"Where you at?" Drama asks J.V. "Round Dale with Hova." Replies J.V. "It's some money out there." Drama says.

"Yeah, I been out here a couple of times but look I won't gone tell yall this but I might be leaving to go to work with my daddy." Replies J.V.

"When?" Asks Drama as G-way passes him a blunt. "Friday." Replies J.V.

"Why you ain't tell a nigga nothing?" Asks Drama.

"Cause, I mean I won't gone go but I can't sell drugs all my life and this is a multi-million-dollar company that I'm gone own." Say J.V.

"Well I can't hate you for that cause everybody don't get a chance like that, so I think you should go for it." Replies Drama.

"For real." J.V says as he serves friends and Hova walks back up the block counting some money.

"Yeah, and we gone throw you a little block party." Replies Drama. "Jasmine ain't going cause I guess she don't wanna leave da hood so can you watch out for her for me?" Asks J.V.

"Yeah, and you can have my car as a present from me." says Drama. "Your car? How I'm gone get dat shit to L.A?" Asks J.V.

"Damn, I forgot dat nigga lives all the way out in L.A, well I don't know, give it to yo girl or something." Replies Drama.

"I'll think about it, but I think Trigger might want da joint." Says J.V. "Man, dat nigga got enough doe to get a whip, where that niggas at anyway?" Asks Drama.

"I don't know, hold up I'm gone call him." J.V says clicking over and using the three-way.

"Hello?" Trigger says picking up on the first ring as J.V clicks back over.

"What's up nigga?" Drama says to him. "What up, who dis?" Asks Trigger.

"It's Drama and J.V nigga you know who it is." Replies Drama.

"Oh, what's up niggas hold on I'm on the phone wit Vel." Trigger says clicking back over and saying "hello?" "Yeah." Replies Vel.

"A, Drama and them on the other end you want me to put you on da three way?" Asks Trigger.

"Naw, I'm straight. I'm bout to get in the shower and get myself together." Replies Vel.

"Alright well I ain't gone hold you up, it didn't sound like you wanted to talk to me anyway." Trigger says.

"Gone wit dat bullshit, I told you I just woke up and I'm still tired as a motherfucker." Replies Vel.

"Well gone wash yo ass then nigga, I was about to go look for these niggas anyway so I'll holla back. alright my nigga. one." Trigger says before clicking back over to Drama and J.V.

Mechanicsville Rd East End

Laying back on the bed, Jovanda who is naked except for the sheet covering her, wraps her arms around Vel as they go back to sleep.

Q ST East End

Getting on the block Trigger sees Varsity sitting in a Lex.

"What's up nigga?" Trigger says running up on the driver side of the car and hitting the hood as Varsity plays with the E.Q.

"Damn nigga you scared the shit out of me, what's up?" Replies Varsity still adjusting the bass.

"Shit, just got off the phone wit Drama and them, while I was on my way over here." Replies Trigger as Varsity yawns.

"Damn nigga you look tired as a motherfucker." Trigger says looking at Varsity's blood shot eyes.

"Shit, I'm getting money fuck sleep and we put in some work yesterday." Replies Varsity.

"Yeah, I know, we gang banging now, they told me when I was on the phone walking up here." Trigger says twisting his fingers making gang signs as Varsity lets out a slight chuckle.

"Did you see G-Way when you was walking up here?" Asks Varsity.
"Naw, why?" Asks Trigger.

"Cause da nigga supposed to went and got me something to eat from the store and come right back damn near forty minutes ago,

I hope he ain't get tore off in that hot ass caddie." Replies Varsity.
"Speaking of cars, where you steal this joint from?" asks Trigger.

"I brought it, bout an hour ago while yo young ass was still in the bed sleep." Replies Varsity.

"Well I'm out dis bitch now and that's all that matters. I was with my girl yesterday anyway." Trigger says as a fiend walks over to them and he makes the sell.

"You sucka for love ass nigga." Replies Varsity turning Trick daddy up in the car and nodding his head to the song.

"I know you ain't talking, the way you cried and got all emotional when Cynthia broke up with you." Trigger says as Varsity looks stunned from the remark.

"Damn yo that was fucked up, why you bring that up for you know how I felt about shorty." Replies Trigger with a hurt look on his face.

"There you go, it's too early in the morning for this shit.

Fuck dat bitch, I told you she won't shit no way." Trigger says seeing Varsity ready to get into his emotions. Taking a deep breath Varsity shakes his head and says "you know what, I ain't even gone trip off dat shit. Just remember, everybody go through shit like that and you'll see watch what I tell you."

"Whatever yo, I ain't ever gone let no bitch get me like that." Replies Trigger serving another friend.

"Alright, will see." Varsity says rolling up a blunt as Trigger ignores his comment while he leans on the car and yawns.

"Damn! that shit slipped my mind that fast, you know some niggas ran up in Nobles crib and snatched his ass up?" Asks Trigger.

"Hell, naw dat's my first-time hearing about that, when the fuck dis supposed to had happen?" Asks Varsity.

"Earlier this morning, Drama told me." Replies Trigger.

"Joe and them know bout dat shit?" Asks Varsity lighting his blunt as more fiends make their way over to them.

"Yeah, they was there. They trying to figure out what's going on now." Replies Trigger as Varsity's beeper goes off.

Looking at it he says to his self, "that's what's up, where Drama and them at?"

"He was on his way-out Henrico to go around Dale road with Hova and

J.V in case niggas out their started tripping cause they took the strip." Replies Trigger.

"Well look dat was shorty dat work at the jewelry joint and we gotta get their before they open so is you trying to roll or is you gone sit out here?" Asks Varsity.

"I'll roll with you." Trigger says walking over to the passenger side and getting in as Varsity shuts his door and starts the car up and pulls off.

Henrico

When they get out Dale they see Drama, J.V, Hova and G-Way standing on the block. Stopping the car, he sees them all look at the whip as if they are about to shoot it up before G-Way lets them know who it is.

Rolling down the window he yells "Is yall niggas ready to go take care of this business?"

"What you talking bout? What's up?" asks Drama.

"Da Jewelry Joint." Varsity says in a you already know tone.

"Yeah, I'm riding but where Vel at?" Asks Drama as they all walk out into the street where Varsity has stopped.

"I don't know, but all us can't go anyway." Replies Varsity.

"Shittt, I'm going and where you steal this car from?" Asks Drama. "I brought dis shit, hurry up and come on man were on the clock." Varsity says as Drama gets in the back seat.

"Why yall keep trying to leave me." J.V says wanting to go.

"You can take my spot yo." Trigger says getting out of the car as J.V goes over to the passenger side and gets in as Varsity beeps the horn and pulls off.

"Why you ain't wanna go?" Asks G-Way.

"We splitting the shit anyway so fuck it." Replies Trigger while they walk back to the side walk.

"Where's Vel at? I know that nigga ain't still in the bed." Says Hova. "Yeah, he still in da crib laid back, he said later on he gone go try to sell them car's Lil One had left to him." replies Trigger.

"What's wrong wit da shit's, he could give them to us." says G-Way. "I don't know, but we can holla at him and tell him we want them." Replies Trigger.

"A look yo, we ain't doing nothing but standing around out here shaking niggas up so I'm trying to bounce." G-Way says to them.

"I'm trying to see what Vel talking bout with those whips." Replies Hova.

"Well look I'm bout to go to da crib and take a shower and shit so call me if something come up." G-Way says giving them five and walking toward a black grand Cherokee getting in and starting it up with a screw driver and beeping the horn before pulling off.

"You strapped?" Hova asks Trigger. "Yeah, why what's up?" Asks Trigger.

"Ain't shit just making sure you had something on you in case these pussy niggas try to trip and I gotta smoke another niggas ass out here." Hova says as Trigger says" let's go try and get one of these whips."

Venable St East End

When Varsity and them get back around the way he parks behind a black Oldsmobile. "Look everything in the whip right there, so when we get in put them gloves and Masks in the back on, I just stole the joint from out Chesterfield so it shouldn't be hot yet so let's hurry up and do this so won't shit go wrong, we got an hour before they open so come on." Varsity says as they all get out of the Lexus and get in the Oldsmobile.

As Varsity starts the car up they put on the gloves and masks which look like Halloween Michael Myers masks as he pulls off.

Broad Street

When they get to the Jewelry store on Broad Street he parks on the side street where the store sits on the corner.

"Damn, yo bitch works at Swarths Child. "We bout to be platinum rich." J.V says as they get out the car and quickly makes their way to the front door seeing very few people on the block it is sitting on.

When they get to the glass door the blinds are still down and the closed sign is on the door.

"You sure dis shits open?" Asks Drama.

"Yeah and my girl said she gone disable the alarm so we good." Replies Varsity pulling the door open and locking it as they walk right in with their backs turned.

"I'm sorry, we're not open yet; an old white lady says as she places jewelry in the display case.

"Shut up bitch and bring yo ass from behind that counter!"

Varsity says turning around with a forty-five, with an inferred beam pointing at her while J.V and Drama runs and checks the back of the store.

Bringing four more people from out the back including Varsity's girl they walk everybody in the back and tape them up with some grey duct tape that was sitting around.

"Which one of yall the owner of this bullshit?" Asks Drama but nobody says anything so he gets upset and starts pistol whipping the old white lady who was behind the counter. As blood starts to gush from her wounds a bald head fat white guy with glasses says "It's me, it's me, please stop hitting her!"

"Yall niggas go get da shit in the display cases while I get the combination to the real shit." Drama says to Varsity and J.V as they make their way to the front.

"Don't break nothing either." Yells Drama.

"By the time you get the safe open the police will be here and all of this will have been for nothing." The cocky store manager says as the other employees sit in silence scared to death as the old white woman lays sideways crying and bleeding badly.

"Well let's just see, what's the number and bitch you need to shut da fuck up for I HIT yo ass again!" Drama says kicking her and knocking the wind out of her before smacking the cocky store manager with the pistol and leaving blood from the old woman's face on his face before he quickly gives him the safe combination.

After getting the number he drags them all one by one to where the safe is before opening it and pulling a black trash bag out of his pocket and dumping the contents from the safe into it.

"Mary are you OK?" One of the female workers asks the old white woman who is starting to shake.

"We need to get her to the hospital!" The female says starting to cry as Drama ignores her while he continues putting diamonds and jewelry in the bag.

"She be alright, she just cold." Drama pauses and says before getting back to what he was doing.

"What kinda human being are you, this woman is laying here dying and you don't even care!" The girl screams again which makes Drama laugh.

"Pretty much." He replies not even bothering to turn around.

When he finishes he looks at the manager and says "unless you're the police I guess they ain't here yet, now where the video tape at?" Asks Drama.

"We don't use video." He replies.

"Oh, OK." Drama says turning like he's about to walk off before kicking him in the face and breaking his nose.

"Why you lying, I should smoke yo ass!" Drama says in a harsh tone.

"Please don't hurt anybody else, the old lady is bleeding bad enough."

Varsity's girl says as tears fall from her eyes as well.

"Then stop playing fucking games and tell me where the fuck the tape at!" Yells Drama.

Looking at the old woman bleeding badly as well as his self the manager says "behind the first door on the right," as J.V and Varsity comes back with trash bags full of jewelry and Drama walks past them to the room and flips everything upside down before seeing the VCR and snatching it out of the wall with the tape still in it and walking back out with it cuffed under his arm.

"Come on maine, let's be out." Varsity says going toward the back exit as Drama says "thank you for your cooperation and have a nice day." As they all make their way out of the back exit and into the alley where they take their masks off and calmly walk out of the alley to the car and Drama gets in the front seat throwing the VCR in the back seat with J.V before starting the car up and pulling off.

"Damn yo why the fuck you do that to that old bitch, she was bleeding like a motherfucker." Says J.V.

"So, fuck dat bitch." Replies Drama as they drive through the back roads of Shocko bottom back to Church Hill.

"Look we gone stash dis shit for a couple of days, so don't nobody start trippin bout not getting nothing." Says Varsity.

"We can keep it at my crib." Says Drama. "Why you say that?" Asks Varsity.

"Cause nigga you live wit yo girl, J.V lives wit his girl, Hova lives with his mama, G-Way lives with his mama and grandma, Trigger lives with his grandparents and Vel lives with his pops, who is a crackhead and I live by myself. Unless yall saying yall don't trust me." Replies Drama.

"Naw it ain't nothing like that, I was just asking but we still gotta separate da shit anyway." Says Varsity.

"Fuck all that, do you know how much shit we got all together from yesterday and today. It's time we lay back and chill cause we rich and one false move can set shit on fire especially as crazy as this week done started off." Replies J.V.

"Naw yo, that's hot, cause if we all of a sudden switch up dat shit gone look funny as a motherfucker." Drama says as he drives.

"I mean both of yall got a point but I gotta go with J.V cause we do need to tone it down a lil bit." Replies Varsity.

"Man, fuck dat shit, I know what I'm talking bout." Drama says to himself.

"I know you need to speed up, driving all got damn slow. I see people on the side walk walking faster than us." Varsity replies as he looks out the window.

Mechanicsville Rd East End

"Who is it?" Asks Jovanda looking out the peephole but whoever it is on the other side has their finger on the peephole while laughing.

Turning around and going to the bathroom door where Vel is inside taking a shower she says "I asked who it is but they ain't saying nothing and they got their finger on the peephole."

"Hova the only nigga that do that shit, he alright you can let him in."

Replies Vel from in the shower.

"You sure?" Asks Jovanda.

"Yeah it's cool." Vel says as she walks back to the door while Hova knocks, Opening the door Hova says "yo " surprised as he sees Jovanda who runs from the door and Trigger says "I know that won't my bitch."

"Dawg, I don't even know." Replies Hova as they both walking in the apartment. As Hova shuts the door Vel comes out the bathroom wrapping a towel around his waist.

"Who da fuck answered the door?" Asks Trigger. Surprised Vel says "Huh? Oh, dat was Honey."

"Dat looked like Jovanda." Says Trigger. "Man, your trippin." Replies Vel.

"Well let me go look in yo room then." Says Trigger.

"Come on then I gotta put some clothes on anyway." Vel says as they walk to his room.

"Where she at?" Asks Trigger as they get in the empty room.

Looking around Vel says "I don't know, maybe she left out the back, she said she was late for work."

"Hell, naw I ain't going for that." Trigger says as Vel gets some clothes and boxers out his closet and dresser.

"Well I'm bout to go get dressed so if you find her you ask her who she is." Vel says walking past him and going in the bathroom.

"Was that Jovanda for real man?" asks Trigger holding the bathroom door open looking inside.

"Naw nigga damn!" Vel says in a upset tone closing the bathroom door. "Why you ain't tell me he was out there?" whispers Jovanda from in the shower.

"I ain't know he was with Hova." replies Vel starting to put his clothes on.

"Well tell them to leave." Jovanda whispers again.

"I'm gone do that, just chill." Replies Vel putting his pants on and going to the bathroom door and opening it.

"Man, who you was in here talking to? Trigger says pushing the door open and walking in the bathroom pushing Vel out of the way.

Snatching the shower curtain back and seeing Jovanda he pauses in shock before Vel says "nigga don't be walking up in here like that, what the fuck wrong with you?" As he tries to grab Trigger who turns around and punches him in the face. As they start fighting Jovanda jumps out of the tub and runs out of the bathroom. Getting, Hova they both come to the bathroom door and she tells him 'don't just stand there do something." As she feels tears forming in her eyes.

"You do something, its cause of you they're fighting." Hova replies shutting the bathroom door as they continue to fight in the bathroom.

"So, you just gone let them fight each other in there?" Asks Jovanda as tears roll down her cheeks.

"If you open the door and break it up they won't be fighting." Replies Hova in a cool and calm tone.

"I ain't going in there." Says Jovanda.

"Well me either then." Hova says hunching his shoulder as Jovanda gets mad and storms off to Vels room slamming the door behind her.

Taking a deep breath Hova opens the door and sees both of them squaring off and breathing heavy. As Hova grabs Trigger and goes to swing him around Vel swings and punches Trigger in the face.

Breaking loose Trigger tackles Vel in the tub and starts punching him. "Man, yall break dis shit up. Yall fighting over a bitch."

Hova says laughing as he grabs Trigger and pulls him up off of Vel and walks him out of the bathroom.

"Nigga get the fuck off me!" Trigger screams struggling to get loose as his nose bleeds everywhere.

"Yeah, let that bitch ass nigga go so I can finish beating the shit out of his ass. He can't fight no way." Vel says through busted lips as he gets up out of the tub.

"Man, yall chill wit dat shit." Hova says laughing as he walks Trigger outside.

"A yo man fuck dat bitch, she ain't worth fighting yo nigga over." Hova says to Trigger who snatches away from him.

"Get the fuck off me, fuck all yall motherfucker!" Trigger replies holding his shirt on his nose as he walks off the porch and up the street.

"Where you going?" Hova yells to him but he just ignores him and keeps walking so Hova goes back in the crib and shuts the door.

Shokoe Bottom Broad Street

"Maine, you drive like an old ass lady, we supposed to been back round the way." Varsity says to Drama.

"That's good then, cause they ain't gone pull over no old ass lady and it's too much shit in here for us to have to bail if we get chased." Replies Drama.

"There goes that girl that we saw over Lil One's crib." JV says as they all look to where he's pointing and they see them getting out of a station wagon and walking off toward an Oldsmobile jeep as they sit at a red light.

"I wonder what them bitches are up to." Drama says noticing the black tennis bags their carrying as the light turns green and the person behind them beeps the horn and Drama pulls off.

"You wanna go say what's up?" Asks J.V.

"For what, them bitches ain't spoke to me since Lil One got killed, so I ain't got nothing to say to them hoes." Replies Drama.

Them hoes in mourning you know how emotional bitches is." Varsity says as the car starts to jump, cough and sputter.

"What the fuck is going on?" Asks J.V from the back seat.

"Dis nigga done stole a getaway car with no gas in it. That's what's going on." Drama says looking at the gas gauge that is pass E.

"You're the one driving all fucking slow, we should've been back round the way." Replies Varsity as Drama pulls over and the car stops by its self.

Pulling the car in park Drama looks over at Varsity and shakes his head before reaching under the seat and getting the screw driver.

"Wipe dis shit down before we get out." Varsity says taking his shirt and wiping everything down he touched as they all do the same thing before grabbing the bags and getting out of the car.

Looking around at the people and cars driving up and down the street they act like their talking to each other as they wipe down the door handles and safely walk off without drawing any attention to their selves.

"Damn, the VCR." J.V says before turning back around and jogging toward the car as they stop and wait for him.

"I'm glad he remembered that, cause I won't even thinking about that shit." Varsity says looking around to see if anyone is watching them.

"Why you keep looking around like that? You got me paranoid." Drama says staring at the ground.

"Shit nigga, anybody but you. Not O-Dogg." Varsity says with a smile, as Drama doesn't smile or reply as J.V jogs back toward him with the VCR in one hand and a bag in the other.

"Now that's hot as a motherfucker. Come on and let's get a car before I have to kill somebody out here for being nosey." Drama says as they start walking again.

Q St East End

In his crib ripping up and breaking everything Jovanda gave him, Trigger breath's heavily from his mouth with tissue in his nose to soak up and stop his nose from bleeding.

Taking off his blood-stained shirt and tossing it on his couch, he sits down and tries to calm down. "I can't believe this bitch." He says to his self with his hands covering his face.

Laying back on the couch he stares at the ceiling and ignores the phone as it rings Hanging the phone up Hova says "I don't think he is in the crib and if he is he ain't picking the phone up." As he looks at Vel.

"I don't, give a fuck I ain't tell you to call that nigga." Vel says before putting a wet rag back over his mouth as Jovanda sits beside him with her head on his shoulder.

"I'm just trying to help, you dead wrong for fucking with his girl anyway." Replies Hova.

"I ain't his girl." Jovanda says in a smart tone. "Whatever shorty I ain't even talking to you." Replies Hova before getting up and walking toward the door and leaving with no words for either of them as he shuts the door, walks to his car, gets in, starts it up and pulls off.

"While driving past Jefferson park he sees G-Way sitting on the hood of a car drinking a forty-ounce talking to a female in some tight jeans that's shows off how fat her butt is.

Slowing to a stop Hova beeps the horn and says "what's up my nigga I see you over there."

Looking at him G-Way throws his hands up and asks "damn nigga, where the fuck yall been at?" As he gets off the hood and walks to the driver side of Hova car and gives him five.

"Who is that right there?" Hova asks looking at the female.

"Lay Lay, she phat as a bitch ain't it?" G-Way asks looking back at her as she stands there waiting for him to come back over there.

"What's up with her?" Asks Hova.

"I don't know I'm gone find out though." Replies G-Way.

"Well my bad, I ain't gone hold you up." Hova says giving him five before pulling off and beeping the horn.

"Who was that?" Asks Lay Lay.

"My nigga Hova, I was busy though." Replies G-Way as she smiles and asks "what you busy doing?"

"Giving you my undivided attention." He replies with a smile. "Boy stop." She says blushing.

"I'm saying though, you still trying to go in the crib so you can show me you know how to cook?" Asks G-way.

"If you want to, I don't care." She says as she continues to blush as he slides off the hood and follows her into her crib.

When he gets in the house he notices baby toys and children's toys scattered around a room to his left.

"So, you gotta lot of nieces and nephews huh?" Asks G-Way as they make their way toward her kitchen.

"Why, what made you ask me that?" Asks Lay Lay.

"I saw some kids toys in that room we just passed." Replies G-way. "Those are my kid's toys." She says as they get in the kitchen.

"Oh yeah, damn. So, where they at?" Asks G-Way.

"With their daddies" she replies.

"Their daddies? Damn, how many you got?" Ask G-Way sitting down at the kitchen table.

"Five, three boys and two girls." She says smiling and going in the deep freezer.

"Damn shorty you nineteen with five kids, you must got some fire." G-Way says making her giggle from the remark while she moves stuff around in the deep freezer and he stares at her ass.

"Wet, as a river." She replies instantly turning G-Way on. "I don't know that." G-Way says with a smile.

"You act right, you might find out one day." She replies pulling some bacon and frozen hamburgers out of the freezer and shutting it.

"Tomorrow ain't promised so I don't live day to day, I live for the moment." G-Way says as they look each other directly in the face.

"So, what you trying to say?" Asks Lay Lay putting the meat on the freezer and walking toward him and staring down at him.

"You know what I'm trying to say so what you trying to do?" Asks G- Way.

"You gotta eat me first if you want some of this pussy." she says with a seductive smile.

"Shit shorty you ain't saying nothing but a word." G-Way says returning her smile.

Twenty Fourth East End

Pulling up on the block, back in Varsity's car they see Joe and a bunch of Bloods posted on the block.

"Yo, it's too hot to be driving that stolen car round here." Joe says to Varsity running up to the car.

"This is my car, ain't shit stolen on here." Replies Varsity.

"Well look don't go round the strip cause Mee Mee and some other bitches jumped out on Quarter and them and sprayed all them niggas, I mean they wet that shit up." Joe says seriously.

"I just seen. Oh shit. damn bitches crazy." Replies Drama laughing "What?" Asks Joe,

"Nothing, you trying to get in?" Asks Drama.

"Naw I'm straight, I'm just striving to keep yall out of trouble." Replies Joe.

"Alright well look I'm bout to go to my crib and take a shower and get a nap in. I'll be back through later." Drama says.

"Alright, yall niggas be easy. I'll be out here whenever yall come back through." Joe says giving them five as he reaches through the window.

"Alright my nigga." Drama says before Varsity pulls off.

"A yo, I'm bout to do the same thing so I'm gone drop yall off and catch up with yall later on." Varsity says to them.

"Alright, you gone chill at my crib J.V?" Asks Drama.

"Yeah, I gotta finish my season in Madden over their anyway." Replies J.V as Varsity drives his Lex toward Dramas crib

Venable St, East End Later that Night

Waking up, Drama stretches and walks out into the front room and sees J.V asleep on the couch and the male news reporter on TV talking about the jewelry store heist. Blowing some lint off his shoulder he walks over to the TV and listens to what's being said. After realizing they don't know anything he turns the TV to some music videos and walks to and in the bathroom where he takes a piss, flushing the toilet and washing his hands, he walks out of the bathroom shaking them dry.

"A yo J.V he says loud enough to wake him up. "Yo." he says with sleep still in his voice.

"Get yo ass up, it done got dark outside and everything." Replies Drama as J.V yawns and says "Varsity called and said we left da shit in the trunk and he going out their wit Joe and them."

"When he call" asks Drama.

"Bout an hour ago! Replies J.V rubbing his eyes. "Did you eat all the tacos?" Asks Drama.

"Naw it's still a lil bit left in the pan." Replies J.V as Drama walks in the kitchen and he pick up the remote from beside him and turns back to the news but a commercial is on.

"Ain't nobody else call?" Drama yells to him from the kitchen. "Some bitches, but dats bout it." J.V yells back before he gets up and goes in the bathroom and shuts the door.

Twenty Fourth St East End

Standing on the block getting drunk with Joe and a bunch of other Bloods who are drinking while some post up and watch the block Varsity talks about a female to Joe.

"Fuck dat bitch though, she'll never find another nigga like me anyway." Varsity says before taking a swig from his forty ounce.

"Damn my nigga. I ain't know that bitch was like that. I just thought you stopped fucking with the bitch and she found another nigga, shit I know the nigga, his name Seven." Replies Joe.

"What Seven, from HP?" Asks Varsity.

"Yeah that nigga, tall light skin nigga with green eyes." Replies Joe. "Yeah I know that nigga." Says Varsity clearly drunk as well as Joe who sparks a Newport.

"A yo be on point." One of the Bloods say to everybody as they watch a Lincoln slowly make its way up the block as Joe and Varsity both stand up and back away from the curb as the car slowly drives by them and all five of the occupants of the car stare hard at them and start throwing up their sets identifying their selves as Crips as they return the exchange of mean mugs and throw up their different Blood sets as the car keeps going.

"What da fuck was that?" Asks Varsity.

"Niggas set trippin cause their niggas keep getting smoked." Replies Joe before he spits on the ground.

"So, what that mean, yall ready to go to war or something?" Asks Varsity.

"Them niggas don't want no problems." Replies Joe before returning to the curb and sitting down as Varsity follows.

"You sure them niggas ain't had shit to do with what happened to Noble?" Asks Varsity.

Honestly dawg I don't even know cause his body ain't popped up and ain't nobody called bout no ransom and we been on the prowl all day and I still don't know what the fuck going on." Replies Joe drinking his beer.

"Well you know if something pops off we gone ride with yall regardless." Varsity says as Joe smiles and says, "chill my nigga it ain't even that serious, but it's some foul shit going on and I figured that out when we was looking for Noble."

Shit ain't adding up, but I think I know what's going on." Replies Joe. "What?" Asks Varsity.

"I ain't gone speak on it, but I'm gone give you something to think about. Keep yo enemies close but watch yo homies." Joe says to Varsity who thinks about it before asking.

"What dats supposed to mean?"

"If you don't know you need to be on point then, but take heed to what I said and that's all I'm gone say." replies Joe as Varsity sits and tries to figure out what he is talking about.

"Do anybody else know what you talking about?" Asks Varsity after a few minutes of thinking.

"I don't know dawg, that's something you gotta ask yo self." Joe replies giving him a serious look.

"Fuck it, I don't know." Varsity says drinking his beer and wonder what the hell Joes talking about.

Ring Ring Ring Ring Ring Joe phone goes off and he picks it up and gets up and walks off as Varsity looks at his back and wonders what the hell is going on before taking out his phone and dialing JV cell phone.

"Hello?" J.V picks up and asks after a few rings. "A yo where you at?" Asks Varsity.

"We on our way round there." Replies J.V. "Who?" Asks Varsity.

"Me and Drama. You is still round there ain't it?" Asks J.V.

"Yeah, A yo you heard from Hova and them today?" Asks Varsity. "Not since this morning why?" Asks J.V.

"I was just wondering, cause I been calling niggas since I woke up and you're the only one that been picking up and Drama been sleep so he don't count." Replies Varsity.

"What's going on?" Asks J.V.

"I don't know, matter fact, I'll holla at yall niggas when yall get around here, alright one." Varsity says hanging up and drinking his beer as he watches Joe walk back toward him.

Chapter 13

Chamberlayne Ave North side
Da Next Day Wednesday October 19,1999

Sparking a blunt while driving around in the stolen whip he had yesterday, G-way notices a car that's been following him for a while. Making a left at the corner he notices the driver does the same so he makes another left at the next corner and so does the other car.

"This can't be the police. Man who da fuck is this?" He asks his self while looking in his rear-view mirror. Stopping at a gas station G-Way gets out and goes in the store.

Looking out the window he sees that the car that was following him pulls up on the other side of the gas pump and a tall skinny dark skin young dude with his hair half done gets out of the passenger seat and walks to the pay phone by the off ramp while looking in the store.

Seeing a small family leaving out of the store G-Way walks out with them and quickly gets in the car which he left running.

As soon as he gets in the car the dude that was on the phone just walks away from it toward G-Way as the driver stays in the car looking around.

Seeing dude go under his shirt for what might be a gun G-Way pulls off as fast as he can almost hit a person coming out of the store as the young male runs to the car trying to catch him before screaming to the driver of the car he was in," what da fuck you let him get in the car for!" As he runs to the passenger seat of the car and gets in as they start to chase him.

Making a hard-right G-Way almost crashes as he slams on the breaks barely missing a car stopped at the red light. Looking out the back window he sees the car coming out of the gas station.

"Come on." G-Way say to his self before going around the car in front of him and through the red light making a right into the oncoming traffic as cars slam on the brakes as he keeps going and the driver of the other car follows right behind him.

"Man, fuck dis shit." G-Way says taking his gun off of his waist as he drives. Slowing down and rolling down the window he waits for the car to get close enough to his before he slams on the brakes and turns toward them hanging out the window and starts shooting POP POP POP POP POP POP POP POP POP POP before he pulls off spinning the wheels as the other car is stopped with shots in the windshield.

When they pull off they almost catch up with him as he sits stuck at another red light.

"Damn! These niggas still behind me." G-way says to his self as the light turns green and he cuts in front of a car getting in the turning lane.

Leaving them stuck in traffic G-Way makes the first left he sees and gets back on the main street while they are a few blocks back stuck in traffic.

"Finally, I shook them motherfuckers." G-Way says to himself keeping straight this time and blending in with traffic.

While going through a green light a police car turns behind him. "Man, please don't fuck wit me." He says before as if they heard him they throw the lights on.

"Shit, fuck this." He says speeding up.

"Why the fuck is everybody fucking with me." He says swerving back and forth through lanes cutting in front of cars. Just beating the red-light G- Way flies through it without stopping as the cop is stopped by the cars that slammed on their brakes.

Shit flying through the streets, G-way bends a corner and slows down as he gets on a back street. "Let me hurry up and get the fuck out dis car." He says to himself going back around the way.

George Mason Square

"Well if it ain't my lil gangsta's, where you been at all yesterday and today?" Jasmine says to J.V as him, Varsity and Drama get out of Varsity's Lex and walk toward the porch where her and one of her girlfriends are sitting.

"Fucking wit Drama and Joe we got fucked up and sat on the block wit them niggas before we went to one of Joe's niggas cribs and fell asleep." Replies J.V.

"What's in the bags and what's up with that VCR?" Asks Jasmine.

"Just some boot leg movies we trying to watch." Replies J.V as the three of them walk in the apartment.

When they get in J.V bedroom they sit the stuff on the bed and sit, down.

"Take that tape out that VCR so we can stop toting this big ass VCR around." Drama says to J.V who picks the VCR up and goes to a wall socket to plug it in so he can eject the tape.

Laughing to himself Varsity says "you and Joe some funny motherfuckers."

"Man, I know you ain't still talking bout dat shit wit da drunk dude we beat up." Replies Drama.

"Man, yall beat dude up cause he said Joe can't rap, you and I both know Joe can't rap, he sounds like one of them old school rapper. Plus, dude was walking and minding his own business till yall called him over there and yall could see he was drunker than we was." Replies Varsity as Drama laughs at the memory while J.V puts the tape in his VCR and starts rewinding it before coming back over to the bed and grabbing the remote as he sits down.

When Drama and Varsity starts taking the jewelry out the bag J.V looks at the jewelry on the bed and says "we millionaires."

"Naw, not yet. we gotta chill and let shit settle down first remember." Drama replies sarcastically as he takes watches, diamond bracelets, charms, ear rings, rings and chains out of the bag, pressing play on the VCR remote and fast forwarding to the part where they came in as they watch it while unloading the jewelry onto the bed.

"I can imagine them playing this shit on America's Most Wanted, we need to get rid of this shit." Varsity says watching the tape play.

"I am I'm gone break da shit. I just wanted to see it first. Cause I ain't never seen myself on camera." Replies J.V.

"Well if the wrong person gets it or see it, you gone be on everybody TV in America." Varsity says as Drama smiles at what they're doing on the camera and says "look at yall Retarded ass niggas" as Varsity and J.V run around the store like kids in a candy shop and J.V is dancing like he just scored a touchdown in a super bowl game.

"We cleaned that bitch out though." Varsity says laughing and rewinding the part where J.V trips "a somebody pulled the door. I guess they was coming to work but seen the door was locked with the closed sign on the door but when they pulled the door dis nigga hauled ass so fast he tripped over his own feet." As they watch, Varsity hold his stomach laughing at J.V who gets up and goes back to emptying the display case he was at.

"A look, I gotta go get my car from round Dale road you forgot all about that shit last night." Drama says to Varsity who says "It ain't even twelve O'clock yet, I'll still take you round there later on though."

"Naw yo, I don't trust them niggas round there. Look keep dividing this shit and put everybody shit in an individual bag.

Where dat screw driver at?" Asks Drama as J.V pulls it out his pocket and gives it to him.

"A yo I be right back and don't let nobody see dis shit, matter fact cut da tape off." Drama says grabbing the remote and cutting the tape off.

"I'll be right back." Drama says before leaving out the room and shutting the door behind him as Varsity starts thinking bout what Joe said to him yesterday but didn't bring it up when Drama and J.V got there.

"You got some big sandwich bags?" Asks Varsity.

"Yeah, I got the zip lock joints that you could put plastic Tupper wear in." Replies J.V.

"Well let's hurry up and bag dis shit up." Varsity says as J.V cell-phone rings and he pick it up and only answers questions in yes or no answers as Varsity doesn't look at him but ear hustles on the conversation before the TV catches his attention as J.V turns to the news and the Mayor is on TV once again speaking about the shootings and the gang violence that is going on in their community and how he plans to put a stop to it.

"He talking bout us." J.V says hanging the phone up.

"Well as long as he don't know who we is we straight and as long as he keeps getting on TV and telling us what he gone do we already know what to look out for. " Varsity is saying before the Mayor says "and in compliance with the enforced curfew, today we will do a dry run sweep of the community and try to see how many of these thugs we can get off of our streets to make our neighborhoods safer."

"You hear dat shit?" Asks Varsity.

"Yeah, Joe's homie just told me to turn to the shit to let yall know what's going on cause ain't nobody else picking up they phones." Replies J.V as Varsity checks his phone to see if he's lying and sees that his battery is dead.

"A yo we gotta let niggas know what's going down." Says Varsity. "Damn, what the fuck is all this?" Asks Jasmine coming in the room with G-Way.

"Some fake jewelry we gone try to sell." Replies Varsity quickly. "Dat shit don't look fake to me." Jasmine says walking over to the bed and picking up some rings.

"Chill out girl." J.V says knocking the rings out of her hand as G-Way sits down on the bed.

"Why you trippin for, he said the shit was fake." replies Jasmine in a confused tone.

"Well it ain't, look." J.V says pressing play on the remote showing the tape.

"What the fuck is you doing, you know ain't nobody supposed to see that shit." Varsity says taking the remote from him and cutting the tape off.

"Yall crazy. So, you mean to tell me that's yall they keep talking bout on TV?" Asks Jasmine.

"Yeah, but keep dat shit to yourself, I mean don't tell nobody." J.V says giving her some diamond earrings the size of M&Ms.

"Thanks boo." She replies focused more on the huge diamond earrings with a huge smile on her face as she sits on his lap and gives him a kiss.

"Did you hear me?" Asks J.V.

"I swear on my mama, I heard you. You know I wouldn't gossip bout something like that." She replies before J.V takes the earrings back and says "well you should understand we gotta keep this stuff on the low right now." As she sucks her teeth.

"A yo listen, tell that nigga what you just said." Varsity says to J.V and G-Way.

"Some niggas chased me and shit but I dipped on they ass after I shot at them. I don't know who the fuck it was but I know they was trying to kill my motherfucking ass." Replies G-Way.

"A yo we gotta go look for these niggas and let them know what's going on." Varsity says getting up and G-Way does the same as they make their way toward the bedroom door.

"What's up man come on." Varsity says to J.V who's still sitting on the bed. "We can't leave dis shit on the bed and somebody's gotta be here to let Drama know what's going on when." J.V saying before they ignore him and leave.

Fairmount Ave East End Getting Around the Way

While driving they see Trigger walking up the street with a pissed off look on his face.

"A yo Trigger, come here man and get in the car." Varsity says to him from the driver side as he stops the car.

Walking to his side of the car Trigger says "either one of yall got a pistol?"

"Why what's going on?" Asks Varsity.

"Nothing, it's just a lil something I gotta take care of." Replies Trigger.

"Naw yo it's too hot for whatever you bout to do." Varsity says as Trigger sucks his teeth and says "I need a pistol." as G-Way reaches over Varsity and gives him his gun.

"What's going on, you alright?" Asks G-Way as Varsity sits back shaking his head.

"Yeah I'm straight." Trigger says before walking off.

"Why the fuck you give him a gun and you know what's going on?" Varsity asks a bit upset.

"Yeah, I know what's going on, but you don't know what's going on wit him and neither do I so why shouldn't I gave it to him." Replies G-Way matching his tone.

Sucking his teeth, he says "A look man go with dat nigga and make sure he don't do nothing crazy." As G-Way gets out the car and Varsity pulls off as G-Way runs to catch up with him.

"What's wrong dawg?" G-Way asks him when he catches up with him. "Nothing, I don't even know why you got out the car." Replies Trigger.

"You ain't ask for that pistol for nothing." G-Way says but Trigger doesn't say anything as they keep walking.

Turning the corner, they see Jovanda walking to Vels house and when she sees Trigger she starts running the opposite way.

"What's up with her?" Asks G-Way as Trigger starts chasing her. "Help, stop!" She screams as Trigger gets behind her, grabs her hair and picks her up and slams her.

Seeing Trigger stomping her G-Way runs to break it up.

"Yo! what da fuck!?" G-Way says pulling him off of her as she gets up crying and bleeding.

"Man get the fuck off me!" Trigger says snatching away from G-way and punching Jovanda in the face dropping her before he starts stomping her again as G-Way grabs him and pulls him away from her.

"Man, I told you to get the fuck off me!" Trigger says snatching away from him and pulling the gun out on him.

"Man, what the fuck, you pulling a gun out on me!" G-Way says to Trigger.

"Look, gone bout yo business nigga!" Trigger screams at him before seeing Jovanda running away from the side of his eye as he backs up.

Shooting in the air, she balls up and stops running and he runs behind her and starts pistol whipping her. Not even attempting to try to break it up again G-Way watches and shakes his head before turning to walk off.

Hearing a car slam on its brakes, he turns around and sees Vel jump out of the passenger side of Varsity's Lex. Seeing Vel, Trigger points the gun at him stopping him in his tracks before he backs up and takes off running.

Making sure Jovanda isn't dead, Vel says "take her to the hospital." As he helps her into the back seat of the Lex before he takes off running after Trigger.

"Vel! Awh fuck it, come on man hurry up." Varsity says to G-Way who jogs to the passenger side and gets in as Varsity pulls off to take a bleeding and beaten Jovanda to the hospital.

Thirty Seventh St East End LATER THAT DAY

At Varsity's crib G-Way sits on the couch drinking a beer while Varsity smokes a blunt and watches TV.

"Where the fuck is everybody at?" G-Way says in a frustrated tone.

"I don't know, but something is going on and J.V knows, that's why he ain't in the crib and ain't wanna leave with us earlier." Replies Varsity.

"Even if something is going on we done drove damn near everywhere and called everybody and still don't know shit, so the question is where the fuck is they at?" Says G-Way as Varsity's cordless phone rings.

Looking at the ID he sees its Vel so he picks up and says "A yo man what the fuck is going on?"

"What you talking bout, I already told you bout that." Replies Vel. "I'm not talking bout you and Trigger, I'm talking bout everybody else." Says Varsity.

"Everybody else? What da fuck you talking bout?" Asks Vel. "So, you don't know what's going on?" Asks Varsity.

"Man, I don't even know what the fuck you talking bout." replies Vel.

"Listen, other than me, Trigger and G-Way have you seen anybody else today?" Asks Varsity as Vel thinks before saying I saw Hova."

"Where?" Asks Varsity.

"Down by Joe's crib, but that was earlier today." Replies Vel hearing Varsity sucking his teeth.

"So, what's up with Trigger?" Asks Varsity.

"I don't know, I couldn't catch him so I came home and then Jovanda called me to pick her up from the hospital so I had to go get her and when I saw yo number on the caller ID I called you so I could make sure you was still there before I came over."

"You know that bitch pregnant, well she was pregnant." says Varsity.

"What! Who told you that?" Vel asked Varsity before asking Jovanda. "That's what the doctor said after he finished his little check. But I don't see how I got pregnant that fast so I'm gone get a second opinion." Replies Jovanda.

"Did he say if the baby got hurt or anything during the fight?" Asks Vel. "Are you even listening to me, I don't think I'm pregnant, I can't be and even if I am he didn't tell me anything about any problems." Replies Jovanda as Vel smiles.

"Nigga is you listening to me?" Varsity asks Vel.

"A look dawg I'm on my way over there." Vel says not even thinking bout what Varsity is saying being so focused on Jovanda as he hangs the phone up.

"Come with me right quick." Vel says as they leave out of the house. Getting in the car he checks to see if his guns are under the seat before he pulls off. While riding he asks Jovanda who's baby does she think it is.

"Even if I am pregnant, which I doubt I am, it might be yours or it might be his. Honestly I don't know." She replies.

"Well we gone take a test to see if you are and find out who's it is and if it ain't mine I'm gone still look out for you even if you back with Trigger." Vel says as she smiles and gives him a kiss on the cheek before leaning back in her seat and look out the window.

When they get to Varsity's crib him and G-Way are out on the side walk.

"Look at these two motherfuckers." G-Way says about Vel and Jovanda as they get out the car.

"You picked her from the hospital in that hot ass car?" asks Varsity. "Yeah fuck it." Replies Vel walking up to him and giving him five. "How long yall gone be right here?" Asks Varsity looking at his watch. "Why what's up asks Vel."

"Ain't shit I'm just trying to catch dude selling these rims." Replies Varsity.

"We ain't doing shit round here, come on it will give us something to do." G Way says as he walks to his car and Vel and Jovanda get back in the stolen Buick he pulled up in before he pulls off behind Varsity.

While riding Jovanda asks "Can you drop me off at home?"

"Alright let me let these niggas know." Vel says beeping the horn and waving for Varsity to back up and pull beside him.

"Yo?" Varsity asks pulling beside him.

"I'm gone take shorty home and meet yall where ever yall going just tell me where it's at." Replies Vel.

"Shit, we can all go round there. Dude ain't even get off work yet anyway." Varsity says while on his cell phone.

"Alright, come on then." Vel says leading the way. When they get there, they see Trigger sitting on the steps of her house.

Stopping the car, as he's pulling over Jovanda asks in a panicked tone "Why are you pulling over for, you see the nigga sitting on my steps."

"Stay in the car." Vel says getting his guns from under the seat and putting them on his waist as he gets out of the car and Trigger stands up.

"Awh shit, here we go again." Varsity says parking as fast as he can. "What's up man, why you still fucking wit shorty for. You done already beat her ass, so gone wit dat crazy shit yo." Vel says to Trigger.

"Nigga, fuck both of yall." Trigger says pulling out and shooting at him as Vel runs on the other side of a car pulling out his twin nines from under his shirt and shooting back as they both shoot it out with each other.

"A yo chill wit dat crazy shit, yall got dat pregnant bitch in the car and everything." Yell's G-Way from his car as he stares from a distance.

"Fuck you mean chill, dis nigga shooting at me." Vel yells back crouched down behind a Yukon Denali.

Getting low Trigger pulls out another glock as he runs up on the car Vel pulled up in.

"Bitch get in the driver's seat and pull off!" He scream's at Jovanda as he opens the passenger door before pointing the gun back in Vels direction and shooting. Scared Jovanda gets in the driver's seat as he gets in.

"Now pull this motherfucker off!" He screams as she pulls off so fast she almost hits the car parked in front of her as Trigger ducks down as they fly past Vel knowing if he shoots he might hit her.

Running to where Varsity is Vel jumps in his back seat and yells "man chase his ass." As Varsity speeds off.

"I don't know what type of Thin Line Between Love and Hate shit yall niggas on but if I wreck my motherfucking car I'm gone kill all yall ass." Varsity says trying to catch up with Trigger.

"Whatever nigga just speed dis motherfucker up." Replies Vel.

"Dis niggas catching up wit us, you better speed dis motherfucker up!" Trigger says to Jovanda pointing the gun at her.

"I can't drive that good and we gone wreck. Why is you doing this to me?" Jovanda asks crying and upset as she barely makes some turns and not slowing down for stop signs as some cars slam on the brakes to keep from hitting them.

"Why am I doing this to you? Bitch, I gave you my heart and you turn around and start fucking my friend and niggas saying you pregnant! Fuck wrecking, you need to be worried about me killing yo ass in dis motherfucker!" Screams Trigger.

"I ain't know you felt that way about me and it might not even be your baby if I'm even pregnant." Jovanda says crying.

"Bitch what! What the fuck you just say? What the fuck you mean it might not be my baby, you been fucking wit dat nigga that long. You know what, if we won't going so motherfucking fast I'd shoot yo ass." Screams Trigger before she slams down hard on the brakes and he flies into the windshield as the car spins around.

Picking her face off the steering wheel dazed, bloody and still crying she looks over at Trigger who's knocked out as she opens the door and stubbles out of the car.

Getting herself together she gets up and runs down the street crying.

Seeing her running Varsity slows down and Vel yells to her to get in the car while he gets out and runs past her toward Trigger with his guns out.

Opening the car door and falling out to the street, Trigger looks up and sees Vel coming right up on him, but his gun is somewhere in the car so he just sits there. Walking up on him Vel smacks him with his pistol and says "nigga what the fuck wrong wit you?"

Vel

Looking up bleeding Trigger says "how you gone fuck my girl dawg?" "Nigga you did all dis shit over a bitch. A bitch! Come on now." replies

"It don't even matter now, you got da-bitch and you got the gun pointed at me so shoot." Trigger says spitting out blood wit tears in his eyes.

"Here come the motherfucking police." G-Way yells as siren's can be heard as people stare out of their windows.

Looking at Trigger, Vel shakes his head before walking to the driver side of the Buick and getting in as he pulls off toward Varsity's car leaving Trigger in the street as G-Way pulls up beside Trigger.

"I can't leave him in da street." Says G-Way opening the door and saying "Jovanda in the car wit Varsity so don't start acting crazy either nigga, get in." G-Way says to Trigger as he gets up and gets in the car as some of the police stop and chase Vel.

"These my motherfucking streets yall niggas can't catch me." Vel says to his self with police cars behind him.

After a short chase Vel looks back and doesn't see the police. He parks the car on a side street gets out and walks. When he gets around the way all he hears is niggas shooting.

"It's da Bloods and Crips, they've been having shoot outs a lot lately cause somebody keeps shooting at them." Hova says to a fiend he is serving.

"Yeah, I know, I heard Joe got killed earlier." Replies the fiend. "Get da fuck outta here." Hova says.

"I'm dead serious." Replies the fiend.

"Here we go again, if des niggas keep dis shit up its gone be too hot to sell anything around here." Drama says to himself stopping the car as he sees Vel coming down the street.

"Dis niggas crazy." J.V says getting out after Drama parks the car and sits on the hood as they see Hova coming out of an alley across the street putting money in his pocket.

"A yo a fiend just told me Joe got smoked earlier." Hova says as Drama slides off the hood and says "what?"

"I don't know what the fuck is going on out here no more." Replies Hova as Drama still has a fucked up look on his face as Vel comes over and sits on the hood next to J.V without saying a word.

"You trying to go round Joe's crib and see what's up?" ask Drama. "I don't care." Replies Hova as they get in the car. "You getting in?" J.V asks Vel.

"Naw, I'll be right here." He replies as Drama pulls off. "What da fuck wrong with him?" Asks Drama.

"I told you man its some crazy shit going on." Replies Hova.

When they get to Joe's crib they see the door open so Drama gets out first as they make their way to the door. Stepping in they don't see anybody as they walk slowly through the front room. Hearing shit being thrown around in the back room they peek around the corner and see dudes in Joe's room flipping it upside down.

"Who da fuck is dat?" Whispers Drama trying to make out who the people are but all he sees is a big brown skin dude with his back turned in the door way.

Creeping up slowly behind him Drama pulls out his forty-four and puts it to the back of dude's head as he is just about to turn around.

"What da fuck is yall niggas in my nigga house doing?!" Drama says catching them by surprise, before one of the dudes looks up and he sees its Noble.

"What da fuck? What the fuck is you doing? Where's Joe at?" Asks

Drama as Noble stands up and walks toward him.

"Nigga you ain't heard, Joe got killed earlier." Noble says pulling out a Beretta.

"Nigga hold da fuck up, I will shoot dis nigga ass if a nigga don't tell me what da fuck is going on in here." Drama says holding the gun on the big brown skin dude.

"Look nigga you need to gone put dat gun down." Noble says to him. "I'm not putting a motherfucking thing down until I get some motherfucking answers." Drama says looking around Joe's room which is flipped upside down.

Smiling Noble says "so you feel like you in control of this situation?" "Man fuck what you talking bout where Joe at and why yall in here flipping his shit upside down?" Asks Drama as they are all in the room now with guns pointed in both direction.

"So, this is the Lost Souls huh? Yall ain't no gangbangers and yall sure as hell don't know shit bout da streets. You just making it hot for everybody else with that dumb shit yall keep doing. And too bad yo little guardian angel Joe ain't here no more cause can't nobody save yo ass now." Replies Noble.

"Why the fuck you doing this for?" Asks Drama.

"Money!! Motherfucker! You ain't heard, money lasts longer than love, especially when it ain't no loose ends attached." Replies Noble.

"So, you saying you killed Joe?" Asks Drama.

"Did you hear me say I killed Joe? Nah, I told you Joe was dead but all this talking ain't gone change the fact that you need to be putting dat gun down for you end up in the same situation your brother did." Replies Noble. POP.

"What the fuck you say about my brother?" Drama says shooting dude in the side of the temple and now pointing the gun at Noble as the whole room stands still as J.V who is visibly shaken looks at the dude on the floor with his brains leaking out feeling like he is about to throw up.

"Hold up look, I don't want to hurt you and I know you don't wanna hurt me cause you or your little team is not built for that kinda war. And the bottom line is Joe is dead simple as that and you ain't got shit to do with that so you need to mind yo business and keep doing what you was doing, I'll keep hitting you off and well keep doing it like dat, But dis right here, this ain't gone get you nowhere." Noble says putting his gun down.

As tears fall from Dramas eyes he says "my brother always told me a man has to make his own decisions in life and if you allow somebody else to dictate those decisions you better off dead because someone is living your life for you."

Getting tired of talking Noble says "well if your bother would have lived by all that dumb ass shit he kept talking then he would've still been here and if he was so damn smart he would've seen what I was doing, so now I'm gone be able to say I killed both of yall cause like him I guess I'm gone have to smoke yo ass too." Noble says as Hova yanks Dramas arm down as Drama shoots at him which knocks his shot off course but still hits Noble in the arm before Hova puts the gun to the back of Dramas hat and tells J.V to take the gun from him which he does while Noble is saying "I don't believe this nigga had the heart to shoot me."

"What the fuck is yall niggas doing?" asks Drama to Hova in a confused tone.

"Shut da fuck up." Hova says before pointing the gun at Noble and shooting him in the face catching him completely off guard.

"Bitch." Hova says to him before saying "now yall niggas come the fuck on." Hova says as him, Drama, J.V and the niggas that was with Noble walk out of the crib with Drama at gun point as they get into a burgundy Caravan and pull off."

"I mean if yall niggas gone kill me why yall ain't just kill me in there?" Asks Drama.

"Cause somebody wanna holla at you. Don't worry about it though, you'll be dead soon enough." Replies Hova.

"Well since you gone kill me can you at least tell me what I did." Drama asks in a calm tone as if it doesn't matter which scares Hova who had expected a more frighten posture.

Swallowing hard as the van stops and Vel gets in Hova says "cause you in the motherfucking way that's why. Niggas trying to get money and all you wanna keep doing is that dumb ass hot shit."

Slightly chuckling Drama asks "So this whole time yall been laying on me? That's alright cause all I'm gotta say is yall better kill me and make sure I'm dead."

Now, Hova who's frightened beyond belief by Drama attitude toward the whole situation like he can't die blurts out "I ain't scared of you yo, so all that crazy shit you talking I'm not trying to hear it. You brought dis shit on yourself cause I had already squashed dat shit wit Rah Rah and them and you kicked it off again for no reason."

"Whatever. You could've at least let me kill Noble for that comment he made." Replies Drama unconcerned with anything Hova just said.

"Naw, I ain't trusting that nigga as far as I could throw him. Shit for all I know he would've shot me for you shooting him. Hold up make a right here and pull behind where that Honda Accord parked." Hova says to the driver after answering Drama as he looks out his window as the caravan comes to a stop and Drama is taken from the van at gun point.

Walking up to the house they all look around to make sure no one is watching them as Hova knocks on the door and waits awhile.

"You sure they here?" Asks J.V before a female comes to the door with a camcorder in her hand. Seeing Hova she lets them in as they all walk in the house and go to a room where Mee Mee and some other girls are eating each other.

"What the fuck is going on in here?" Asks Vel. We were in the middle of making a porn movie and yall messing our money up cause we do get paid off selling this." Replies the girl with the camera.

"Why you ain't call before yall came over here?" Mee Mee says wrapping a robe around her and wiping her, mouth with a towel as so does the other female while they all stare on.

"I ain't know we was gone catch the nigga out there like that, the shit just happened." Hova says still not blinking.

"Well yall niggas gotta hold up cause I gotta put some clothes on." Replies Mee Mee putting her hair in a ponytail and leaving out the room.

"Why are we over here?" One of the dude's whispers in Hova ear.

"Cause nigga des bitches gangsta and she smoked Quarter and she told me she wanted to get down wit us so I told her she had to prove her loyalty by smoking Drama ass." Hova says coming out of his little trance. Noticing their all turned on the girl with the camera asks "yall ever made a porno flick?"

"Naw." They reply smiling.

"Well after we take care of this yall trying to get down?" She asks.

"Hell yeah, that's what's up right there." One of the dudes says as the small five-man crowd laughs and starts to talk amongst themselves as they sit Drama down on a couch and surround him.

"Damn Chyna, you too?" Asks Drama to the dark skin girl on the bed who just ignores him while rolling her eyes.

"I would have never thought I had this many people wanting me dead?" Drama says to himself looking at the crowd the girl with the camera and Chyna.

"Did yall know that yall would be able to get him today that's why yall pick today?" Asks Chyna.

"I ain't know it was gone be this easy, but yeah we planned it to a T. So, it had to go down today regardless, we just had to catch da nigga." Replies Hova as J.V and Vel both stare at Drama without saying a word.

Coming back in the room in some tight blue jeans a black shirt and some black Air force ones Mee-Mee says "alright, I'm ready."

"Took you long enough." Replies Vel as he hands her a Forty-five. "What you give me this for? Umm Umm we not doing this in here we taking this shit somewhere else." She says holding the gun.

"Gat damn Mee-Mee is you gone do the shit or what?" Asks Hova. "Yeah, but not in here fuck wrong wit you." She replies smartly looking him up and down.

As some of the dudes in the crowd suck their teeth someone knocks at the door.

"Shhh." Hova says trying to quiet everybody down. "Who da fuck is that?" Asks Hova.

"How the fuck I'm pose to know. I'm in here with yall." replies Mee-Mee walking to the door with Hova behind her with his gun ready as whoever it is knocks again.

"Who is it?" Asks Mee-Mee.

"Ma'am it's the police department; you have a stolen vehicle parked in front of your house and several of your neighbors said they saw several of the occupants of that vehicle holding weapons as they entered your home now can you open this door or it will be kicked open." The police man says as Hova looks out the window and sees the police man behind the door.

"We going out the back, just hold him out there for a few seconds."

Hova says jogging away from the door as Mee-Mee says hold on I gotta get the key to the lock on the door."

"The police out there we gotta bounce yo, pick dat nigga up and come on." Hova says as J.V and Vel pick up Drama and they make their way to the back door.

"See if anybody out there." Hova says to Chyna when they get to the back door which has no peep hole.

Going to open the door it flies open and a mausberg pump is aimed at the crowd as the police man says "Put ya motherfucking hands up." And the crowd does as they are told as Hova puts his gun in Dramas back pocket.

"Everybody against the wall, hands up." The cop says as Mee Mee and a bunch of dudes with red shirts and or bandannas come into the kitchen where they're lined up with their hands up.

"What da fuck is this?" Asks one of the dudes as they all turn around. "Drama, J.V and Vel yall come over here and anyone of yall niggas over their put yall hands down its gone get real ugly in here." The policeman says but as they take a closer look they realize that that's not a policeman its Joe dressed like one.

"Awh shit, yall niggas done fucked up now." Drama says taking the gun Hova tried to plant on him out of his pocket and standing beside Joe.

"Takes des niggas, check'em and put'em in da trunks." Joe says to the Bloods who has guns drawn on Hova and the other two dudes who do as their told and one by one take them out of the back door.

"Noble won't with them was it?" Asks Joe. "Naw, Hova killed Noble." Replies Drama.

"Well he did me a favor." Joe says lowering the mausberg as Hova is taken out the back door.

"You don't see no shit like this every day, so can one of yall tell me what the fuck is going on here." Drama asks Joe who's giving Mee Mee a hug.

"I'll tell you when we get in the car yall come on," Joe says as they walk out into the back yard toward one of several cars that's parked in the alley.

"Look, one of yall move that van from in front of the house and take me to get rid of this outfit and I'll meet yall at the spot. Joe says to a group of the Bloods.

"Ride wit them and I'm gone ditch this shit and meet yall there." Joe says to JV, Vel and Drama before him and one of his homies walk off and they all get in the cars and pull off.

"Can one of yall niggas tell me what the hell is going on?" Drama asks J.V and Vel as they sit in the back seat as Scarface blares from the speakers.

"Let me tell him." Vel says to J.V as he is ready to speak. "Don't get mad, cause everything was done for a reason. Hova was crying bout how you was making shit hot so some how him and Noble got clicked up to where they would only deal with each other but not us. So, one day out the blue Hova tells us Noble said he wanna talk to us so we meet him round his crib and he tells us how you and Joe are in the way and will be getting removed from the picture. He told us we could get down or be placed in the same boat as yall and if we told someone about what was going on no one would believe us and we would be killed in so many words. Anyway G-Way said hell naw and left and we said we'll think about it but went and told Joe." "Why the fuck yall ain't tell me?" Drama asks cutting him off.

"Hold up I'm gone tell you." Replies Vel before getting back into the story.

"Like I was saying though we went and hollered at Joe and he said not to tell you cause if you had killed Hova, Noble would know Joe knew and he would've bounced and if you would've killed Noble the same would have went for Hova he told us to play along, and everything they plotted out we would go and tell Joe and them about to figure out how to catch them slippin so when the date was set that we would move on yall we already had something waiting in the cut. So, when Hova sent us to find you and Noble sent his so-called niggas to get Joe we had already had it set up, I almost missed it though fucking wit dis nigga Trigger but dat's another story.

Anyway, a nigga did get killed; but it was a nobody nigga, but niggas made it seem like it was Joe.

So, when the police and ambulance left that's when the shoot outs popped off to make dat shit look even better like niggas was riding for Joe, but niggas was shooting out of beef the whole time and somehow

J.V stole a police car."

"Yeah I did dat yall gotta step yall car game up now." J.V says "and anyway gat damn, that's where I guess the uniform and gun came from Joe had on. I ain't know it was gone go down like that though cause I was back and forth fucking with Trigger so, I don't even know how J.V got it."

"He left it sitting there so I took it and hide it and Joe did the rest." J.V says smiling.

"Damn, yo can I finish. We was just supposed to stall everything and try to get them away from the guns when and where ever we caught you and took you. Da shit even caught Mee Mee off guard but everything worked out and now I guess we going to kill they ass but I don't know where the fuck we going." Vel says finishing his story.

"Damn, so you mean to tell me that all that shit was going on and I ain't know shit, man I'm slippin like a motherfucker." Replies Drama.

As long as you got us you ain't ever slippin my nigga cause we gone always be there to catch you." J.V says reaching over and giving him five.

When they get to where Joe told his niggas he would meet them at, it is pitch dark outside as the afternoon has turned into midnight.

Getting out the car stretching Drama looks around as the cars all line up and the place even though its dark looks very familiar to him.

"Homie I gotta be honest with you, I have never seen this place before in my life." Replies Vel.

"Man, I know I been here before." Drama says as they cut the lights on, on all the cars and start pulling Hova and them out the trunks of the cars and placing them in front of the high beams as they stand in front of them guns drawn.

"Look man, I got fifteen G's if you let me go man. I'll pay you and leave from round here yo that's my word." Hova is pleading with one of the dudes as he is seated on his knees on the ground squinting his eyes from da bright high beams.

"Man, I know where da fuck we at, I know I knew where the fuck we was at." Drama is saying to his self as they walk over to where Hova and the other two dudes are on the ground and Joe is still nowhere to be found.

Yawning and rubbing his eyes J.V says "I know I'm tired as a bitch and

I gotta piss." He says walking off looking for some place to piss as Vel and Drama do the same.

"I know you hear me talking to you yo why you ignoring me, if I get up to run I bet you'll pay attention to me." Hova says still trying to talk to dude.

"That's what I want you to do, get up and run." Replies dude with no trace of humor in his words.

"Oh, you can talk to me when you talking bout killing me." Replies Hova as he gets no reply but hears a car pull up.

"A Skinny and Black Mike." Hova says to the other two dudes but get no answer as they sit there too afraid to move or speak because they already know what it is and one of them has a visible piss stain that can be seen through his blue jeans.

"Come on Drama." Joe says to Drama as he has changed into a red shirt and black jeans with some wheat trims. Coming over to where Joe is he hands Drama a Mausberg while he holds a Machete and says "do you."

"Talk to them niggas man." The dude who has pissed his pants says to the other dude.

"Joe, dis me Skinny yo, you know where my." is all Skinny got out before Joe swings the machete and not only decapitates him, but almost decapitates the dude next to him as well as he screams in pain from the large gash the machete makes in his neck while Skinny's decapitated body lays in front of him.

"Gat damn Jason Friday the Thirteenth where ya hockey mask at?" Vel says to his self as him and J.V watch on while one of the Bloods put a bullet in the screaming dudes fore head and it gets silent.

"What you gone do Drama?" Asks Joe cutting the two dudes into several pieces as he continues to hack away at them.

"I mean I was just waiting for yall to finish." Replies Drama with the chrome mausberg in his right-hand staring at Joe hack away at the lifeless corpses.

"Drama maine, Look man I'm sorry yo." Hova says.

"You're sorry, sorry you are. A Joe dis shit called a mausberg right I like da way that sound rolling off my tongue. Matter fact nigga open ya motherfucking mouth." Replies Drama.

"Open my mouth? Hold up hold up." Hova says closing his mouth before the barrel sits on his face.

"Come on now Hova. I can put it in ya mouth or ya ass. They cutting niggas up out here so I gotta do some exotic shit, I can't let them show me up." Drama says to Hova.

"Just hurry the fuck up and kill the nigga ass so we can get da shit over wit." One of the Bloods say making Drama a little mad as he starts dumping knocking Hova's face off with the first shot and taking him apart with the rest as shit flies everywhere until the mausberg is empty.

"I just saved yall the hassle of Cutting him up." Drama says looking at dude before throwing down the mausberg and walking off as J.V and Vel both look at Drama and then look at Drama and then look at each other before looking back at Drama with their mouths hung open.

"What the fuck is wrong wit yall?" Asks Drama walking over to them. "Ain't nothing wrong we alright, you feeling alright." asks Vel. "Yeah, I'm alright, and I remember where I know this place from this where came after we burned Quarter shit down. Joe told us to meet him here." Replies Drama.

"I need a blunt." J.V says rubbing his hands on his face.

"Come on, yall niggas ready to bounce?" Joe says as they start to pile back into the cars.

"Hell yeah." Vel says as they walk to the cars and get in as some stay while they pull off.

"My lil motherfucking Solja, you crazy for real, it ain't no doubt about that, But I love you to death lil nigga." Joe says to Drama as they sit in the back seat of the car.

"I love you too maine." Replies Drama with a smile happy that he makes Joe proud as Master P blares through the speakers of the car as they all make their way back to the hood with a feeling of happiness, love and loyalty for each other.

CHAPTER 14

Thirty Fifth St East End
Da Next Day Thursday October 20,1999

Knock, knock, knock, knock "man who the fuck is it this early in the motherfucking morning?" G-Way says getting up and walking to the door.

Opening the door and seeing its Vel he smiles and says "man where the fuck you been at?"

"Naw, where the fuck yall been at?" Asks Vel coming in the house and yawning seeing Varsity and Trigger knocked out on the couch.

"Where Jovanda at?" Asks Vel.

"Varsity took her home, but man we got chased like a motherfucker yesterday. I had to bail out the car and everything; We just got back to the crib a little while ago." Says G-Way as Trigger sits up and yawns.

Looking at Vel he's kinda scared but he still says what's up to him. "What's up dawg." Replies Vel before him and G-Way sit on the couch and G-Way tells him what happened.

"Man, when you started driving toward the police I was telling myself this nigga crazy and then I got Trigger in the car and the police car that didn't chase you got right behind me. So, when Varsity turned left I turned right and it's like them motherfuckers chose to chase me so I'm flying and shit and Trigger screaming slow down like a lil ass girl but I'm like fuck dat shit. I'm telling you man them people chased us out into the middle of nowhere, so I'm like fuck it I ain't trying to get lost, so I make some lefts and bring the chase back round the way. But I fucked up and got on the highway and now it's some shit of cops behind us so after they see they can't fuck wit me some state troopers got in the chase and I'm like I gotta get the fuck off the highway. So, the first exit I see coming I get in the lane and blend into the shit, I'm telling you I was fucking dat shit up, but anyway the way I turned some of the police cars tried the shit and hit the safety rail blocking the rest of them off so now it's only a few police behind us. But these motherfuckers was dumb as a bitch cause I put my left turning signal on and act like I was gone turn left but I bent right and the cops was so close he spent out and the other cops hit his ass So when we got close to round the way I parked and we got out and ran. We hide for bout an hour and we started walking and seen a bike so I stole that shit off the porch and Trigger got on the handle bars so we riding and shit and the police slow down beside us and start staring in our face so Trigger hop's off the handle bars and starts running, I start speeding that motherfucker and the chain popped.

Man, I flipped everywhere, but I got da fuck up and hauled ass then I see Varsity so I jumped in the car wit him and then we started looking for Trig and guess where this nigga was at. dis nigga was hiding under the car in front of that bitch Valorey house dat Drama use to fuck with this nigga seen us drive past and he damn near picked da car up trying to get from up under it.

So, after riding past yo crib and not seeing yo car we came back here. That nigga Varsity claim he got chased too but that nigga shit won't sweeter than mines." G-Way says.

"Yeah, I got chased too but look, them niggas Hova and Noble tried to set niggas up, but yo we flip dat shit on they ass and laid all them niggas down." Replies Vel.

"What you mean they tried to set niggas up?" Asks Varsity sitting up and getting in the conversation.

"They was trying to get niggas to kill Joe and Drama. Replies Vel. "That nigga was serious, I thought he was joking or testing niggas loyalty." Says G-way.

"You been with me all day and you knew what was going on and ain't say shit? That's fucked up." Varsity says to G-Way.

"I ain't think them niggas was serious, so why would I bring it up?" Replies G-Way.

"So, what's up now? Is niggas straight?" Varsity asks Vel.

"Man, that shit was funny as a motherfucker and everybody knew what was going on. I don't know why Hova would tell us and not you." Replies Vel.

"Cause he know Joe and Drama my niggas and I wouldn't have went for it. Who was all in on it though?" Asks Varsity.

"Everybody from me down to Mee Mee and her little click. But don't feel bad cause Drama didn't know either and Joe told us not to tell nobody." Says Vel.

"So, J.V was in on it to huh?" Asks Varsity.

"Yeah and I was shocked! Shit J.V been running round all day setting shit up." Replies Vel.

"So now what?" Asks Varsity.

"Nothing, we done already found the weak link and broke it, we can lay back and get this money now." Replies Vel. Shaking his head Varsity says "yall know that's fucked up, all this shit been going on and ain't nobody tell me shit."

"We couldn't and I thought you probably already knew but just won't saying shit so you could see who sides niggas was on." Replies Vel as G-Way gets up and walks toward the kitchen.

"So, where Drama at now?" Asks Varsity.

"I left him wit Joe, went and got some breakfast at Mickey D'S and came over here. I ain't even know where yall were at but I seen yo car and figured you was probably in here sleep." Replies Vel as Trigger listens and looks on in silence.

"Yall sure them niggas dead cause Hova know too". Varsity is saying as Vel cuts him off by saying.

"Yeah, my nigga they dead, Joe had dis big ass Jason knife and you know Drama Mr. Overkill so if them niggas still breathing we might as well roll wit them cause they some bad motherfuckers." As he chuckles from the remark.

"Damn yo, you can't trust nobody no more." Varsity says after thinking about everything Vel just told him.

"You can trust me dawg, and I know you trust me cause after everything I just told you. You still ain't called Drama to verify if I was lying or not, so you know you can trust me." Vel says as Varsity smiles. Coming out of the kitchen eating a bowl of Captain Crunch G-Way sits between them and says "We family yo, we was the Ones who cared about each other when no one else did. Hova was new to the circle so that lets us know we need to be more careful bout who we invite into what we established." As they all nod in agreement.

Looking at Vel and then looking at Trigger Varsity asks, "so is yall niggas done acting all stupid and shit, Cause me and G-Way gone beat both yall ass if yall don't hug or something." Looking over at Trigger Vel grins and leans over to him and gives him five and hugs him.

"My bad dawg, I was wrong for fucking wit yo shorty. ° says Vel. "Yeah dawg, and I was wrong for shooting at you and stealing yo car."

Replies Trigger still hugging him "and kidnapping shorty and beating." Vel says before Trigger cuts him off and says "alright, I get the point. I'm sorry" and starts laughing.

"Well look, since shorty pregnant and don't know who baby it is me and you gone go round her crib and tell her to make a choice on who she wanna be with or we both just leave the bitch alone. And who ever baby it is the other one gone be the Godfather, bet. And after that we gone go to this party." Says Vel.

"Alright, we can do that. But I already know she gone pick you after what I did to her." Replies Trigger as they chuckle and Vel says "yeah, you did fuck her up".

We gone throw the party later on, I got Joe and them helping me set the shit up, I'm going to get the food and shit now so we wont run out of nothing." Drama says over his phone while driving talking to J.V at his crib.

"Alright, well we gone go around G-Way's crib and see what them niggas doing cause that's where Vel told me he was going before we split up." Replies J.V as Jasmine looks over from under the cover on her side of the bed and asks him "Do yall ever go to sleep?"

You ain't even been in the house two hours yet and you ready to leave out again!" As he hangs the phone up and gets off the bed.

"I'm taking care of shit." J.V replies.

"Well you need to be trying to take care of home first cause I'm tired of doing everything around here." says Jasmine in a smart tone.

"Tired of doing everything? All you do is cook and clean, and work and I pay for every motherfucking thing so I ain't trying to hear that shit early this morning." Replies J.V in a smart tone before walking out of the bedroom and slamming the door behind him as she jumps out the bed mad and follows him saying "he done lost his damn mind this morning, JERELL!" She yells to him opening the bedroom door and sees him leaving out the house before she turns back around to put her house slippers on.

When J.V gets on his porch he hears a male voice say "yo J.V!". "Yo." Replies J.V before his heart jumps when he recognizes who it is calling him.

"Where Drama at?" Asks the dude leaned against a Mercury Sable with Rah Rah in the driver seat and another dude in the back.

"I don't know, why?" Asks J.V trying his best to show he isn't scared "He knows what's up!" Replies dude before pulling a nine millimeter from his waist and shooting in the air then getting in the passenger seat before Rah Rah hangs this mac eleven out the window and J.V dives back in the house as Rah Rah sprays the automatic shots at him as he pulls off.

"JERELL!" Jasmine screams in a scared tone as bullets fly in the house hitting stuff and she ducks but continues to run to her man's aid as he gets back up and says I'm alright. As he watches the car drive down the street with a mean mug and his fist balled up before looking back at Jasmine and walking out the house and down the stairs.

"Boo come back in the house." She says to him in a scared tone.

Coming on the porch in her robe and house shoes.

"Naw, you go back in the house and lock the door, I'm bout to straighten this shit! ° J.V says angerly.

"Well you come back in the house too then, don't go messing with them boys." Replies Jasmine as tears start to fill her eyes as J.V keeps walking before looking back and yelling "go back in the damn house!" Before he gets to the corner and turns it.

Angry, scared and frustrated Jasmine goes back in the house and slams the door before storming back toward their room and falling on the bed crying as she worries about J.V.

Accidentally hitting the TV remote on the bed with her elbow and cutting the TV on she hears the male news reporter speaking about what has been happening all week concerning the violence that has mostly erupted in the East End of the city. Getting herself together she looks up just in time to see and hear the announcer say "we are offering a ten-thousand-dollar reward if anybody has any information on the events that took place this week the number is " The man is saying as Jasmine crawls on the bed over to the night stand and opens the top drawer reaching for a pen and some scrap paper as she listens to the reporter talk and writes the number down before cutting the TV off and going to her dresser taking out a pair of socks, bra and panties putting them on her bed before going to and looking through her closet for an outfit to put on.

When J.V gets to and in G-Ways crib they're already talking about what was on TV

"I missed that shit, but look some niggas just came to my crib shooting at me and shit." J.V says sitting on the couch next to Varsity as him and G- Way both ask "Who?" at the same time.

"Rah Rah and two other niggas. They was waiting outside my crib when I came out and one of them asked me where Drama was at and when I said I don't know they just started dumping." Replies J.V still visibly shaken pissed off.

"Do you know where Drama's at? Cause we gotta let that nigga know them niggas looking for him." G-Way says picking his phone off the table and calling Drama.

"I don't know, when I last talked to him he said he was going to get the food for the block party." Replies J.V rubbing both of his hands on his face.

"We need to worry about this right now fuck dat party and this nigga ain't picking up so we need to go see if we can catch up with the nigga before they do." G-Way says as they get up and all walk out the house to the car.

Oakwood Ave

"Why the fuck you bring that nigga over here!?" Jovanda screams at Vel as they stand in her front yard while Trigger who waited for Vel to get her from out of the house and in her yard steps out of the passenger seat of the car and makes his way toward them.

"Stop screaming, damn. Look yo ass pregnant and you don't know who the daddy is, so until you find out you gone have to deal with both of us and you gone have to make a choice on who you wanna be with."

Replies Vel as Trigger stops and stands beside him.

"You know I don't wanna be with that nigga, I don't need no nigga hitting on me!" Jovanda says with a smart upset tone which irritates Trigger who replies "I wouldn't have been hitting yo ass if you wouldn't have done that fucked up ass shit." In a calm tone through clenched teeth as he tries to keep his composure.

"Nigga! I won't even talking to you so shut the fuck up!" Jovanda snaps at Trigger who balls up his fist and matches her tone as he steps toward her saying "Bitch who the fuck you think you talking to like that, I'll smack the shit out yo ass out here!"

"You won't do shit to me nigga." Jovanda says in a scared tone getting behind Vel and pushing him in front of her.

"Get the fuck from behind me, I ain't trying to get hit cause he swinging at you." Replies Vel moving from in front of her which makes her mad so she pushes him and screams." That's fucked up you gone just let him hit me and shit! I ain't fucking with " POP POP POP POP POP POP POP POP POP gun fire erupts from a car parked across from them before Rah Rah steps out of the driver seat holding a Mac eleven and walks toward them as the dude who shot in the air at J.V earlier slides over into the driver seat.

Kicking over Trigger who's laying on the ground in pain, Rah Rah shoots him in the face.

"Yeah, yall niggas thought we was gone let that shit slide." He says spraying Vel with the Mac and then Jovanda who wasn't even shot, but laying on the ground scared, as she now screams from feeling the bullets tear through her back.

Grabbing Vel, Rah Rah drags him out into the middle of the street as the dude in the driver seat pulls out of park and drives into the street before putting the car in reverse and backing over Vel as Rah Rah gets in the passenger seat and dude pulls off rolling over Vel again as he drives off and turns right at the corner.

Crying and coughing up blood Jovanda looks around and sees Trigger and Vel both dead before she tries to crawl her way toward her house as pain shoots through her bullet riddled body.

Coming back down the street from circling the block Rah Rah and them see Jovanda trying to crawl to her steps.

Jumping out of the back seat, one of their homies runs up on her as she screams "Ma" as she sees him coming.

Standing in the doorway traumatized with the phone in her hands her mother stands completely frozen in fear as the dude raises the gun toward her and opens fire knocking her back in the house from the shots as her leg hangs out on the porch shaking.

"We ain't do nothing to " Jovanda cries as dude grabs her by her hair and says "bitch shut the fuck up!" As he shoves the gun in her mouth and pulls the Trigger causing the back of her head to explode.

Letting her limp body go he jogs back to the back seat of the car and gets in as they roll over Vel again as they speed off.

Thirty First St East End Around the way

After riding around the entire Church Hill, they still don't find Drama but they do see the niggas who hang with Rell and Rah Rah standing out on the block deep in several groups as some mean mug the car as they drive by them.

Turning his head away from them J.V sucks his teeth and says "we gone get them niggas." As a police car turns the corner in front of them and slowly drives up the block and past them.

"Man, them motherfuckers is everywhere." G-Way says about the police as he looks out the back window from the back seat.

"Shiitttt, niggas been dropping all week and that curfew shit ain't working. I'm just surprised they ain't got the national guard out this bitch yet." replies Varsity as he drives.

"They gone bring the feds out here again watch what I tell you cause this shit round here done got way worst then it was when Big Bro was alive,

R.I.P my nigga." Varsity says again before making the sign off a cross. "Call Drama again, this nigga gone pick his phone up." J.V says.

"We done called this nigga a million times and got the busy service. I don't know what the fuck this nigga doing." Varsity says pulling his phone from his waist and dialing Drama number and letting the phone ring.

"Yo????" Drama asks loudly over "No more pain" by 2 Pac coming from his speakers as he picks his phone up while he continues to drive.

"A nigga, you know we got Ten thousand dollars looking for us and

J.V got shot at?" Asks Varsity.

"Who shot at J.V?" Asks Drama in an upset tone. "Rah-Rah and them peoples." Replies Varsity.

"Oh, word. Alright, I'm gone take care of that shit." Drama says speeding up a bit.

"Did you hear me when I said them people offering ten G's for some information bout us?" Asks Varsity.

"So, where yall at anyway?" Asks Drama.

"We riding around looking for you, where you at?" Asks Varsity.

"I was going to go get this food but now I'm on my way to kill one of them niggas. Replies Drama in a Serious tone.

"Naw man chill don't do that shit, I just told you we hot as a motherfucker so just get the food and everything, alright."

Varsity says as Drama replies "You sure?" Which catches Varsity off guard.

"Yeah, yeah everything straight." He says.

"Alright, well look I already done paid some ma fuckers to help set da shit up for the party and Joe said he gone make sure shit get set up right. I'm gone go get this food and shit and meet yall at the party." Drama says as Varsity asks "Where the fuck is this block party at anyway?"

"On Z street, Vel ain't tell you yet?" Asks Drama.

"Hell Naw, all that nigga thinking bout is dat bitch. I'm gone holla at you when you get their though alright. one." Replies Varsity hanging up.

"So, what's up?" Asks J.V. you know that nigga was ready to go nuts but shit too hot right now for that shit so I told the nigga to chill and we gone deal with it on a later date." Replies Varsity as J.V thinks about what he said and sees that it's the best decision to chill and let it go.

"A yo J.V ain't that Jasmine?" G-Way says looking out the window as they drive right pass her as she walks down the street.

"A Varsity, back up yo. I told her ass to stay in the motherfucking house." J.V says as Varsity puts the car in reverse and backs up until he's right beside her.

Rolling his window down J.V says "I thought I told you to stay in the house."

"Nigga you don't own me and I was looking for you anyway." Jasmine says walking to the car as J.V opens the door and she gets in the back seat with him.

"I wrote that number down off the TV." She says opening her small purse as everyone asks "For What????" Looking around after she jumps from the response she says "to give it to yall and let yall know what's going on."

"What the fuck we want the number for, we already know what's going on." Replies G-Way reaching back, getting the piece of paper with the number on it, reading it and asking "you ain't call this shit did you?" As he turns back around in the seat.

"What the fuck I look like, did you call it motherfucker. Don't carry me like that?" She replies in an upset tone crossing her arms. "It was just a question, damn." G-Way says before J.V cuts in saying "yall cut that shit out." As he puts his hand over Jasmines mouth as she mumbles still talking shit.

"A, do her ass like Trigger did Jovanda," G-Way says laughing.

"Get yo motherfucking hand off my mouth and he ain't- gone do shit to me." She says knocking his hand away.

"Shut the fuck up then." Screams J.V.

"Don't be screaming and cursing at me, who the fuck you think you talking to. Let me out dis fucking car, stop the car Varsity." Jasmine says angry as Varsity stops the car and she gets out and slams the door behind her.

"Why the fuck you stop for?" J.V asks in an upset tone. "Cause yall motherfuckers is crazy." Replies Varsity laughing.

"Gone let her cool off cause I ain't trying to argue with her this whole ride." G-Way says to J.V who tells Varsity to "pull off." As he watches her walk the other way.

"She gone be alright." Varsity says to J.V as he looks at him through the rear-view mirror before cutting the stereo on and turning it up a little bit.

"A, stop at the store right quick so I can get some blunts." G-Way says as Varsity slows down and pulls to the curb of the store on the corner and G- Way gets out and jogs into the store.

"You gone tomorrow?" Varsity says with a smile striving to start some type of conversation.

"Yeah, I need a break from all this crazy shit anyway." replies J.V.

"That ain't no joke, I wish my daddy had some shit like that I would've been gone." Says Varsity with a slight chuckle.

"I could've been gone but I ain't wanna leave yall, especially not Drama after what he's been going through. And somehow I just figured as long as I stayed here I could keep things in order." Replies J.V.

"I feel that, but you gone have to understand that everything happens for a reason and you can't stop what's meant to be whether you stay here or not cause if it's gone happen its gone happen you feel me." Varsity says turning the stereo down some.

"Yeah I feel you and you right but I love yall niggas yo and I don't want to be off somewhere living good while yall here struggling to survive." Replies J.V.

"See you missing a point though cause as long as you their living good you can always make a way for us to come out there and do the same thing, so it ain't like you leaving us, you just going to set it up to where we can all eat." Varsity, says as G-Way gets back in the car and they both end the conversation with silent nods before Varsity pulls off.

Z Street East End

By the time Drama pulls up to the block party Joe's homies have everything already set up as people dance to the music coming from the huge show speakers, eat and drink.

"Shit." Drama says to his self with a car full of food as he looks around and sees people enjoying their selves.

Smiling he grabs his tape case holder gets out of the car and walks to the house where everything is set up at, grabbing the microphone and stopping the music Drama asks "Yall ready to wild the fuck out?" As some people scream yeah and Drama goes in his tape case holder and pulls out one of the mix tapes he made and says "This block party right here is dedicated to my nigga J.V, he round here somewhere and just like me I know he'd want yall to enjoy yall selves so yall have a good time."

Drama says sticking the tape in the stereo and turning it up some more before music blasts through the speakers after a short pause and people continue dancing.

Looking around in the crowd Drama yells "yo. J.V." and walks in the crowd toward J.V who's sitting on the curb drinking a beer looking at the ground.

"Nigga get yo ass up and come get on some of this ass out here." Drama yells to him as J.V happy to see him smile and gets up as Drama walks toward him giving him five and a hug.

"Bout time you got here." J.V says to him. "Yeah, my bad you alright?" Asks Drama. "I'm alright now? Replies J.V.

"Well come on, let's go get on some of this ass out here then." Drama says as they walk in the crowd and both get behind some females wearing very short dresses.

"I see yall niggas." G-Way says with his hand down the front of the girl he is dancing with pants.

"Nigga this yo party, do what the fuck you feel like." Drama yells to J.V while dancing with a girl and looking at what G-Way is doing.

As more and more people come the wilder Drama gets and J.V being so drunk feeds right into it.

"Money ain't a thing nigga." Drama and J.V scream back and forth throwing money at each other like their having a food fight while the people around them scramble to pick it up as they chase each other back and forth through the crowd.

"What the fuck is wrong with them niggas?" Varsity asks his self out loud and laughing as he watches them while he dances and drinks a Corona.

Seeing Drama have a good time Joe and a few others who were standing on some one's porch making sure everything was straight decides to leave.

Going to the coolers Drama and J.V find the beers after going through two coolers of juice and sodas.

"Watch this." Drama tells J.V as they grab beers out of the cooler and Drama starts shaking his up.

"Which one of des bitches been tripping?" Drama asks J.V.

Smiling J.V says "dat bitch right there." Pointing at a female who is dancing by herself and acting as if she is better than everybody else.

Walking toward her, Drama gets up on her he asks her "dis shit off the hook ain't it shorty?"

Looking at him and rolling her eyes she replies "It's alright." "Damn, what's the little attitude for?" Asks Drama.

"I have a man." Replies the girl as she continues to dance by herself.

"I ain't ask you all that, but since you over here dancing and shit you want me to get you something to drink?" Asks Drama as she makes a face as if he's bothering her before saying "I said no, I'm alright."

"But I insist." Drama says opening the beer can and spraying beer all over her then dumping it on her laughing as she stands there in shock.

"You bitch ass nigga, I'm gone get somebody to fuck yo ass up the girl says walking away angerly.

"Shut up bitch, these niggas know what it is." Drama replies throwing the rest of the beer toward her and then hitting her in the head with the can.

"Yeah nigga!" J.V says as he watches laughing before shaking his beer and letting it shoot in the air.

"Whoo!" He screams again as loud as he can before he sees Jasmine standing to the right of him with a few of her friends. Putting the bottle down as him and Jasmine start to approach each other, giving each other a hug when they get close enough.

"Boo, I'm sorry." He says as she replies "me too." before she gives him a kiss.

"You wanna dance?" Asks J.V. "If you want to." She replies.

"Come on." J.V says walking her to the crowd and dancing with her while Drama gets G-Way and they chase people around the party squiring beer on them.

Looking into Jasmine's eyes J.V says, "I love you girl." and she replies, "I love you too."

"A Drama! Where Joe and them go?" Varsity grabs Drama and asks looking a bit scared.

"They supposed to be meeting some nigga to get some more guns why?" Asks Drama as he stands there and continues throwing beer on people as some people throw it back.

"A nigga just told me Trigger, Vel and Jovanda got killed."

Varsity says as Drama looks at him and asks "huh?" before gun shots ring out and people start scattering revealing Rell and a small group of his friends looking around.

"Where that bitch ass nigga Drama at!" Rell say with authority in his voice looking around as they start walking.

"I'm right here Motherfucker!" Drama yells to them before shooting his forty-four, doom doom doom doom and knocking one of his niggas clean off their feet as well as hitting and spinning around a male who was just trying to get out of the line of fire.

Scattering Rell and the rest of his crew continue to chase Drama through the crowd as Rell catches up with him and starts shooting hitting everything but Drama as he ducks before grabbing a girl and putting her in front of him as shots knock her down.

"I'm gone kill yall niggas!" Drama yells as he runs through Someone's yard and gets away as Rell and them run off leaving behind their friend.

Standing on someone's porch Varsity, G-Way, J.V and Jasmine stand in shock as they see at least a dozen people shot screaming and bleeding in the street and on the sidewalks.

"Look at dis shit!" G-Way says out loud.

"Do yall see Drama anywhere out there?" J.V asks looking around but not seeing him.

"Naw, but fuck dat we better bounce cause its bout to get real hot out here." Varsity says walking off the porch as they follow hearing crying, yelling and screaming from the people who were at the party.

"Look I'm gone grab his tape case so they won't get his finger prints, yall meet me at the car." Varsity says jogging to get Drama tape case as they walk to his Lex around the corner and get in, shocked to see Drama ducked down in the back seat holding his bleeding arm.

"Oh shit! You alright?" Asks J.V as fear stabs him in the heart.

"Yeah, I'm alright, it just grazed me." Replies Drama with his black rag tied around his wound to try and stop the bleeding.

"We gotta get you to the hospital before you bleed to death." Jasmine says watching blood make its way through and down the cracks of his fingers.

"Hell, naw if I go to the hospital I'm going to jail and I'd rather bleed to death first." Replies Drama in a serious tone as he rocks back and forth and G-way looks on from the front passenger seat as Varsity gets in the car with the tape case and shuts the door not even paying attention to J.V. Drama and Jasmine sitting in the back seat as he starts his car up saying "we gotta find this lil nigga man, I hope he ain't hurt."

"He sitting behind you bleeding to death." J.V says as Varsity turns around.

"Oh shit! We gotta get you to the hospital." Varsity says with concern. "Fuck the hospital, I'm not going to the hospital. Just take me home." Drama says balling his face up as he rocks from the pain.

"Let's take him to my house I got a first aid kit and we can at least try."

"Pull off!" to do something to stop the bleeding." Jasmine is saying as J.V yells for him to pull off and he does as G-Way watches police start to dramatically speed to the block party and slam on their brakes.

"They kill me with that shit." G-Way says about the police as Varsity drives carefully to J.V and Jasmine's crib "

Sir did you see who it was that shot you?" A detective asks Rell's shot half dead friend who police have hand cuffed on the side walk bleeding while waiting for an ambulance, as more people point to him as being one of the guys who initiated the shoot out that took place.

"Sir do you hear me? I need to know if you know who it was that shot you.

"A nigga name Drama." He replies clearly in pain.

"Drama? Do you know his real name? Could you pick him out of a photo line up?" Asks the detective loudly so he can hear him.

"Look at me I'm dying, where the fuck the ambulance at? I'm bleeding to death." Replies dude.

"They're on their way I promise you. But right now, you need to tell me who this Drama guy is." Says the detective.

"I don't know his real name, I just know that ever since his brother got killed he been shooting up the apartments and he killed my nigga Tragedy, and Lil J and he be stealing cars and shit." He is saying as pain is surging through his body while the detective thinks before his eyes get big and he asks "Is it Darell Drakeford? He had a brother Ralph Drakeford who died last month in a drug related killing?" But dude doesn't reply.

"Come on Corey answer me, an ambulance is on the way." the detective says to the dude who isn't responding as he sits slumped over in his lap.

Touching him he falls over dead and the detective says "shit! Look! I need a APB put out on a Darell Drakeford and he's wanted for questioning in a string of homicides." As police place the order through on their walkie talkie and computers inside the cars "

George Mason Square

"I told you the shit just grazed me." Drama says sitting in J.V room with no shirt on as Jasmine wraps a white bandage around a white pad on his upper left arm as they all sit around staring at her bandage him up.

"That's not a graze that's a gash and you might need stitches but this should stop the bleeding for now." Replies Jasmine as she finishes wrapping his arm.

"I'm gone kill these niggas kids and everything that's my word." Drama says out loud looking for his shirt and putting it on when he finds it.

"We need to lay low." Replies G-Way. "Fuck dat, its war!" Drama says.

"Naw yo, he right, we gotta chill." J.V says to Drama who stands up.

"Naw fuck that you go pack and get ready to go get that money." Drama says looking at him.

"He right boo, get packed I don't need you in the middle of this." Jasmine says getting up.

"Do you need some help?" Varsity asks turning the TV off and getting up.

"Not really," replies J.V worried about Drama

"You gone be alright?" G-Way asks Drama who's now staring into space.

"Yeah, I'm alright." Replies Drama before he looks at everybody and slowly turns and starts walking to the door.

"A yo man, you sure you alright?" Asks G-Way again as he gets a real eerie feeling that makes him shake a little.

"I'm straight, I'm bout to go home and change then look for Joe and I'll catch up with yall later." Replies Drama as he leaves out the crib with them a little ways behind him as he walks down the street and they watch him until he turns the corner before they get in Varsity's car and Varsity starts the car up and pulls off.

"You don't think he bout to do nothing crazy do you?" G-Way asks out loud.

"I hope not." Replies Varsity thinking about how crazy Drama has been acting lately as he continues to drive.

Twenty Fourth St East End That Night

Leaning up against Joe's car smoking a blunt as Joe and a few Bloods stand little ways away from the car having a conversation, Drama is into his own thoughts as he thinks about his brother, Trigger, Vel, Tyron, Pooh and Yummy and all the things they use to do together.

"Drama, did you hear what I said?" Asks Joe breaking Dramas concentration.

"Huh?" He asks looking up.

"The police coming hide dat blunt. Replies Joe as Drama looks and sees a police car slowly creeping up the street.

Putting the blunt out in the street and standing back up Drama takes a deep breath as he looks up and stares off into the night sky.

Thinking about his friends makes tears well up in his eyes and roll down his face wiping his face with his arm he looks over at Joe and them who are having what sounds like a personal conversation.

When the police car slowly rides pass them and flashes the light on them while it drives by nobody really pays it any mind and continues doing what they were doing when it turns the corner.

Sparking his blunt back up, Drama looks over toward Joe once more before walking off and outta sight without Joe or any of the people he's talking to even noticing it.

As he walks along the dark streets he starts to feel like he's running out of people who love him and the more he thinks about it the more and more the burden weighs heavily on his heart as he walks smoking his blunt and staring at the ground.

Nobody says anything to him as he passes them and neither does he bother to acknowledge anyone he walks past.

When he gets to where the block party was held he walks over to his car takes out his keys, unlocks the door, opens it and sits in the driver seat.

Taking another deep breath, he shuts the door, Starts the car up and pulls off.

Turning his set all the way up he zones out to the music as Pac's lyrics makes him madder and madder.

As a tear of frustration falls from his right eye he cuts the music down feeling like its making him feel as if he's ready to snap and blackout.

Ring ring, ring, ring, ring "Hello?" Drama asks picking his phone up. "A yo dawg, where the fuck you at??" Varsity asks very fast with a hint of fright in his voice.

"Why? What's going on now? asks Drama as his heart thumps hard in his chest thinking something has happened to J.V.

"Man, you all over the fucking news, they got your picture and everything. Where ever the fuck you at you need to bounce and I mean now cause they trying to involve you in everything!"

Varsity says with general concern as he looks at the news talk about everything that had been happening and showing a picture of Drama and repeating "Darrell 'Drama' Drakeford is armed and extremely dangerous."

Pausing, Drama lets it all sink in as he drives and Varsity repeatedly asks "Hello? Drama?"

"I'm still here, I was just thinking bout something. Good look on the tip though." Replies Drama.

"No problem my nigga but you need to get ghost. alright. one." Varsity says still watching TV as they both hang up and his phone immediately starts ringing again.

"Hello?" Asks Varsity.

"A yo you looking at the news?" Ask G-Way.

"Yeah, I just told Drama about the shit." Replies Varsity.

"Did you tell that nigga he need to lay low somewhere?" asks G-Way as his phone beeps.

"Hold up." G-Way tells Varsity and clicks over. Hearing a male and woman crying G-Way asks

"Hello?"

"A yo man, they got my nigga on TV" the male voice says as he cries. "Who is this, J.V?" Asks G-Way.

"Yeah yo, what the fuck we gone do. We can't let them lock our nigga up and I bet you Rell or one of them told on him." J.V says in anger, pain and tears.

"Look yo I got Varsity on the other end, are you still in yo crib?" Asks G-Way.

"Yeah," replies J.V.

"Well look we gone call you on three-way alright." "Alright." G-Way says before clicking back over to Varsity.

"Hello?" he asks.

"Yeah, I'm still here." replies Varsity.

"A look that was J.V, I'm bout to put him on three-way so hold on again." G-Way says clicking over and dialing J.V number and waiting for him to pick up.

"Hello?" Asks J.V.

"Hold on." G-Way says clicking them both over to Varsity. "Hello?" Asks G-Way.

"Yeah." Varsity and J.V reply.

"Hold up, Drama on the other line." J.V says clicking over. "So, what now?" G-Way asks Varsity.

"I don't know." Replies Varsity as they both hear the click. "What the fuck is that nigga doing?" Asks Varsity about J.V.

"I don't know, that nigga losing his motherfucking mind." Replies G-Way as they hear Drama ask "who yall talking bout?"

"OH shit, what up nigga." Says G-Way.

"Man, I don't know, I know I ain't turning myself in though." Replies Drama as J.V can be heard striving to get it together.

"A yo where the fuck you at anyway?" Asks G-Way.

"It don't even matter, as long as it ain't in hand cuff's so fuck it." Replies Drama.

"A look yall tell Drama he should come with me tomorrow." J.V says to everyone.

"Shit that's a good idea." Varsity says as Drama says "hell naw, cause I ain't for having to jump out no air plane." As they all laugh.

"Well you gotta do something you just can't sit around here." J.V says seriously.

"Don't worry about it dawg, I'll think of something." Drama says in a calm tone striving to keep J.V calm as the battery on his cell phone starts to beep showing the battery is low.

"What the fuck is that, who's phone bout to go out?" Asks Varsity. "That's me yo, so look yall make sure J.V make his flight tomorrow and don't worry about me " Drama is saying before his phone dies.

"Hello? A yo Drama?" They all seem to ask but get no reply just static before J.V clicks the line off and start crying again as he says "Man fuck dat shit, I ain't going no where tomorrow. I gotta make sure my nigga O.K."

"Man, you trippin, you heard Drama say make sure you go to the airport. If you had something to say, then you should've said it when he was on the phone so don't even try dat bullshit!" Replies Varsity as J.V hangs the phone up.

"I know this nigga ain't just hang the phone up, that's an emotional ass little motherfucker." Varsity says to G-Way.

"Man fuck that shit, we going round there tomorrow anyway and it ain't no need to sit up stressing bout Drama when we don't even know where he at." Replies G-Way.

"You right, we got to get up early anyway tomorrow, so we need to be trying to go to sleep. I'll holla at you at J.V crib tomorrow, alright One"

Varsity says hanging up.

CHAPTER 15

**George Mason Square East End
Da Next Day Friday October 21, 1999**

Pulling up to J.V crib, Drama gets out of the car and walks to the door.

Ringing the doorbell, a male voice asks "Who is it?"

"It's me nigga." Replies Drama as G-Way opens the door and he sees Jasmine placing two suit cases on the floor in front of the door as their faces light up when Drama walks in.

"I see you all ready huh nigga?" Drama says to J.V who was walking behind Jasmine with some more suit cases. After hugging G-Way he walks over to and gives J.V a hug and sees Varsity sitting on the couch drinking some Sunny Delight.

"Damn dawg I been worrying about you all night." J.V says to him while they hug.

"I'm alright nigga." Drama replies before giving him the keys to his car. "Thank you." J.V says as they give each other five.

"A yo, I thought you'd be outta state by now, what the hell you doing over here?" Asks Varsity getting up and giving him five and a hug.

"You know I had to see my nigga off." Replies Drama.

"Shit, I'm trying to give you my ticket and see you off." J.V says before walking to get the rest of his bags.

"I know you crazy for real now, you even got the news people looking for you, you done took some of the heat off the niggas on America's Most Wanted." G-Way says trying to bring some humor to the situation.

Laughing a little bit Varsity asks. Where did you go yesterday? Drove around and did some self-reflecting and I snuck in the crib took a shower, ate and changed right before I came over here." Drama replies.

"Shit, I'll be in Kentucky somewhere by now. Fuck that, you a better man than me." G-Way says turning channels as he sits on the couch and J.V comes back with two more suit cases.

"A yo man for real, you say the word and the ticket yours." J.V says. "Nigga you better carry yo ass and get that money." Replies Drama.

Jasmine who's been avoiding Drama since he came in walk's directly in front of him, puts her hands on his face and says °I prayed for you last night and I hope if you somehow get out of this that you learn a lesson from it because you've been nothing but real to us and I'd hate to see anything bad happen to you." And with that said she gives him a kiss on the cheek and a hug before going back in the bed room.

"Damn, I never knew she felt like that." Drama says looking over toward J.V.

"Man, we both been up crying and worrying about yo ass last night." Replies J.V.

"For what? I told yall I'm good. And I still gotta smoke them bitches ass niggas before I bounce and since I'm already looking at the electric chair a few more ain't gone hurt nothing." Drama says with a laugh but nobody else finds it funny as they just stare at him.

Looking at his watch J.V says "I gotta put this shit in the car, is yall niggas gone help me or what?" As he opens the door and they all get up and grab some of his suit cases and Jasmine comes back out of the room as they walk out the crib to the car Drama just gave J.V.

"You coming with us to the airport?" She stops and asks Drama as he stands in the door way.

"I would, but I got something I need to take care of. He replies as he goes in his pocket and pulls out a clear zip lock bag full of jewelry and gives it to her.

"What's this for?" She asks staring at the bag.

"It's a lil something from me to yall cause I just gave J.V a used car." Replies Drama as G-Way, J.V and Varsity make their way back past them to get the rest of the suit cases.

"You gave him your Infinite?" Jasmine asks surprised.

"Yeah." Drama says as they walk back past him with the last of the suit cases. Then "what are you going to drive to get from around here?" She asks.

"I got something in the cut, I'm alright." Drama says as J.V says "yall come on if you coming."

Walking on the porch Jasmine shuts and locks the door as J.V walks ahead of her.

"You rolling wit us?" Asks Varsity as him and G-Way stand by Varsity's car.

"Naw yo, I got somethings I need to take care of before I bounce." Replies Drama giving them both five and a hug one by one before they get in the car and Drama walks over to J.V and says "I'm sorry about your party."

"It's cool, you just don't do nothing stupid while I'm gone." Replies J.V as they give each other five and a hug.

"You know I am." Drama says breaking loose from the hug and starting to walk away not wanting J.V to see him tear up.

"I love you nigga!" J.V says to Drama.

"I love you more." Replies Drama as he walks without looking back and

J.V sits in the car Drama just gave him and watches Drama walk away until he turns the corner and is out of sight.

Starting the car up he pulls off as Varsity pulls off beside him. "Boo, I'm gone give you the car." J.V says to Jasmine noticing how excited she looks from being in it.

"Me, why?" She asks surprised.

"Cause I love you, and how am I gone get this to L.A?" asks J.V.

Thank you boo." She says leaning over and giving him a kiss and then turning to look out of her passenger tinted window to hide the fact that she is blushing.

"Where did Drama say he was going?" Asks Jasmine.

"He didn't say." Replies J.V now thinking about what Drama said before he walked off While walking Drama sees the police so he puts his head down and turns onto a side street as he continues to where he's going.

When he gets to his apartment complex he walks over to a parked Bonneville and gets right in it. Opening the glove compartment and pressing a button he opens the trunk.

Getting out the car he walks to the trunk and pulls back some junk to reveal a mac eleven and two extended clips. Taking them out the trunk and shutting it he walks back to the driver side and gets in.

Shutting the door, he puts the mac and the clips in the passenger seat before going under the driver seat and getting a screw driver, starting the car up and pulling off.

While driving he drives right pass Rah-Rah who's standing on the corner catching sells. Seeing him, Drama drives to the end of the block.

Making a U-turn at the corner he drives back down to the middle of the block and parks.

Watching Rah-Rah stand by his self on the corner serving fiends Drama puts the clip in the mac and pulls the slide back before he puts the other clip in his pocket.

Getting out the car and ducking down he shuts the car door enough to where it wouldn't lock before he creeps toward him.

When he gets close enough he Jumps up and screams "Yeah Motherfucker, What's Up Now!!" And letting the mac spray TAT TAT TAT TAT TAT TAT TAT TAT TAT TAT TAT TAT TAT TAT TAT TAT.

Seeing Rah-Rah drop and not move he takes off running back toward the car but the police hearing the machine gun fire fly around the corner and see him running toward their squad car with the mac in his hand.

"OH SHIT!" Drama says feeling his heart drop in his stomach before he sprays the mac at the police car and runs across the street and through someone yard.

Richmond Virginia Airport

"Now boarding to L.A." A lady says over a loud speaker as J.V sits with his head in his lap.

"That's you my nigga." Varsity says standing up stretching as G-Way does the same before giving him five and a hug and Varsity does the same before J.V turns to Jasmine who says "I'm gone miss you baby." Before giving him a kiss and a hug.

"I'm going miss you too, and I'm gone make sure you don't need for nothing plus I'm gone come back for the holidays and your birthday." J.V says holding her in his arms.

"You gone miss your flight dawg." Varsity says watching the last few people walk through the entrance way.

"Alright Boo." J.V says giving Jasmine another kiss and a hug before giving G-Way and Varsity a hug and saying "Lost Souls" and throwing up the sign they made up as G-Way and Varsity say and do the same thing before he turns and walks toward his flight entrance with his bags.

The closer he gets to the entrance way though the more he thinks about Drama.

"Fuck dis shit!" He says stopping at the door and turning around. Seeing him coming back they all walk toward him.

"What, what's going on?" Asks G-Way with tears in his eyes.

"I gotta make sure my nigga O.K." J.V says speed walking toward the parking lot right past them like he doesn't even notice them.

"Wait for us then, shit." Jasmine says as her, Varsity and G-Way run to catch up with him as he walks toward the doors without bothering to look back "

Venable St East End

"Give up you are surrounded!" One of many police say to Drama through a bullhorn with the others standing behind their car doors with their guns out as Drama is ducked behind a parked car.

"Fuck yall motherfuckers" Drama yells as he puts the other clip in the mac.

"Put the gun down or we will be forced to shoot you!" the police man warns him.

"Yall gone have too!" Drama yells before shooting over the hood of the car and the police scatter to take cover.

"Open Fire!" The police with the bull horn yells ducked behind the door of his car holding his neck as blood gushes from it from being shot.

Running a couple of parked cars up as shots tear through and bounce off of the cars he's behind, Drama sees a police car stopping at the corner and he sprays the mac at it shattering the car windows and riddling the car with bullets killing the officers inside.

"So, what if we don't even see him when we get around there?" Jasmine asks J.V.

"Then I'll know he ain't doing nothing crazy and I'll leave with a clear conscious." Replies J.V as Varsity who has G-Way in the car with him tries to keep up with J.V.

"The plane done already left though, and you need to slow down before you kill us in here." Jasmine says holding on tight to the door handle.

"I can get another plane ticket, that's nothing. But you ain't gone find too many niggas as real as my nigga." replies J.V going even faster.

"Well if you kill us in the car you'll never find out." Jasmine says bracing herself as he flies around a car in front of him as he continues to speed through the streets.

Venable St East End

As the police keep people as far away from the shoot out as they can, Joe and his niggas stand at the front of the crowd as Joe silently cries for Drama as the exchange of gun fire rips through the air over the sound of police and ambulance sirens as people duck from it sounding so close.

Hoping for the best for Drama, Joe prepares for the worst as he says a Prayer for Drama as Rell and a few others angerly leave the crowd and get in a Pathfinder as Rell pulls off "

"I ain't going alive!" Drama yells as he's ducked behind a semi shot up car as shots continue to tear the car apart. "Alright, alright, I give up just stop shooting!" Drama yells as the shots continue and he lays on his stomach to duck the shots.

"I said I give up!" Drama yells again this time being heard as he smiles when he hears the police yell "hold fire." to each other and slowly they stop shooting.

"Put your hands where we can see them." Another police says through the bull horn ducked behind his shot-up squad car as the officer who originally yelled through the bull horn lay dead up against the car.

"Hell naw, cause I know yall gone shoot me!" Drama yells back as blood from his chest wounds stain and soak his white T-shirt as he sits up and breaths hard as his mind races trying to figure out his next move.

"Are you OK?" Asks the officer.

"Just stay back!" Drama yells putting the mac on the hood to show he will start shooting again as they remain where they are.

"Do you notice that we been flying like we on a race track but ain't seen one cop car yet?" G-way asks Varsity as they get around the way and lose track of J.V.

"I was about to say the same thing, I know this nigga done did something crazy." Replies Varsity bending A corner and seeing J.V car going through a stop sign without stopping just a few blocks up as he speeds up on the straight away to catch him before seeing him hit a black Pathfinder.

"Oh shit, da nigga wrecked!" Varsity says with concern in his tone as he slows down and stops at the stop sign on the corner of the block he's on and looks both ways before he pulls off and sees the occupants of the Pathfinder get out and he instantly recognizes Rell and Noet. Speeding up he says "Oh shit!" As they walk to the driver side of J.V's car and yank the door open and Varsity watches Rell start shooting into the driver side.

"Fuckkkkk!" He screams flying toward them trying to get there to save J.V.

"Last time, put your hands up!" The police man yells at Drama who's sitting behind the car holding his stomach as he spits out blood and thinks about J.V and his friends as he feels his self, getting light headed.

Smiling after a few thoughts he says to himself "fuck it." and laughing as blood drops out of his mouth.

"Alright, I'm gone put my hands up. Just don't start shooting." Drama yells to which the black police man assures him "just be calm, no one's going to shoot you."

Laughing Drama tightens his grip on the mac and with all his strength he jumps up and screams "LOST SOULS MOTHERFUCKA!!" As he sprays the mac which kinda catches the police off guard before they return fire.

With every bullet that strikes Drama his weak body jerks back, but he refuses to fall as he screams and continues to shoot causing police to drop and sparks to fly off of cars from the volley of shots until Drama's life less, bloody, bullet riddled body falls to the ground.

As G-Way pulls Jasmine out of the car, he notices that she's been shot in the leg and hurt badly from the wreck but still alive as she cries while G-Way holds her in the air in both of his arms while looking at J.V who is dead from multiple gun shots including several in the back of his head as he lays stretched out across both seats.

"He died saving me. He covered me up and died saving me." Jasmine cries in G-Ways ear as G-Way and Varsity stand on opposite ends of

J.V car speechless staring at J.V who lays dead in the car as tears leave Varsity's eyes while Rells Pathfinder sits abandoned in front of J.V' car with none of them anywhere insight.

"Come on dawg, we gotta get her to the hospital." G-Way says solemnly with tears running down his face before walking off back towards Varsity's car still holding Jasmine as people start to crowd around while Varsity who's consumed with anger, shock and sadness continues to stand there staring at J.V with tears falling from his eyes "Damn."

A black cop shakes his head and says while he stares at Drama's now unidentifiable lifeless body.

"It was him or us." A cop assures him while looking out over at the officers in black body bags and receiving Medical attention before continuing with, "and a couple of dead officers who were damn good cops proves it." As he then looks down at Drama's lifeless body with disgust on his face and a strong urge to spit on him crossing his mind before his thoughts are broken by the sound of his walkie talkie and the dispatcher informing all officers about calls received from the incident involving J.V.

"See, they just wanna kill each other anyway. So, like I said. It's better them then us." The white cop repeats to the black cop once more before putting him on his shoulder and then walking off. If my theory isn't correct, then the point of it has been made because every day we are at war even if you don't see it. The world is a big place and when the fighting, the racism; the egos and the gun shots do finally stop, there will be no one else breathing, not just in certain hoods or nations but the whole world as we know it. So, believe it or not, we are going to see crime until the end of life as we know it IN EVERY NATION!!!

www.ingramcontent.com/pod-product-compliance
Ingram Content Group UK Ltd.
Pitfield, Milton Keynes, MK11 3LW, UK
UKHW021312180426
11947UKWH00015B/1183